Christmas Elf

TIELLE ST.CLARE

ELLORA'S CAVE
ROMANTICA PUBLISHING

An Ellora's Cave Romantica Publication

www.ellorascave.com

Christmas Elf

ISBN 9781419955495
ALL RIGHTS RESERVED.
Christmas Elf Copyright © 2005 Tielle St. Clare
Edited by Briana St. James.
Cover art by Willo.

This book printed in the U.S.A. by Jasmine–Jade Enterprises,
LLC

Electronic book Publication December 2005
Trade paperback Publication October 2007

Content Advisory:

S – ENSUOUS
E – ROTIC
X – TREME

Ellora's Cave Publishing offers three levels of Romantica™ reading entertainment: S (S-ensuous), E (E-rotic), and X (X-treme).

The following material contains graphic sexual content meant for mature readers. This story has been rated S-ensuous.

S-*ensuous* love scenes are explicit and leave nothing to the imagination.

E-*rotic* love scenes are explicit, leave nothing to the imagination, and are high in volume per the overall word count. E-rated titles might contain material that some readers find objectionable—in other words, almost anything goes, sexually. E-rated titles are the most graphic titles we carry in terms of both sexual language and descriptiveness in these works of literature.

X-*treme* titles differ from E-rated titles only in plot premise and storyline execution. Stories designated with the letter X tend to contain difficult or controversial subject matter not for the faint of heart.

Also by Tielle St. Clare

໙

About the Author

~ ~

Tielle (pronounced "teal") St. Clare has had life-long love of romance novels. She began reading romances in the 7th grade when she discovered Victoria Holt novels and began writing romances at the age of 16 (during Trigonometry, if the truth be told). During her senior year in high school, the class dressed up as what they would be in twenty years—Tielle dressed as a romance writer. When not writing romances, Tielle has worked in public relations and video production for the past 20 years. She moved to Alaska when she was seven years old in 1972 when her father was transferred with the military. Tielle believes romances should be hot and sexy with a great story and fun characters.

Tielle welcomes comments from readers. You can find her website and email address on her author bio page at www.ellorascave.com.

Tell Us What You Think

We appreciate hearing reader opinions about our books. You can email us at Comments@EllorasCave.com.

CHRISTMAS ELF

ဢ

Trademarks Acknowledgement

80

The author acknowledges the trademarked status and trademark owners of the following wordmarks mentioned in this work of fiction:

BMW: Bayerische Motoren Werke Aktiengesellschaft Company

Prologue

ဆၢ

Marlie hunched her shoulders and slunk around behind the painting factory foreman. There was no chance of slipping in unnoticed, but if she could avoid making eye contact, she wouldn't have to see the gentle reproach on his face.

She was late. Again. It was becoming harder and harder for her to make it to work on time.

She slid into her chair and forced a tight smile at Teresa who sat across from her. Teresa had to take up the slack when Marlie wasn't there, but Teresa never complained. *No one here ever complains.* Too cheerful, Marlie thought with a grimace. She picked up her red paintbrush and began haphazardly applying a thick layer of red to the toy fire truck in front of her.

"Good morning, Marlie," Teresa greeted with a bright grin. "Can you believe it? Only fourteen days until Christmas. I'm so excited. I can hardly wait."

Marlie's fingers squeezed the end of her paintbrush. *Here we go again.*

Voices from all sides chimed in as the factory burst to life at the sound of the word "Christmas".

"Is only two weeks? But there's so much to do…"

"Think of all the children on Christmas morning, opening their new presents."

"We'd better get busy if we're going to make it on time."

Marlie's taut nerves stretched to the point of snapping. She didn't know how much more of this she could take.

The deep voice of the factory foreman erupted into a rousing version of "Here Comes Santa Claus". Seconds later, several other workers joined in perfect harmony. Teresa bounced in her chair as she painted a bright blue beach ball, her body moving with the perky rhythm of the song. Marlie glared across the table.

She gripped her paintbrush tightly between her fingers, resisting the almost overwhelming urge to pitch it at Teresa's smiling, cheerful face. Although the brush stayed in Marlie's hand, the words didn't stay in her mouth.

"Do you have to do this *every morning*?" Marlie's peevish tone echoed through the workshop.

Immediate silence blanketed the room, as if her angry words had sucked the cheer and joy from the factory. Several heads drooped forward and stayed low as they returned to their work. Teresa's bottom lip trembled, her eyes filling with tears. All eyes turned to Marlie—not in anger, but reproach and sadness. Sighing, she dropped back into her seat and waited. Any moment the factory foreman would come over and have another little "chat" about working with others and how they all had to try to get along.

"Marlie!" *Uh-oh.* She slid further into her chair. "In my office, right now!"

She should have known *he'd* be watching. A guilty conscience made her look at the faces of her coworkers as she walked down the aisle to his office. She deserved their scorn, their anger, but it wasn't there. Teresa's tears disappeared and she looked at Marlie with sympathy and support. In fact everyone at the table smiled encouragingly as she walked by. Even that irritated her.

Why can't they be smug when I'm getting in trouble?

She stopped outside the closed office door and waited. The silence of the workshop and the weight of each pair of eyes made the hair on the back of her neck stand up. Taking a deep breath, she tapped quietly on the door.

"Come in." Marlie entered at the brusque command. She tried to smile at the man waiting for her, but he would have none of it. The cheerful twinkle in his eye was gone and the rosy red in his cheeks seemed a little too florid.

Most people would have thought it was impossible. But she'd done it. She'd pissed off Santa Claus.

The door had barely closed behind her before she jumped into her defense.

"Now, Santa, I can explain." She paused. "Well, maybe not explain, but I can apologize. I promise I'll do better. I have been doing better, haven't I? I haven't thrown my paintbrush at Teresa in weeks. And it's not as if I haven't wanted to but I remembered what you said and…" The stern lines of Santa's face hadn't changed and the solemn look in his eye stopped her stream of words.

He folded his arms across his chest and leaned back in his chair. Even underneath the snowy white beard Marlie could tell he wasn't smiling. He shook his head sadly.

"Not this time, Marlie. You're a Christmas elf with no Christmas spirit." He stood up behind his desk and began to pace. "You're grouchy. You're late for work. You hate Christmas carols—" He ticked off each item on his fingers.

"I don't hate them," Marlie interrupted. "But do we have to sing them *all* the time?"

"And your attitude is beginning to affect the other elves," Santa continued as if she hadn't spoken.

"They've complained?" Marlie stared at the man in red.

Santa gave her a disgusted look. "Of course they haven't complained," he said.

"Of course not."

"And you're sarcastic," Santa added. "Now, did I forget anything?"

Marlie reviewed the list.

"No, that about does it," she agreed with a sympathetic wince.

"Something's got to change, Marlie."

"I really am trying, Santa."

"I know," he answered with a resigned sigh. Shivers skipped down her arms. Something was really wrong. "You're not going get your spirit back if you stay here," he concluded.

"You're moving me to another part of the Workshop?" That wasn't so bad. In fact, that was great. It was better than she'd dreamed. It was chance to do something different. Something besides paint red on fire trucks and little red wagons.

"No, Marlie. You need something more. The best way to help yourself is to help someone else. So you're going help someone else revive their Christmas spirit."

Marlie scanned the office, waiting for this person to appear, someone in more trouble than she was. After long moments, it was clear no one was popping out of any secret door. "But, Santa, everyone else has their Christmas spirit."

"I'm sending you away from the Workshop."

Air locked in Marlie's throat. Her heart pounded at double speed. Cold drenched her body from the top of her pointy ears to the soles of her curled up shoes.

Like every elf, she'd heard tales about the Outside World. Whispers really. Many of the elves who left were never seen or heard from again. No one talked much about their fate, but it had to be horrible. The elves who did return spoke about it only in hushed terms, warnings to the other elves.

This was her punishment for being a little crabby? She folded her arms across her chest and sunk into a pout. It was a little extreme.

"You will leave the Workshop—"

"But Santa—"

"You will leave the Workshop," he repeated, "and help a human of my choosing revive his Christmas spirit. You have less than two weeks." Her mouth bobbed open and closed. Santa held up his hand to stop her protests. "I'll send the information to your room. You'd better go pack. You have until Christmas Eve."

She desperately wanted to ask what would happen if she failed, but she couldn't get the words to leave her mouth. She wasn't sure she wanted to know. She didn't even glance at the elves in the painting room as she walked past.

The Outside World. She stopped in the dormitory hallway. *The Outside World. Beyond the Workshop doors.* A repressed sense of adventure fluttered in her chest. She could do this. She was an elf after all—and she had the power to grant wishes. She could certainly convince one human that Christmas was the most wonderful time of year and all that other junk. Santa expected her to fail but she would do this and prove to him that she was a true Christmas elf.

Her heart thudded with excitement. She brushed her hair over her shoulder and skipped down the hall. All she had to do was convince one old and crabby human to like Christmas. She'd have an adventure and be back in the Workshop in time for Christmas.

Chapter One

&&

He's supposed to be old and crabby, Marlie thought as Jacob Triumph entered his office reception area. She whipped the magazine up to cover her face, hoping he hadn't noticed her yet. She needed a few minutes to study him before contact was made.

"Ms. Benson, I thought I made it clear I want no decorations in this office. It is a place of business after all."

Marlie flinched at the rough, cold sound of his voice. Well, she'd been half right. He was crabby.

She peeked beneath the magazine and sought out the offending decoration. A small snow globe starring none other than Marlie's boss and reindeer friends sat on his secretary's desk. The tiny flakes of fake snow swirled through the water and began to sink to the bottom.

Great, I get the role model for Ebenezer Scrooge.

Santa obviously wanted her to fail. He clearly wanted her out of the Workshop forever, she thought with a mental snarl.

"It was a present from Eric in Accounting. I'll take it home tonight," Terry Benson answered in a soothing, slightly mocking voice. Her assurance had no impact on Jacob's scowl.

"Fine," he said, the subject clearly closed for him. "We're close to an agreement on the Henderson buyout. We need to set up a meeting next week with everyone involved."

While his secretary scanned the pages of her calendar, Marlie took the chance to observe her charge, doing her best to keep her internal dialogue clinical and cold. She'd read his file on the way here but it was different seeing him in person. The dossier she'd received had given his height, hair color and eye color. But six feet tall with brown hair and green eyes wasn't nearly descriptive enough. Tipping her head to the side, she let her eyes wander across his beautifully cut suit—even beneath the elegant jacket she could see hints of broad muscles and strong arms. With Jacob unaware of her perusal, she continued, letting her gaze drop down. The slacks did a better job of hiding the lower half of his body. Disappointment fluttered through her chest. His jacket completely covered his backside.

It would be intriguing to see him in a pair of tights like the elves wore at home. She licked her lips and considered wishing the coat gone, wishing all his clothes gone for that matter. She had the power but it seemed a bit unprofessional. No doubt Santa wouldn't approve. Still, she did very much want to see his body, maybe even touch it, trail her fingertips along the lines of his back, the rise of his ass. Her palms started to tingle so she rubbed her hands down her thighs—willing away the sensation. The other elves had never understood her desire to touch things, to sample the world with her fingers. From what she'd read, humans were less opposed to physical contact but somehow she didn't think that meant walking up to a stranger and running her hand along his butt. So until she learned the rules, she'd just have to keep her hands to herself.

Too bad. It was a beautiful body. A foreign warmth curled in her stomach and sank lower, heating that space between her legs. She squeezed her thighs together but that only made it worse. Pressing up on her toes, she slowly rocked forward and back. The heat began to spread, seeping into her limbs, making the tingling in her hands stronger and warming her whole body. Marlie smiled. She hated the cold. Being warm—even by this strange fever—was better than shivering.

Savoring the heat inside her, she watched her charge as he talked quietly with his secretary.

He was a delicious-looking man. His deep brown hair reminded Marlie of the summer coat of the reindeer. The short, above the ear haircut he wore was similar to the typical male elf hairstyle—though personally, she'd always thought they should wear their hair a little longer, over top their pointed ears—but on Jacob it looked wonderful. It gave a clear view of his high cheekbones and strong jaw. He was lovely, and she was spending the next two weeks with him.

It doesn't matter what Jacob Triumph looks like, she reminded herself with a little jolt. She was on a mission—get back to the Workshop by Christmas Eve and prove to Santa that she was worthy of the title "Elf".

Not that she hadn't enjoyed her first experiences in the Outside World. The toy section in Triumph's would make Santa proud. And she didn't mind the cup of black liquid Terry had offered her while she waited for Jacob. She took another sip from the paper cup.

"It looks like next Thursday is the best bet." Terry's comment brought Marlie's attention back. "You're in meetings Monday and Tuesday."

Jacob leaned over his secretary's desk.

"What's wrong with Wednesday?" he demanded. "It's completely clear."

"Mr. Triumph, that's Christmas day."

Marlie stifled a bit of laughter at the appalled sound of Terry's voice.

Jacob shook his head. "Why are the holidays right in the middle of our busiest time?" he muttered.

"It's our busiest time *because* of the holidays," his secretary pointed out.

"Fine," he brushed away the valid point. "Set it up for whenever you can." He turned and started toward his office door when Terry's call stopped him.

"Mr. Triumph, this young lady is here to see you." She indicated Marlie waiting silently in the large leather chair.

Realizing she finally had his attention, Marlie froze. What did she say now? "Hi, I'm an elf and you need to get some spirit so I can go home?"

Marlie hadn't been in the Outside World long but she knew that wouldn't get the appropriate response.

She dropped the magazine and stood, surreptitiously wiping her hands on her trousers before offering one to Jacob. "Hi, I'm Marlie."

He stared down at her hand then up at her face. A tiny light of curiosity flickered deep in his eyes but was extinguished almost before she saw it. Hope surged in her heart. He was in there somewhere. She just had to find a way to bring out the true and loving Jacob Triumph.

She smiled. And waited.

The skin at her temples tightened when she realized he wasn't going to shake her hand. Santa might have gotten rid of her because she lacked spirit but he should have added stubbornness to the list. She pushed her hand forward and silently dared Jacob to take it. With a sigh, he pulled his hand from his pocket and clasped hers in his firm grip. Heat skittered up her arm, racing from the center of their bound palms. As if he felt it too, Jacob gave her hand one brusque squeeze before releasing her and stepping away.

Marlie stared at her hand. His heat was branded on her skin.

"What can I do for you, miss?" he demanded.

Marlie shivered at his cool voice, such a contradiction to the warmth of his palm. She rolled her fingers over her thumb, amazed that she could still feel his touch.

"Miss?"

"Hmm?" She looked up. His green eyes were waiting to capture hers. Another strange sensation curled into the center of her body. What would it be like to feel that delicious heat all through her body? "Yes."

"Did you need something?"

Warmth. She needed his warmth. She blinked and realized he'd asked her a real question.

"I-I needed to see you," she blurted out, her mind still adjusting to the strange sensations moving through her body. Not unpleasant. Just new and unusual.

"Is there a problem in the store? Did you have a complaint?"

"Complaint? Oh, no." Marlie shook her head. "It's fine. Wonderful. Great toy section."

"Thank you." Jacob looked over his shoulder at his secretary. She shrugged and he returned his gaze to Marlie. "I'm rather busy. What can I do for you?"

"I'm here to help. To help you." Her voice hit a desperate squeak as her mind searched for a coherent thought and found none.

"Thank you." He took a step away. "I don't need any help. If you're looking for Personnel, it's down the hall." He leaned toward his secretary's desk, never fully taking his eyes off Marlie. "Ms. Benson, could you explain this?" he asked in a hushed voice.

These pointed ears have some benefit, Marlie thought, listening to the whispered conversation. She knew eavesdropping was wrong but she needed all the help she could get. This was turning out to be harder than she'd thought. She didn't know how to approach a human. They were much more complicated than elves. If she'd told an elf she was here to help him, he would have thanked her and set her to work.

"She came in here looking for you," Terry whispered. "She was shivering. She didn't have a coat. I couldn't very well turn her away. I just gave her some coffee and let her warm up."

"We're running a business, Ms. Benson, not a shelter for the homeless."

"But, sir, it's Christmas."

Marlie waited as both humans looked at her. The grim look on Jacob's face told her what she needed to know—she'd failed.

She was going to be trapped forever in the Outside World. Alone. And cold.

"Here." The harsh word jerked Marlie from her depressing thoughts. She looked to Jacob. "Here," he said again.

She followed the direction to his hand—a hand holding a single slip of green paper. Money had been covered in her orientation—page three of the "Elf in the Outside World" handbook—but she hadn't expected to see it so soon. She cautiously accepted it from his grip, turning the multicolored paper over in her hand and inspecting it.

"Get yourself something to eat and maybe some warmer clothes," he commanded. Turning on his heel, he started toward the inner office door.

Marlie stared at the bill. One hundred dollars. If she showed up at the Workshop doors saying Jacob Triumph had learned the true meaning of Christmas because he gives money to strangers, Santa would boot her butt right back to where she was.

"No. This won't work," she called to Jacob's back. He stopped at the door and slowly turned. One eyebrow was raised as he looked at her.

"Pardon me? Isn't it enough?" The chill in his voice had reached glacier level.

"What?" She flushed, realizing he'd misunderstood. "No. I just really need to speak with you."

"I don't have time, miss. Now, I'd like you to leave."

"I can't." It was the truth. She had nowhere else to go. Her heart started to pound.

Things weren't working out the way she'd planned. Not that she'd had a plan.

Of course, *he* hadn't helped the situation. He wasn't what she'd expected. He was handsome and something inside her wanted to stay with him, touch him, look at him. The thoughts confused her. She'd barely noticed the other elves at the Workshop. Why would she suddenly become obsessed with a human's physical features? *Odd, very odd.*

Jacob stepped close to Marlie and placed one hand in the air behind her back, not quite touching her. Curious about where his hand was heading, she turned around. Again, he stepped to her side, one hand behind her back, one hand toward the door. He seemed to be herding her that direction.

"I appreciate that you want to help me," he spoke in soothing, nonthreatening tones. "Now, is there someone Ms. Benson could call to come pick you up?" he asked in that calm voice. "A doctor perhaps?" He took a small step forward. Marlie inched along.

"But you don't understand…" she protested.

They were halfway to the door and if she didn't gain control of the situation, she'd end up in the hallway. She stopped. Jacob's hand whapped into her back.

"Do people usually go away after you've given them money?" she asked.

The question jolted his face out of its calm, understanding veneer.

"Yes," he answered after a moment of thought. Marlie shook her head in sympathy. His spine stiffened and he backed away, his eyes turning to stone, the moment of vulnerability gone.

"You don't understand," she said with a sigh. "I don't need any money and there isn't anyone to come get me. I…" The impatient look on his face stopped her words. Pleading wasn't getting her anywhere. Her teeth snapped together. She'd had a very challenging day so far and he wasn't helping the situation. "Now listen." She stalked forward, her index finger pointing and wagging in time with her words. "I'm here to help you and I'm going to whether you like it or not. I want to go home and you're my ticket, buddy," Marlie finished through clenched teeth.

The temperature in the room dropped twenty degrees as Jacob pulled himself to his full height. The crinkles at the edges of his eyes deepened and Marlie had the distinct impression that people didn't talk back to Jacob Triumph very often. They probably only did it once before they learned their lesson.

Even Terry seemed to shrink in her chair as if she didn't want to be included in Jacob's wrath.

Great. She'd pissed off her charge.

Jacob's voice was cool and controlled but the power behind it made her shiver. "Listen, Marlie, I'm going to ask you to leave one more time before I call security and have you thrown out."

Marlie's brief indoctrination into the Outside World had covered the usual topics — money, food, lodging, security officers, police, stalking charges. It was obvious that elves sent on similar missions hadn't known when to go away.

And it looked like she was going to be one of them. She just had to try one more time.

"Before you —" The jangling of the phone interrupted.

Terry grabbed the handset and brought it to her ear as if it were a lifeline to safety.

"Mr. Triumph's office." Her voice wavered slightly as she spoke. "Oh, hello Mrs. Butterstone. Yes? Really?" Her eyes widened and Terry smiled up at Marlie. "Now I understand. We were a bit confused for a moment."

Marlie stared at Jacob, who hadn't taken his eyes off her. The strength of his gaze drew Marlie to him, the green depths silent, betraying no emotion, no hint of feeling. If she succeeded, Jacob's green eyes would sparkle with laughter. The very idea gave Marlie a new reason to stay.

"Do you want to speak with her? Okay. Well, have a Merry Christmas." Terry replaced the phone and stood up, her hand reaching out to Marlie. "You should have said something." Terry turned to Jacob. "This is Mrs. Butterstone's niece. She's filling in while Mrs. Butterstone is off with her daughter over the holidays."

"Mrs. Butterstone is leaving?"

"Remember I told you about this? Her daughter is about to give birth. She was going to find a replacement housekeeper for you for a few weeks." Terry indicated Marlie. "And that's who this is. You could have saved us some worry if you'd said who you were. I was starting to think you were some kind of nut," she said with a laugh.

Marlie laughed along with her, at the same time trying to look as efficient and as nonthreatening as possible. Santa had said he would help her get access to Jacob. This must be it.

The straight line of his lips and slight tightening of skin around his eyes didn't bode well for their future interactions. "You're Mrs. Butterstone's niece?"

"That's me," Marlie answered. The upped-perky quotient in her voice made the "me" come out in a squeak. *Tone it down, and you're home free.* "How is Aunt…uh, my aunt?"

"Fine. You say her daughter is about to have a baby?"

"Anytime now," Terry answered. Marlie nodded wisely, trying to give the impression that she knew the whole story.

Jacob continued to watch her. She shifted uncomfortably, uneasy with his steady gaze. "You don't look anything like your aunt," he said finally.

"Oh, I wouldn't." Marlie scanned through her mind for a good excuse. "We're related by marriage." Warming up to the idea, and wanting to sound credible, she continued, "My father, who's married to my aunt's sister, married her after I was already born."

The look in his eyes went from suspicious to confused and it was enough to warn her to stop talking. She'd just get

24

herself in trouble if she said anything more. At least, that's the way it worked at the Workshop.

"It would have helped if you'd introduced yourself as Mrs. Butterstone's niece."

Marlie shrugged and gave him what she hoped was a sweet smile.

"Yes, well, I guess, that's it then." Jacob moved back to his office door. "I'll be home around seven."

"What should I do until then?" Marlie asked, blocking his escape.

"I don't know," Jacob answered in an exasperated voice. "Whatever it is housekeepers do."

"How do I get there?"

"Get where?"

"To your house."

He sighed. "How did you get here?"

"Reindeer?" she offered with a light laugh. Jacob didn't respond. "Just a little Christmas humor there," she muttered.

"I get it."

"Can I just hang around and ride with you?" That was good, she thought. It would give her a chance to spend some time with him and work on that Christmas spirit thing.

"That's five hours away," Jacob replied. Marlie nodded. "I'm going to be in meetings all afternoon." Again she nodded. "You can't come with me to the meetings." Marlie joined him as he shook his head. He waited.

"Oh." Marlie jerked back from the hypnotic movement of his head. "Well, I guess I'll just wander around the store, then. I'll be back up here later."

"Fine," he answered. The frustration was subdued but still there and Marlie had to wonder if the confused look on his face was normal or if it was something she'd inspired. "Dinner should be served by eight." He opened the door to his inner office.

"Dinner? Great. You cook?"

"Marlie, that's your job."

"Oh, right. It was a joke."

"You can cook, can't you?" His voice regained the hard edge. "Tell me Mrs. Butterstone didn't send someone to me during the holidays who can't cook."

"Of course I can cook. I'm a fine cook. A wonderful cook, in fact."

"Fine," Jacob finished abruptly. He turned and stormed into his office closing the door with what would have been a slam if the perfect acoustics in the room hadn't muffled the sound to a thud.

All the energy drained out of her body and her shoulders drooped forward. It had been a hard won struggle but she'd gotten her foot in the door. What was she going to do now?

Terry flashed her a sympathetic smile and said, "Cookbooks are on the fourth floor."

Chapter Two

∞

Jacob stared at the computer screen, watching the flashing cursor bounce before his eyes. He had to focus. This note needed to get to the Board of Directors tonight. Then they would have two days to think about his proposal before the dinner this week.

Providing the information to the board was almost a formality. Between Jacob and his parents they owned a majority of the shares and he knew his parents were in favor of the buyout. The board had its uses and Jacob had no intention of offending them by point blank telling them they had little choice in the matter. The email had to be a fine balance of information and coercion so they understood what was happening but weren't under the impression they could stop it.

But the words just wouldn't come.

It was fear that stopped him. Not of the board or their reaction. But of *her*. Marlie. Any moment she was going to pop into his office and interrupt him. It had been—he glanced at his clock—forty-five minutes since her last appearance so her next arrival couldn't be far off. And he knew, just as soon as he got into crafting the note, she'd appear, tipping her head and asking in that come-fuck-me voice if he was ready to go home.

It was the voice that got to him—well, along with the body. Physically she reminded him of cheerleader—energetic, cheerful, tight ass, strong legs. But the voice was pure smoke and sex. Wicked combination. A sweet smile countered by the husky sensual sounds coming out of her mouth. It made him wonder what she would be like in bed, how that energy would translate and what it would be like to hear her plead ever so sweetly in that voice—beg him to fuck her, drive himself deeper into her pussy.

He shifted in his chair, trying to ease the growing erection. He'd been fighting it all afternoon. He'd just get the damn thing willed away and she'd walk in again.

Put it aside. Concentrate. Ignoring sex was a new sensation for him. Despite most reports in the media, he did not spend much of his workday fantasizing about his coworkers. Work was work. Sex was something completely outside of the building.

The words on his screen came into focus and he realized he'd typed the word "sex" into the email to the board. He laughed without humor and moved his mouse to click undo. After only five hours, she was screwing up his—

"Ready to go?"

At the sound of the cheerful, feminine voice, his finger twitched and the screen went blank. He looked up. His mouse had been over the send button.

He'd just sent an unfinished note to the Board of Directors that ended in the random word "sex". How the hell was he going to explain that?

Biting down to keep control, he moved back from the computer and sought the source of the voice.

It was leaning into his office.

Marlie. As expected.

He turned in his chair and rested his elbows on the surface of his desk. Fingers clasped together, he peered over his hands. He'd had years of practice intimidating people— employees, competitors, paperboys. It was a skill he'd learned from his father and he used it well in his business.

"Marlie, it's considered polite to knock before you enter someone's office," he said, pleased to note he sounded stern and disapproving. It was a tone that quelled the most eager intruder.

Marlie looked at the door like it had committed the offense then pushed it the rest of the way open. She moved into his office as if she had every right to do so.

"You'd have just growled at me to stay out, like you did earlier," she said, dropping into the chair in front of his desk. She placed a shopping bag at her feet before stretching her arms above her head and yawning broadly. Jacob's eyes fell to her chest as she arched her back, pushing her breasts forward and into the soft material of her T-shirt. A voice in the back of his head warned that this was a lawsuit in the making but Jacob couldn't look away. She moved with such unconscious sensuality. Not grace but pleasure—like each movement of her muscles was a treat.

She closed her eyes and let her head fall back. Her breasts shimmied beneath the shirt, soft and round, and clearly unrestrained. They weren't large so he supposed she could get away without a bra. The tight nipples poked against the thin material. Her low groan teased him with the idea of the sounds she would make if he sucked on those pretty little nipples. Preferably while his cock was deep inside her.

The tightening of his trousers reminded Jacob where he was. He snapped his eyes up, back where they belonged. Her innocent gaze met his. She smiled with no awareness of his lustful thoughts. For a moment, he considered the idea that she *wanted* him to stare—that she was out to seduce him. That idea faded as quickly as it came. If she was bent on seduction, she wasn't very good at it.

"What do you want?" he demanded, hoping professionalism and irritation would come to his rescue. Marlie didn't seem to notice the harsh tone to his voice.

"It's late. Are you ready to go home?" She swept her shoulder-length blonde hair back. "You really need to keep perspective about your work."

He deliberately stared down the line of his nose, glaring at her intrusion.

Marlie didn't notice. Hell, she wasn't even looking at him any longer. She'd turned her attention to his office. He knew what she'd see. Dark wood furnishings provided the somber air necessary for a CEO. The heavy wood desk had been in his family for years, lovingly polished every week by the cleaning crew. Not a scratch on it. Everything in the room had been selected or designed to match his personality and the overall effect was powerful, quiet strength. The same aspects he displayed during business.

"You need to redo this office. Brighten it up a bit," she finally said. "It's kind of dark and it doesn't really feel like you," she concluded with a shake of her head.

Jacob opened his mouth to protest—this office was perfect for him—then she smiled.

Warmth washed over him like the waves on a sun-drenched beach. The smile brightened her whole face. Her eyes sparkled with laughter and wisdom. Unable to stop himself, he started to lean forward, captivated by her eyes, the blue depths drawing him closer. She watched him with an intensity and openness that warned she might see into his soul if he didn't guard against it.

But he couldn't look away. Blood rushed through his body, quickly abandoning his limbs and sinking into his groin. His eyes drifted to her lips, imagining the feel of her mouth beneath his. He slid his tongue over his bottom lip. He wanted to taste her—her mouth, her breasts, that sweet hot place between her legs. The fantasy quickly changed to her writhing beneath him as he pounded his cock into her pussy—her cries filling his ears as she begged for more.

In the past few years, his lovers had been decidedly restrained. It had been a conscious choice made when he'd taken over the leadership of the company. Restrained, vanilla sex fit his image as the corporate executive—even if he did sometimes crave something a little…more. Natalie, his current occasional bed partner, was a perfect match to his present lifestyle. She liked to fuck and then talk business. Since those were the only two things they had in common, the relationship worked for them.

He'd experimented with BDSM in his younger days but found the lifestyle didn't match his professional goals well. He'd ended that portion of his life and willed the urges to dominate from his psyche. At least he had until Marlie had walked in. She would be a challenge. An interesting submissive sex toy. While he enjoyed dominating a woman in the bedroom—he liked spirit and spunk to go along with it. Nothing was more boring to him than an overly submissive submissive. Marlie wouldn't have that problem. He would be able to tie her up, spank her ass and fuck her all night and in the morning, she'd still look at him with those laughing, almost taunting eyes.

He jerked back, physically shaking the thoughts from his mind. What the hell was he thinking? She was his employee. He could not be having sexual thoughts about her. No matter how eager her nipples appeared. He stared at the piles of paper on his desk unwilling to meet her eyes, forcing his mind to fixate on the mundane task of packing his briefcase for the evening,

The heavy weight in his crotch warned him his erection hadn't subsided. If he kept having fantasies about his housekeeper, he was going to be hard all night. Prolonged bouts of celibacy followed by mediocre sex had obviously driven him over the edge.

"Are you okay?"

His head pulled back at her question. "What? Oh, yes. Fine. I'm just, uh, well—" *battling a raging hard-on,* he finished silently. "Are you ready to go?"

"Finally. Yes." She stood up and turned, bending over and giving him the perfect view of her exquisitely shaped ass. The pants stretched, hugging every curve. It had been years since he'd warmed an ass like that with his palm. His mind had just dipped into the fantasy for bending Marlie over the desk and punishing her for interrupting him when she straightened and held forth a lime green and magenta monstrosity. "Like my new coat?"

The fluorescent multicolored stripes etched themselves onto the backs of his eyes and he feared they were permanently imbedded. Not only did the coat look three sizes too big for her, it was ugly.

"So, do you like it?"

"It's nice." The words slipped out of his mouth from force of habit. "Did you buy that here at Triumph's?" he asked. And God help the purchaser who ordered it, he added silently.

She shook her head. "Terry sent me down the street to a discount place." Marlie smoothed her hand down the bright pink sleeve. "Personally, I think it's kind of ugly but it's pretty warm." She shrugged. "It was all I could afford."

He didn't know what he was paying her but he immediately decided that a new coat would be part of her uniform. *That's it. I'll require her to wear a uniform. One that includes a bra.* Before he could picture her in a dowdy "Nurse Ratched-type" outfit, a French Maid costume popped into his head. Complete with ruffles on her ass and a push up bra that created cleavage deep enough a man could lose himself in it.

This is ridiculous. He shoved his chair back and stood.

I should give Natalie a call and spend the evening with her. It would be the perfect solution. A night of restrained fucking to push Marlie from his mind. His cock twitched but it had little to do with the prospect of fucking Natalie and all to do with the sight of Marlie's nipples pressing against her shirt.

"What is that?"

Jacob followed the path of Marlie's pointing finger— directly to his erection. It was time to bluff his way out of this.

"What do you mean?" he asked, pleased with the cool tone he achieved. Completely opposite to the fire racing through his veins.

"That." She pointed emphatically. "What's with all the papers?" she demanded.

Papers? He looked down at the desk. She wasn't pointing at him. An unconscious sigh of relief escaped his lips.

"It's work." He finished gathering the final stack and slid it into his briefcase.

"I thought you were done working."

"There's more to do," he stated calmly. He snapped the briefcase shut and walked to the tiny closet in the corner of his office, trying to ignore Marlie's presence.

"You looked like you were working every time I came in."

The silence waited for a response. Jacob let it hang between them. Too many secrets were lost by someone trying to fill silence. He didn't need to share his secrets. All he needed was a housekeeper who could cook and despite her brave words earlier, Jacob felt sure he was living off canned meat and beanie-weenies until Mrs. Butterstone returned.

He glanced at Marlie. Now would be a good time to ask about her cooking credentials.

"Marlie..." he began.

"Were you playing computer games instead?"

He turned to stare at her. "What?"

"Well, if you were at work all day and you didn't get your work done, I thought you might have been playing computer games instead." She picked up his briefcase and walked across the room until she stood at his shoulder. "We had an el—a fellow who did that once, but he didn't stay around long." Her teeth worried her lower lip as she stared off into space. Finally she shook her head and looked back at Jacob with wide eyes. "Nobody knows what happened to him. He just...disappeared."

Don't ask.

Don't ask, don't tell. It had become Jacob's motto. If he didn't inquire about anyone's personal life, they couldn't expect him to share his own. There was always something they felt compelled to fix, or, at the very least, provide advice on.

Jacob reached into the closet. Marlie was silent again. Jacob tracked through their conversation and realized she was waiting for an answer. Damn, if he could only remember the question.

Computer games. Right.

"No, Marlie, I wasn't playing computer games. I was working. All day." That should have ended it. With any of his *other* employees, it would have. Not Marlie. He pulled on his long black wool coat.

"Then you need to hire more people." Her tone indicated Jacob should have figured that out *long* ago. It was only pure, concentrated self-control that stopped him from letting his mouth sag open as she walked away, leaving Jacob behind.

That little bit of a woman was advising him on his business? The click of his outer office door opening knocked him free of his immobility. He went after her, pausing long enough to run a quick scan of the reception area. The snow globe was gone. *Good.* He checked the rest of the room. He wasn't exactly *looking* for decorations, but the office was his final bastion of peace from the holiday season. Even his home had the requisite trimmings, or it would once he got around to hiring someone to hang the blasted things. If he'd had his way, his house would be as bare as his office, but with the board coming to dinner this week, it would seem strange if he didn't at least pretend to be in the holiday spirit.

A double-ding at the end of the hall indicated the down elevator had arrived and that Marlie was leaving without him. He locked the door and jogged down the hall, catching the elevator just as it was closing. The doors popped back open and he stepped inside, flashing an irritated glare Marlie's way.

"I couldn't find the 'door open' button," she defended before he'd even said anything.

"I'd like that back." He indicated the briefcase she carried.

She shrugged. "I was just trying to help." She let go of the case, letting it thump to the floor as the elevator doors closed trapping them inside. "Must be pretty weighty stuff."

"You don't understand," he said, even as he tried to figure out why he was justifying himself to her. "This is all work that *I* need to do."

"Nobody's that important. What floor?"

Jacob stared at the lighted display, trying to remember where he'd parked his car. He shook his head. The same place he parked his car every day.

"Garage two. And these are all decisions I have to make." He pointed down the case sitting between them.

The mocking cough told him what she thought of that. "You need to learn to delegate."

Jacob watched the lighted numbers change as the elevator dropped.

I'm the executive. She's the housekeeper, he reminded himself. He rubbed his forehead with the tips of his fingers. Another headache was coming on. *What am I doing? I know that. She's the one who's lost perspective.*

"Don't worry." Marlie's cheerful voice penetrated the silence. She straightened and flashed a relieved smile to him. "I know a lot about division of labor. I can help you. That's not the help I was sent to give you, of course, but why not use it?"

"I see. Housekeeper by day, management consultant by night. How lucky can I get?"

Marlie turned her head again. Her "don't get smart with me" glare was spoiled by the smile that burst onto her face. Jacob fought the urge to grin back. The corners of his lips started to curl up, but he forced them to remain in a straight line, tightening the edges to keep them under control. He couldn't start smiling at her now. She was his employee.

The elevator doors opened allowing Jacob to escape her smile.

"Is this your car?" she asked as they approached, her voice full of wonder. His shoulders straightened with pride as he ran his hand over the sleek black BMW Z-4. "They're much bigger than the toy versions, aren't they?" she asked, her words shimmering with awe and wonder.

Jacob stared at her back as she peered in the window.

"Yes, much." He opened her door and helped her into the low seat. Jacob took several deep breaths as he walked to the other side of the car.

The balance between cause and effect, action-reaction, had been lost. Marlie didn't respond the way she was supposed to. To anything.

He grabbed the door handle and took another calming breath. It had been one of those days. He should have known it when he'd had to fire Santa Claus for stealing women's lingerie. He realized now *that* had been his clue to go home.

Casually looking through the window, Jacob observed his latest challenge. Marlie—running her fingers across the buttons on his CD player, the dash, the steering wheel—like a blind person learning the world. Jacob ground his back teeth together. It was too easy to imagine her stroking him in just the same manner, learning his body with that eager fascinated look on her face. Her, kneeling over him, her mouth following the wandering trail of her fingers.

He swallowed and looked around the garage debating how long he could avoid getting into his car. Some of the tension in his groin eased and he realized Marlie was going to become curious about why he wasn't getting in. Not that she'd noticed yet. She was too busy caressing his car.

He jerked open his door and slid his briefcase in the tiny space behind the front seat.

"Oh, Jacob," she sighed. "It's beautiful. And the leather." She rubbed her palm over his seat. A delicate shiver raced through her body as if the sensation had caused a mini-orgasm. "Umm. It's so soft. Don't you just want to strip off your clothes and rub your body all over it?"

She followed her words by a slow sway in her chair. The ugly coat hid most of her form but it didn't matter. Jacob had a good idea of what was happening—the sway of her breasts and the tightening of her nipples.

"Glad you like it." He was pleased his voice was calm and cool as he climbed inside. "Do you have a suitcase?" Jacob glanced around the car, noticing she was empty-handed.

Marlie opened her mouth but shut it before saying anything. She squeezed her lips together and stared up into the far corner of the windshield.

Jacob watched, fascinated at the changing expressions on her face. He'd never seen anyone so obviously thinking up a lie before.

"It's being delivered," she said at last. "I think," she added in a mumble Jacob almost didn't hear.

What is she hiding? Jacob allowed himself one last look before starting the engine. The center of his stomach began to burn. He had a bad feeling about this. It wasn't fear but some sort of ominous sensation that his world was about to change. Marveling at this strange insight, he backed out of the parking spot and drove to the garage exit.

The parking attendant leaned down and greeted them with a cheerful wave. Jacob rolled down his window to say good night.

"Merry Christmas, Mr. Triumph," the attendant said as they came to a stop. "Drive safe. Santa might be on the road with his reindeer."

Jacob felt an involuntary clench of his jaw. He forced his lips into an insincere smile and nodded as he punched the gas pedal and launched the car from the garage.

Santa Claus, Christmas, and the holidays in general. Bah Humbug.

"That was kind of a silly warning, wasn't it?" Marlie's voice interrupted his grim thoughts.

He flashed her a quick glance before returning his attention to the road. Could it be true? Was she like him and disliked the holidays? A glimmer of hope flared in his chest. A kindred spirit.

"Everyone knows Santa is a better driver than that." She turned in her seat to face him. "Can you imagine what it's like to land a reindeer-pulled sleigh, full of toys, on house tops? If he's that good, he can certainly avoid a little vehicle traffic," Marlie concluded with confidence and more than a little irritation.

Jacob stared at the street in front of him. His fingers tightened on the steering wheel. *Why does it sound like she believes in Santa Claus?*

"Ooh, their Christmas lights look so beautiful," she said as they drove by Town Square. "Do you have any lights up at home?" Jacob shook his head slowly. "Don't worry. I'm great with lights. We'll have your house looking like Santa's Workshop in no time."

Jacob's heart fell to his feet. His home, his refuge, was about to be invaded by Christmas.

* * * * *

Marlie shrugged off her new coat and dropped it behind her on the bright linoleum floor as she walked into the large, open kitchen. She'd been in the kitchens at the Workshop a few times, so she recognized the equipment, but wasn't quite sure what it all did. They had a strict division of labor in the Workshop. Elves, who made or decorated toys, didn't do other work. There were too many toys to make. Training classes to attend. New techniques on production and new items each year as toys became more and more sophisticated.

She trailed a careful finger over the sleek polished surface of the stovetop. The cool metal sent shivers up her arm. Clutter was conspicuously missing from the blue and white countertops. Marlie leaned against the kitchen counter and took in the whole room. Everything was perfect, in place and sparkling clean. Who lives like this? she asked herself, then answered her own question. *Jacob.*

Not only was the kitchen clean and excessively tidy, it was devoid of personality. The kitchen elves always had pictures or cute, cheerful sayings pasted to the walls and cupboard doors.

Marlie smiled. Maybe when she returned to the Workshop, Santa would put her to work in the kitchen. *Who knows, maybe I have an aptitude for cooking?*

She made a circle of the room and stopped in front of the refrigerator. Cold air swirled around her as she opened the door and peeked inside. After a few seconds, she shivered, shut the door and continued her tour of the kitchen. If, for some odd reason, she felt homesick for the North Pole, she knew where to go.

It didn't take long to check out the rest of the kitchen and end up back in front of the refrigerator. There had to be something in there she could cook. The cookbooks she'd looked through had been interesting with plenty of pictures. But instead of getting ideas for dinner, she'd gotten hungry and had found herself in the coffee shop on the first floor of Triumph's. After her new coat, the doughnuts and several cups of coffee, she didn't have much left from the money Jacob had given her this morning.

Again, she looked inside the refrigerator. There was milk. He probably had cereal. Marlie shook her head. No, Jacob would want something cooked. Like a slab of nearly raw meat. He'd done nothing but growl at her since they'd started the drive home. He's probably just hungry, she decided with forced cheerfulness. A quick investigation into the freezer revealed a package of steaks. They didn't eat much red meat at the Workshop, but she'd seen enough steaks to know all she would have to do was cook the thing a little and someone would eat it. *Success at last.*

"What the...?"

Marlie turned in time to watch Jacob tangle his feet in her coat and stumble, catching himself against the counter.

"Oh, sorry," she said, leaning on the open freezer door. "Could you hang that up?"

Jacob picked up the jacket and stared at it for a moment then transferred the look to Marlie. She waited. Santa often gave her the same undecided-just-what-do-with-her look.

Jacob sighed and draped the collar of her coat on a hook behind the kitchen door. Great, a neatness freak, Marlie thought with a mental grimace. *If he's that obsessed about tidiness he should hire someone to clean up after him.*

She mentally slapped her forehead. *Right. That's why I'm here.*

"I'll be in my office working. Call me when dinner is ready," he announced but didn't leave. Instead he walked through the kitchen to her side. The faintest hint of his aftershave lingered and Marlie drew in a deep breath. "Is there a reason you've got the door permanently open, or did you just want to cool down the room a bit?" he asked looking pointedly at the open freezer.

Her lips flattened out. "It's all this metal in the kitchen," she answered, tapping the door closed. "It's stopping my X-ray vision." Jacob's eyes tightened.

Marlie winced. That sarcasm gene she'd inherited from some unknown parent tended to reveal itself at moments like this.

Jacob blinked but continued to stare.

"It was a joke," Marlie finally said. "I don't really have X-ray vision."

Jacob pressed his lips together.

This man has no sense of humor.

Another item to add to the list. Having a sense of humor wasn't a requirement for Christmas spirit but it was definitely a benefit. She tried to imagine the Workshop without the laughter and shuddered. It would be like...well, like the Outside World. Suddenly she missed the Workshop. *Home for Christmas. Home for Christmas. I have to get home for Christmas.*

She picked up the package of steaks and walked to the stove. Jacob trailed behind her, stopping just to her right, monitoring every movement as she stacked the meat on the counter. His eyes followed her hand—like he was afraid she was going to grab one of the knives and suddenly turn on him. If he kept hovering over her, she might take up the suggestion.

She walked to the pantry. Jacob followed.

"Do you like rice?" she asked. It was yummy and filling, and she was pretty sure there were instructions on the box.

"Yes."

She leaned in to get a box of rice. Jacob leaned with her. She stepped back. Jacob did as well. When he followed her back to the stove, she pulled to a sharp stop and spun to face him.

"Did you want something?" she snapped. She had to cook dinner and she didn't need the added pressure of Jacob watching her every move. Best if he not see the product before it was completed.

A hint of red crept up his neck and he backed away. "Uh, no. I'll be in my office."

The door swung closed behind him and Marlie dropped her forehead against the microwave. Santa had sent the wrong elf. Jacob didn't need someone like her. He needed a cheerful, pleasant elf who never got annoyed. Someone like Teresa.

Marlie immediately struck down the idea. Jacob had looked ready to throttle the parking attendant. And her own attempts at Christmas cheer had caused his fingers to turn white on the steering wheel. No, Teresa was a bit too perky for Jacob.

Marlie's stomach rumbled reminding her that if she was hungry, Jacob had to be starving. She looked at the frozen lump of meat.

Santa *should* have sent an elf who could cook.

Chapter Three

&

Marlie collected the plate in front of Jacob. *He's a braver man than I thought*, she decided in amazement. The sandwich she'd eaten had been edible, but there was no way she was actually going to try her own cooking. He'd managed to eat some of the steak, leaving only the still frozen section in the middle and the burnt black edges. The rice was mainly gone, although it had turned out a little more brown than it was supposed to. *Who knew rice would burn that quickly?*

Jacob sat staring at the cleared tablecloth, his eyes focused on the pattern. *The man needs some laughter in his life.*

"So, do I just leave the dishes?" she asked, blinking her eyes innocently. "Will someone get them?"

"Marlie." Her name came out of his mouth as a sigh.

She snapped her fingers. "That's right. I do them. Never mind." When he looked up she winked and pushed open the kitchen door. The surprise in his eyes wasn't exactly humor but it was close. She had the funny feeling very few people teased Jacob Triumph.

As the sink filled with water, Marlie reviewed the progress she'd made during her first day.

Uh, none. She had to get moving on this Christmas spirit thing. *How long did it take to recover a failing spirit?*

She dunked her hands into the soapy water. The slippery suds teased the skin between her fingers as she scrubbed on the plates and the few pans she'd used to create the inedible dinner Jacob had consumed.

Focus. She should focus on one aspect of Christmas spirit at a time. If she worked on him from too many sides, he'd become overwhelmed and retreat farther into his shell.

Presents wouldn't work. From the look of the house, he could buy whatever he wanted. Decorations sometimes encouraged people to be in the spirit, but she'd heard his opinion on decorations.

She sighed. In the distance she heard the jingle of bells reminding her of Santa's sleigh harnesses.

Maybe she should just tell him she was an elf and that they could work together to fool Santa. *Great idea. Try fooling the man with the naughty and nice lists.*

As she scraped the burned-on rice from the pan she ran through the qualities of the Christmas spirit. *Joy, peace, sharing…sharing.* She lifted her eyes and stared out the window.

"It's perfect. It's an active thing," she said aloud. From her limited contact with him, Jacob seemed like the kind of person who needed a task, something physical. "I can teach him to share." She dipped a plate into the hot rinse water. But share what? Not money. She'd seen for herself how casually he gave money away. That wasn't sharing. That was buying someone off.

The kitchen door swung open. Jacob entered the room, filling it with his presence. The back of her neck tingled as if she could feel his gaze. She greeted him with a smile.

"Come to help?" she asked. That's it, she thought with a silent laugh. *I could teach him to share my chores.*

"The phone's for you."

"Me?" He held up a cordless telephone.

Marlie glanced down. Her arms were covered in soapsuds up to her elbows. "Could you…maybe…" She tilted her head to show him where to place the phone.

"What? Oh. Yes."

He put the receiver against her cheek and held it there with his hand.

"H-Hello?" Marlie asked.

"Marlie? Is that you?" The voice boomed from a distance. The North Pole if the truth were known.

"San—" She watched Jacob out of the corner of her eye. "Say, is that you, sir?"

"Yes, sorry the line is so bad. Don't have much need for the phone. Just wanted to make sure you got there all right and got situated in his house."

"Yes, yes, I did." The indescribable scent that she associated with Jacob tickled her nose and she took a deep breath, pulling it into her lungs. It seemed to fill her up and flood her body with comfort. The heat she'd experienced earlier returned as a slow pulse deep in her core. Unable to stop herself, she inched closer. Warmth radiated off of Jacob's body, overtaking the cold that seemed to forever lurk inside her.

"How's it going?" Santa asked.

He's asking for a progress report all ready? "Fine. We're moving along." Jacob sighed and shifted, resetting himself into an impatient position. "But, sir, I'm a little busy right now."

"Oh, don't want to impede progress. Good luck, Marlie. I assume I'll be seeing you Christmas Eve."

"I hope so, sir. Bye." She pulled way from the phone and smiled her thanks. "An old friend," she said by way of explanation.

He cleared his throat. "Are you almost finished? I can show you to your room."

She rinsed the final plate and put it in the dish drainer. "All done."

"There is a dishwasher you know," he said. He indicated the appliance under the counter next to the sink.

She shrugged. "I like washing dishes. It's soothing." As she said the words, she realized they were true. She smiled into his eyes, sharing with him her pleasure at the simple touch of her hands in soapy water. It was the first step. She had to show him how to share. Even sharing something so basic as happiness was a risk. It made you vulnerable. It opened you up to the rejection of your gift. She waited.

Almost visibly she could see him respond. A tiny smile started in his eyes. She shivered, waiting for the light to take hold. The infant stages of the smile drew her closer and the urge to touch him returned. Not thinking, she placed her hand on his breastbone...and instantly left five marks from the soap on her fingers.

The smile disappeared from his eyes, never making the journey to his mouth.

"Oops."

"I'll show you where you sleep," he announced. He turned and left the room, clearly expecting Marlie to follow.

She dropped the rag on the counter and sighed as she followed him out. *It's a start. He's in there.* She just needed to find a way to break through the icy barriers around his heart.

He led her down the hall to a small room at the back of the house. Pale lavender flowers decorated the bedspread with matching curtains covering the window and the deep pile carpet tickled the bottoms of her bare feet. Marlie walked into the room and dropped onto the bed. The springs bounced her up and around a few times. The mattress was soft and the room well decorated but, like the kitchen, there was an impersonal coldness about it that Marlie found uncomfortable.

"Where do you sleep?" she asked, swinging her feet off the end of the bed. Jacob's eyes widened. She watched the muscles in his neck convulsively swallow. *What have I done now?*

"Upstairs."

"Can I see?"

"Why?"

"Shouldn't I know where you sleep?" she asked.

Marlie couldn't really blame him for his hesitancy. She hadn't behaved in the most normal, *human* manner today. She was kind of surprised he'd let her into the house at all.

"If I'm going to clean in there, I should know where it is."

That seemed to help Jacob make up his mind. Silently he led her upstairs. He tapped one door. "Bedroom." He tapped the door across the hall. "Bedroom." He pointed to the door at the end of the hall. "Master bedroom."

Marlie stepped past him and opened the indicated door. His chest expanded as his shoulders pulled back, like a cat protecting its territory. She stopped in the doorway but still peeked inside.

The largest bed Marlie had ever seen dominated the room. The black and brown bedcovers were perfectly trimmed at the corners. *Three or four elves could sleep in this bed.*

"You sleep here by yourself?"

A choked cough slipped from Jacob's throat. Marlie looked at him to make sure the dinner she'd cooked wasn't poisoning his system, but he stopped with the one gasp.

His forehead crinkled into a series of tight lines as his eyebrows squeezed together. "Most of the time, yes."

The light bulb lit up above Marlie's head. Of course. This was it. This was the perfect opportunity to teach him to share.

It didn't take long for Marlie to decide who he would share the bed with.

"Don't worry. I'll sleep with you."

"Pardon me?" The words burst from deep inside Jacob.

"I'll sleep with you. I mean, with a bed that big, we could hold a party and invite the neighbors. Besides, no one likes to do it alone. It's so much nicer with someone else. I'll go get my stuff."

She'd made it to the top of the stairs before his voice stopped her.

"You're assuming a lot. What if I don't want to sleep with you?"

"Don't you?"

"Well, that's beside the point."

She smiled sympathetically. "Don't worry. You'll love it by the time it's over. I'll be back in a minute," she promised and raced down the stairs.

Jacob sputtered a few incoherent protests but Marlie kept walking. Learning to share was not an easy thing to do—not for a grown-up—but after a few nights of sleeping together, he'd get used to it.

The thought of sleeping beside Jacob sent a flurry of warm tingles through her body. She'd never liked the cold. She'd been the only elf at the North Pole who'd gotten an electric blanket for Christmas. And even without cuddling up to him, she was sure his natural body heat would warm the bed.

In the room Jacob had shown her downstairs, the suitcase she'd packed at the North Pole had mysteriously appeared on the foot of the bed.

She unpacked her nightshirt as she thought about Jacob.

He wasn't pleased with the idea of sharing his bed but that was just fear, she was sure. She had to show him that it wasn't bad, that sharing didn't make him weak, but if he kicked her out, she'd never get the chance. Well, she'd just have to give him a little nudge.

She closed her eyes, squeezing them tight and gathering the magical power into her heart. "I wish that Jacob will share his bed with me." The wisps of magic slipped from inside her and floated out into the cosmos. There she'd done it. It probably wasn't the best use of her power but she had to start somewhere.

When Santa called again, at least she would have progress to report. Hopefully by then she'd have taught Jacob to share. Another delicate flush of warmth bubbled up from inside her as she pulled the nightshirt over her head and she smiled as she remembered the warmth of Jacob's hand in hers. Somehow, she knew her toes wouldn't be cold tonight.

Jacob watched his temporary housekeeper hurry down the hall. She was going to come back upstairs and sleep with him. Knowing no one else was in the house, so no one would see, he pinched himself on the arm. It hurt and he hadn't startled himself out of any deep sleep. That meant this wasn't a dream.

She wanted to sleep with him. Sheer strength of will had kept her from intruding on his thoughts as he'd worked before dinner. It had given him time to control the physical responses to her mere presence. Now the thought of Marlie in his bed re-ignited the fires he'd spent the evening extinguishing. He groaned and dropped his forehead against the doorframe.

I don't need this right now. It's Christmas, the Henderson's buyout is looming and now Marlie.

No, it isn't Marlie, he corrected himself. He straightened his shoulders and walked into his room. *It's sex in general. It's just been too long since you've bothered.* The trials and traditions surrounding the actual deed seemed less and less worth the effort as he got older.

Maybe I should get married. The idea held some merit. Then when he wanted sex he'd only have to roll over and tap someone on the shoulder. Natalie was certainly in support of the idea. Marriage, that is. Not necessarily sex. She'd started dropping hints a few months ago that she'd like their relationship to take on a more permanent feel. Jacob winced. It just didn't seem like a good idea.

She was the perfect corporate wife—elegant and strong in the boardroom but cool and controlled in the bedroom.

Around her it was easy to suppress the urges to make sex a little more interesting.

Jacob sat down on the edge of the bed. The image of Marlie draping herself over Mrs. Butterstone's mattress and the way her tight breasts had swayed gently beneath her T-shirt—fuck, he was getting hard again. Still. In the eight or so hours since Marlie had come into his office, he'd somehow lost control—of his body, his home, his life.

He fell back against the mattress. There was something about her that wasn't quite right, not normal. Maybe it was the wide-eyed innocence that seemed so real, but no one got to her age without some experience. Some shattering of their dreams. Jacob draped his forearm across his eyes. Innocent but seductive. It was a wicked combination that stronger men than he had succumbed to.

It wouldn't be disloyal to Natalie to sleep with Marlie. We don't have any sort of formal agreement. Jacob stared up at the white ceiling. Where had that come from? What was he thinking? Was he actually considering it? Hell, it was hard not to consider it. She was cute and sexy and damn, she wanted to fuck him.

He looked over at his pillows. She was right. It was a big bed. More than enough space for both of them—no matter how they rolled around. He smiled thinking about the torn up blankets in the morning. He couldn't remember the last time he'd burned up the sheets with a woman.

He groaned and closed his eyes. No matter whether he wanted it or not, it couldn't happen. There was too much risk. Not only was she an employee but there was the added factor that once he had her in bed he wasn't completely sure he could resist tying her up and fucking her long and hard, making her plead for her orgasm. That taut lithe body stretched long, nipples tight and swollen from his mouth, pussy wet and squeezing him as he plunged into her.

He groaned and tried to push the images aside. Too much temptation. When Marlie came upstairs, he'd just send her back to her own room. Reclaim his life. If she wanted to seduce someone, she could find someone besides him.

But you know… Jacob tried to stop the little voice inside his head. It was the voice that always got him into trouble. The one that had convinced him when he was twelve that super-gluing the teacher to her chair would be funny. The one that told him in high school he was suave enough to date the Prom Queen. He tried to block it from his mind.

If you slept with Marlie, you'd work off the sexual tension you're feeling. You'd be more relaxed. Get more work done.

"You're still dressed," her slightly accusing voice interrupted his internal debate.

Jacob took a deep breath and released it slowly. He pushed himself into a sitting position, ready to begin a logical explanation of why they couldn't, shouldn't sleep together. He hoped this logical explanation created itself soon.

Digging deep inside for the strength to send her away, he braced himself and looked at her. *If she's trying to seduce me, she could have worn something more appropriate.* She stood with a stuffed bear clutched firmly in the crook of her elbow and a perturbed look on her face. The oversized T-shirt she wore was decorated with painted-on Christmas lights and the words I Love Christmas Nights. Her legs were bare — strong and sleek. His eyes trailed down her legs, enjoying a few fantasies about her thighs — spread, wrapped around his hips. Even her calves were attractive, and her feet…

Her feet? Her feet were covered by bright red slippers that curled up at the toes, forming tiny loops.

"What's with the funny shoes?" It took him a moment to realize he'd said the words out loud.

Marlie pulled up to her full height. When the edges of her lips tightened, Jacob realized he'd offended her.

"They're very comfortable and they keep my feet warm." She stepped to the edge of the bed, seemingly prepared to climb right over him. Jacob rolled out her way, and stood, his eyes instantly drawn to her backside as she crawled over the top of the blankets to the far side.

Her nightshirt rode up above her thighs as she moved, revealing her sweet, rounded ass. A thin strip of material cupped the curvy mounds but did little to cover them.

Thoughts of protest and that clever logical answer he'd been thinking up disappeared. What would be so wrong with a little—

She looked up at him with unblinking eyes as she leaned against the headboard and lifted the top blanket, slipping her feet under the covers.

"Do I have to cook breakfast for you?"

"No," he answered absently but the reminder of her cooking brought him back to the present. "You can't stay here." *Let her stay. She looks good in your bed. She'd look even better bent over the end of it. Let her stay.* He willed the nagging voice to shut up and watched Marlie situate herself.

She stopped in the process of adjusting the covers and looked up at him with those eyes. Seemingly innocent eyes that held a hint of steel. She was in his bed and it would take a crowbar to get her out before she got what she wanted. *Let her stay.*

"Why not?"

"Because it's my bed and you can't stay in my bed." He had to fight to get the words out, like some invisible force was holding them in.

"There's no reason to be selfish. There's more than enough room. I don't take up that much space."

As if to solidify her position, Marlie wiggled on her butt, scooting farther down on the mattress. The oversized shirt revealed just the barest hint of a tight nipple grazing the underside. She laid the teddy bear next to her and smiled at Jacob.

The teddy bear, the nightshirt. The reality of it finally hit him.

"You really mean 'just sleep' don't you?"

"Of course." Marlie's face showed her confusion. He felt some satisfaction in that. He'd been racked with confusion all day. "What did you think I meant?"

"Nothing." Jacob stared at the wall and hoped she never figured it out. At least he didn't have to find a gentle way to reject her, he thought mocking his own arrogance.

But that didn't correct the problem. She was still in his bed.

"Listen, if you want to sleep here that badly, fine. You take my room, I'll go sleep in the guestroom." Problem solved. He turned to leave.

"But that won't work. I don't want you to *give* me your bed. I want you to *share* it with me. That's sort of the whole point." The disappointment on her face wrenched at his heart and he could have sworn tears were forming in her eyes.

Jacob walked to the side of the bed and sat down. In a gentle voice, he tried to explain. "Marlie, it just isn't right for us to sleep together." *Let her stay. Crawl in beside her.* The voice barely even sounded like his.

"Of course it is. I know how to share," she insisted. "And I won't take up too much space. See?" She held her arms to the side as if to show how much space she wasn't taking up. *What is the big deal anyway? We're both adults. And it's just for one night.*

Let her stay. Share your bed with her. A foreign sensation he couldn't explain seeped into his chest.

"Fine," he said with a resigned sigh, he would figure out what to do with her tomorrow.

Marlie's smiling eyes glowed with happiness and seemed to cause the area around his heart to ache. Before he could say anything that reflected the strange sensations, he headed for the master bath.

Man, you are losing it. What have you gotten yourself into?

And worse, what am I going to wear to bed? He normally slept in his shorts or nothing at all. On the way to the bathroom, he grabbed a pair of gym shorts and a T-shirt from the dresser.

It took him only moments to get ready but he stalled, not wanting to return too soon. Hot blood coursed loudly through his veins, settling in heavy doses in his cock. Being away from her wasn't helping. The pictures were too clear in his mind — naked bodies rocking his headboard against the wall, her ass as he plunged deep into her cunt.

Nerves rumbled through his stomach like rabid butterflies. He felt like a virgin bride on her wedding night, hiding out until the eager groom could wait no longer. *All she wants to do is sleep.*

Damn. He couldn't remember the last time he'd slept with a woman. He'd had sex with Natalie three, no, four weeks ago but he hadn't stayed. He never stayed. The last time he'd *slept* with a woman was…probably college before he'd learned the benefits of a well-timed early exit.

And he'd never slept with a woman without having sex with her first. He didn't like having someone else in his bed. It was too confining. He had to worry about running into them, or snoring too loud, or God forbid, throwing the covers on the floor if he got too hot.

There were three other bedrooms in this house and a pull-out sofa in his office. She could just find somewhere else to sleep.

With that resolve in mind, he opened the door. The bedroom lights were off but he could see her form curled up on the far side of the bed, her head nestled between the pillow and her stuffed bear. Her eyes were closed and her breathing even.

Perfect. He'd just slip out and she'd never be the wiser. He started toward the door.

"Where are you going?" she asked in a sleep-laced voice that found its way around his cock, caressing it like tiny fingers. She groaned softly and rolled over, pulling back the blankets on his side. "Come to bed, Jacob," she said. He fought it but his body seemed unable to resist her command.

She smiled at him as he slipped under the blankets and his heart did a slow roll.

"Good night, Jacob. I'm so glad I'm here." Her words drifted away as she sank into sleep.

Me, too. He kept the sentiment silent, not sure where it had come from. She'd been nothing but trouble since she'd arrived. And how the hell he'd ended up with her in his bed — and neither of them naked — he didn't understand. Marlie was a strangely powerful force.

Well, tomorrow, he would just lay down the law. It was his house and things would be done a certain way.

The edges of Marlie's mouth curled upward as if whatever she found in sleep was pleasurable. In the dark he found himself smiling back. He lifted his hand and brushed the backs of his fingers across the silk of her hair. *Beautiful.*

Jacob slowly brought his hand away. *Now's your chance to escape.* The wise inner voice was distant, drowned out by the steady beat of his own heart. His breath joined the rhythm of hers.

He'd leave, he promised himself. In just a few minutes.

* * * * *

Marlie snuggled into the warm, solid teddy bear that held her safe. She smiled and rubbed her cheek against the soft material of his T-shirt. *Teddy bears don't wear T-shirts.* Her eyes popped open.

All she could see was white. White cotton. Well, she knew where she was. Pressed against Jacob's chest. *Drat.* It had been a habit the other elves had found extremely annoying — her tendency to cuddle. She'd been moved into her own room at a very early age because no matter what elf she slept beside, she ended up snuggled tight up against that elf by morning. Elves by nature weren't big on physical contact.

It had been years since she'd shared a bed with anyone else and she obviously hadn't outgrown the tendency.

She lifted her head and looked around, trying to figure out how close she was and how she could extricate herself without waking him. Well, she couldn't get much closer. She was fully draped across his chest, her breasts pressing against him. She looked down. One of her legs was lying between his, a hard lump pushing against her thigh.

His arm was wrapped around her back, holding her to his body but she knew it wasn't intentional. He was still asleep. If he woke up, while she was so entwined with him, he would be annoyed.

It was convincing herself to actually move that was the challenge. He was warm and smelled delicious. The heat flowing from his skin poured into her. Her whole body hummed with the powerful sensation, from her ears to her toes—especially that place between her legs. It made no sense. She'd never felt any sort of heat there before but now...she wiggled her hips just a little. A wicked sparkle fluttered inside her. She gasped.

Was this some kind of magic she didn't know about? She moved again, pressing down on the leg that seemed firmly lodged between hers. A giggle threatened as she repeated the motion. It was just too delicious.

Jacob moaned from deep in his sleep. Marlie froze even as his hand tightened on her backside. Best to get away now. Somehow she didn't think he would be pleased to find her rubbing herself against him. It had been a fight to get him to allow her to stay. He'd almost managed to throw off her wish-magic last night so she couldn't imagine his reaction if he woke and found her practically on top of him.

Using that resolve, she ignored the interesting flutters between her legs and cautiously twitched her fingertips, trying to figure out where her hands were without actually moving them. One hand tickled her own stomach. That was good. The other rested flat against a broad expanse of skin. She wiggled her fingers. She felt nothing.

Okay, that meant it wasn't her skin. She peeked over the side and saw her hand beneath Jacob's T-shirt, wrapped around his waist. She took a deep breath preparing to move. The tips of her breasts rubbed against him sending new, different shivers into her body. Much like the ones between her legs but lighter. This was definitely something she needed to investigate.

Later. Now she had to get away. She pulled her hand back, unable to resist trailing her fingertips across his skin. The ripple of muscles tempted her to further exploration but she refrained.

But as she tried to move, Jacob's hand held her, keeping her pressed to his side. Using the hand on his stomach, she pushed back, trying to lever herself away. Two inches separated their bodies when Jacob's arm closed tightly around her, pulling her against his chest. The slowly increasing beat of his heart was just below her ear. His nose nuzzled her hair and Marlie thought she'd die of pleasure—but there was no time to enjoy it.

A low groan slipped from his lips as he rolled toward her, trapping Marlie underneath him, his lips pressing against her throat. His legs slipped between hers and a hot, hard ridge matched up to the V between her thighs. Marlie held her breath waiting as he began to move against her, slow, easy pulses. *Ooh, there it is again.* The sensation was just too delicious to resist and she spread her legs and pushed her hips up against his, trying to find that same spot. She gasped as their bodies met just right. Jacob grabbed her backside and held her in position as he moved on her. With each thrust, he firmly massaged the sensitive place, sending waves of the delightful shivers through her core.

Marlie moaned, liking the sound and his weight and the building pressure. She wanted more. He grazed his teeth along her throat, more of a tickle than a bite and Marlie couldn't help but laugh. It felt so good. Jacob lifted his head, his sleepy eyes drifting open. A lazy smile curved his lips. She smiled back.

His hand on her ass squeezed and he rocked her against the growing bulge, guiding her movements as if he knew what she was feeling.

"Oooh, Jacob, right there. That's it."

First his smile widened. Then his eyes popped open and he stared down at her. "What the hell?" he demanded. "What are you doing?"

All the pleasure drained from her body. She'd known he wouldn't like to have her curled around him when he woke but she hadn't expected the anger. She opened her mouth to apologize but her lips were dry and the words wouldn't come.

Tears burnt the back side of her eyes. She pushed on his shoulder and he rolled away easily—releasing her like she was made of fire. Marlie lunged to her feet and leapt for the floor and the door. "I'm sorry," she managed to mutter as she escaped.

She ran downstairs, not stopping until she was locked in the coldly neat room he'd assigned her last night.

This was not working out as she'd planned. She sank down on the edge of the bed.

Drat. All she'd wanted was to encourage him to share.

She'd probably put him off sharing forever. What man would want to share his bed with a woman who rubbed herself all over him?

Chapter Four

🔊

Jacob stared at Marlie's fleeing form, his sleep-fogged, sex-starved brain trying to absorb what just happened. He'd woken up, on top of Marlie, his cock between her legs. He groaned and closed his eyes. The heat of her pussy still clung to his shaft. The feminine scent of her hair, the taste of her skin, the feel of her nails gripping his back—it hovered around him like a cloud of sensation.

What the hell had happened? Last thing he remembered, he was planning to climb out of bed once he was sure she was asleep. The next thing he knew he was about to push inside her.

Fuck. He hadn't meant to yell at her. It wasn't her fault his dreams had been filled with doing precisely what he'd been on the verge of doing. The images were vague but they all included Marlie and him, locked in some kind of embrace—him on top, her on top, front to back. Whatever. Didn't matter.

Fuck. That's what he needed. He just needed to fuck someone. Then he could concentrate. That way tonight when they went to bed—

He sat up. No, this was not happening again. Marlie had a perfectly good bed downstairs. She would be sleeping in it tonight.

The words sounded so firm in his head but then so had his resolve last night and look where he'd ended up—between her thighs, two thin layers from paradise.

Groaning he rolled out of bed and went to the bathroom. The mirror wasn't kind to him this morning. He looked tired. Hell, he was tired. He'd been so busy in his dreams he didn't feel like he'd gotten any sleep.

He stripped and got in the shower, letting the hot water run over him. The idea of turning the tap to cold was considered and rejected. It might work but hot dreams like the ones he'd faced last night, followed by a brief taste of the reality, needed more than just a cold shower. Propping one hand against the wall, he reached down and cupped his cock in his palm. A few quick strokes was all it would take but he couldn't bring himself to do it. He wanted to feel it, to imagine another touch. Marlie.

He closed his eyes and let the fantasy form in his head. Marlie standing beside him, those tight nipples bared and brushing against his chest as she watched him. Her eyes twinkled with sensual promise as her hand curled around his shaft. Light and delicate—she traced her fingers over his skin—the same way she'd stroked his car, exploring his cock before taking it in both hands. Her almost dainty touch tightened as she moved slow strokes, up and down. Hot lavish kisses whispered across his chest sending more heat to his cock.

"Jacob, you feel so good," she whispered, that sexy voice adding power to her touch.

"That's it, baby. Squeeze just a little harder." The grip tightened and he pushed against it, hard, a little deeper.

"Yes, come for me. Let me feel it."

The rhythm increased and he moved with it, pumping his hips, thrusting into the tight grip, wishing it was her pussy he was filling. The tight ass she'd bared last night would fit perfectly against him as he bent her over the end of his bed. He'd fill her and ride her hard, fast. All that vibrant energy directed at him.

He punched his hips forward and bit back the cry as he came, the picture before him shattering. He leaned against the shower wall—his heart pounding in his ears, his lungs almost bursting. Needing a few calming breaths before he could function, he waited until his pulse had slowed and then finished his shower. With that out of the way, he should have no problem making it through the day.

Unfortunately, though his cock was relaxed, the ache remained. Waking up with an armful of warm woman wasn't how he wanted to start his day—not unless he could do something about it. Tomorrow morning he was waking up alone and that meant going to bed alone.

Whatever else happened, Marlie was not sharing his bed again.

* * * * *

Marlie heard Jacob's footfalls on the stairs and wrapped the towel tight around her breasts. She tucked the end in and ran into the entryway to meet him. Their bodies collided with a heavy thump. Jacob reacted first, grabbing her and managing to keep them both upright. As soon as they were both stable on their feet, he released her and stepped away. She opened her mouth to speak but the strange glint in his eyes stopped her. His scrutiny started at her feet and went up, pausing at the lower edge of her towel and continuing higher until his gaze finally met hers. The light in his eyes was blazing with some emotion she didn't quite recognize. She reached out to see if Jacob was maybe running a fever but as she moved closer, he backed up—like she'd waved a snake at him.

I've frightened him. Drat. She hadn't meant to tackle him at the bottom of the stairs but she needed to apologize before he left for work. The day would be pure torture with this on her conscience.

"Jacob, I—"

He held up his hand to stop her. "Marlie, I need to apologize."

She blinked and tilted her head. "You?"

"I didn't mean to yell at you this morning. It certainly wasn't your fault that we ended up…well, that we ended up in the position that we did. I wasn't angry at you. I was just surprised. So, I apologize for yelling at you."

He was apologizing? But it was her fault.

"But Jacob—"

"And of course, for putting you in that position."

Marlie wanted to correct him. She hadn't really minded the position. It had been quite intriguing but it seemed to distress him terribly.

"I assure you it won't happen again." *Drat.* "I need to get to work. Mrs. Butterstone's keys to the house and the car should be on the hook in the kitchen. Call my secretary if you need anything."

"But—" Before she could start again, he was gone. The door closed behind him and Marlie was left alone.

See, this proves Jacob is a kind man. He took the blame even though it was my fault.

She shook her head and walked back to her room. She would have to explain tonight. It wasn't fair that he should think it his fault. Any elf she'd ever slept with would tell him the same thing. She cuddled up to the nearest warm body. She felt the distinct urge to fan her face. Jacob's had certainly been plenty warm. It took a moment for her to brush that memory aside but finally she was able to finish getting ready.

After eating breakfast, she wandered around the house, not sure what to do. She was officially the housekeeper but how dirty was a house going to get in one day?

She had to figure out her next plan of attack. Jacob had reluctantly shared his bed last night. She'd keep working on that. Surely he would be willing if she promised not to end up on top of him again. She wasn't quite sure how she would fulfill that promise but she vowed to try.

But there had to be something else, another aspect of Christmas to work on.

She looked at the bare walls.

Decorations. Perfect. She would decorate and bring the spirit of Christmas into Jacob's home. The image of Jacob's glaring at Terry's snow globe dampened Marlie's spirits for a moment. He didn't like decorations. But surely he wouldn't mind if she bought a few, simple decorations.

Triumph's had a wonderful Christmas display. She'd go there and buy what she needed and maybe she'd have a chance to apologize for this morning.

* * * * *

Marlie tapped her foot and stared at the bubbling pot of spaghetti sauce—her attention unevenly divided between dinner and Jacob. She hadn't seen him all day. He'd been too busy to see her today when she'd stopped by the store—at least that's the message Terry had sympathetically passed along. How was she supposed to inspire a sense of Christmas in him if she never saw him?

When he'd arrived home thirty minutes ago, she'd tried once again to apologize for her behavior this morning, for waking up on top of him but he'd just brushed her aside, gruffly asking when dinner would be ready before he'd barricaded himself in his room. She'd heard the shower running but that had gone silent moments ago. He would be coming downstairs in just a little bit expecting dinner and no doubt an explanation.

She stirred the sauce absently. She didn't want to spoil his dinner...any more than her cooking already would. Apologizing now was probably best. It would only take a second and then they could sit down and enjoy a nice meal.

Big bubbles burst inside the sauce. Well, hopefully an edible meal. It was hard to go wrong with sauce out of jaw.

She cranked up the burner under the water and turned down the heat underneath the sauce.

Spaghetti sauce covered her apron so she pulled it off before she headed upstairs.

It wasn't that she was sneaking exactly—though she did take care not to make any noise on the steps. It was just that if he heard her, he might find another excuse to avoid her and she really needed to get this off her chest. It had been a cloud on her day.

Quietly, she pushed the door open to his room. The breath locked in her throat. He stood with his back to her while he picked up his watch and wrapped it around his wrist.

He was naked. All six feet of him. Naked except for that watch.

His bare back, the etched muscles of his shoulders, the curved, firm cheeks of his backside...her palms heated. She'd never seen any thing more beautiful. But she wanted to do more than look. She wanted to touch, feel those strong muscles move beneath her hands.

She'd seen naked elves before, naturally, but they looked nothing like him—all tight lines and interesting angles. The suit he'd worn yesterday had done a better job than she'd first thought at hiding his form. It was lovely. A work of art. Like a well-made cast-iron train.

Her breasts felt heavy as she imagined playing with Jacob on Christmas morning beneath the tree. She could spend hours on him. The heat between her legs returned in a rush, more of the delicious warmth from this morning. The only problem was it left behind an almost painful ache that had been extremely annoying for much of the day.

Lost in the strange workings of her body and her fascination with his, she walked across the room. The lines of his back were too intriguing to be ignored. She stretched out her hand and traced two fingers along the curve of his shoulder, following the muscle down his arm, skipping over and skimming across his lower back. He straightened but didn't pull away. The heat from his body transferred to hers and thought she would melt inside. Fire spun through her center and spread into her chest, making her breasts tight and tingly.

She trailed one finger up the center of his spine, realizing her hands weren't sensitive enough. If she traced those same lines with her tongue...

Taste him. The idea was more tempting than any Christmas sweet.

Slowly he turned and the sleek lines of his back were replaced by the bold curves of his chest. Her tongue peeked out and skimmed across her upper lip imagining the flavor and texture. She swooped her middle finger down the center of his chest, following the delicious muscles down to the ridges of along his stomach.

"Marlie, are you —"

Marlie didn't hear his question. She was too fascinated, enraptured. Touching him was better than she'd imagined. And it created the most delightful sparkles inside her. She spread her fingers wide across his stomach, feeling the muscles ripple beneath her touch.

She licked her lips imagining the feel of her tongue exploring the dents and curves, learning each muscle inch by inch. He held still as she stroked him, letting her eyes lead the way down his —

She jumped back. What was that? That strange thing between his legs. She snatched her hand back. It had moved — like it was alive. What was it? *She* didn't have one. She tried to recall if the male elves had them but couldn't remember. What could possibly be the purpose for it? It was odd looking but strangely intriguing. Flat against her stomach, her fingers twitched with the urge to touch it. Stroke it and test its weight. Its heat.

Jacob watched Marlie and couldn't decide if she was impressed or disappointed by his cock. What he lacked in extra length, he made up for in width. Well, he wasn't going to stand there and be judged like the latest piece of meat. He grabbed the edge of the blanket and pulled it over and around his hips.

"Perhaps you should wait downstairs," he said. Damn, he sounded prissy.

Marlie blinked and looked up, finally pulling her gaze away from his crotch.

"What?"

"I'll see you downstairs."

Bare emotion transitioned across her face—disappointment, confusion, interest. He couldn't tell which won but he watched her eyes dip down, as if she wanted another peek. If she didn't leave soon, she was going to get it. Between her blatant inspection, the light caress of her fingers, and her breasts pressing against tonight's T-shirt, his cock was on the rise.

If she stayed around, she'd get more than she'd expected...not that he knew what she expected.

"Oh, okay." She turned away, making it to the door before she looked back. Again her gaze fell below his waist. Her lips squished together as if she was considering a weighty matter. After a lingering glance, she sighed and walked away.

Jacob released the breath he just realized he'd been holding. She was driving him crazy. Less than thirty-six hours after her arrival and he was no longer the sane, rational man he'd always been.

She wasn't like any woman he'd ever met. Any other woman would have either backed out of the room when she'd seen him naked or perhaps attempted to seduce him, making some joking remark about his bare ass. Instead, she'd looked at him like she'd never seen a penis before.

And then there was her mouth. The way she'd licked her lips like he was a midnight snack. It had taken considerable effort to resist grabbing her and teaching that mouth to do some real damage.

He forced air into his lungs and willed calming thoughts to his groin. Mrs. Butterstone would be gone for another three weeks at least. He'd never make it. He'd be a quivering mass of hormones by then—and the morning hand jobs weren't going to do it for him.

If it had just been a calm, normal desire for sex, he could have handled it but this was something completely different. Something from his distant past that reminded him what a pleasure it had been to have a woman on her knees, hands bound behind her back as she sucked his cock. He'd left that part of his life behind but something about Marlie brought the desires back.

He dragged on jeans and a shirt, leaving the front untucked to mask his erection—not that she could have missed it.

Through his drive home and his shower, he'd planned what he would say to her. It was time she understood the expectations for the job. It was a conversation he had with all new employees. He should have done it when she'd arrived but fantasies about seeing her naked had taken priority. Now, he had to do it. Tell her what had to happen so he could live the next three weeks in calm, restful sanity.

He didn't have the specifics laid out but the high points were she had to cook decent meals and sleep in her own bed. And she had to wear a bra. That was fast becoming a condition of her employment.

If she didn't do these things, he would have no choice but to fire her.

The thought made his stomach queasier than last night's dinner. Firing Marlie would be like kicking the Easter Bunny.

His reluctance was a revelation as well. He stared at himself in the mirror. He fired people all the time. It was business. There wasn't room in business for personal sentiment. So if Marlie couldn't cut it, she would have to go.

He nodded in the mirror and...realized he'd been giving himself a pep talk.

She's driving me crazy.

Clinging to the final hope for his sanity, he went downstairs, calling to Marlie that he wanted to speak to her.

"I'll be out in a bit!"

No. He needed to talk to her now before something else distracted him—like maybe he'd come upon *her* naked. Naked and spread-eagle on his bed with silk ties holding her bound.

He paused at the bottom of the stairs and almost choked. The erotic fantasy evaporated, replaced by the biggest Christmas tree he'd ever seen—sitting in his living room. Undecorated but huge and real if the pine scent was any indication. When he'd stalked into the house, he hadn't looked around, too afraid that he might see another half-naked Marlie. That memory of her in a towel had haunted his day.

And now this.

She'd brought a tree into his house. He stepped into the living room and saw bags and boxes stacked on every available surface. Silver glitter and red balls sprung from every opening. At least two dozen boxes of Christmas lights sat on the coffee table.

A few simple tasteful decorations. That's all he was willing to accept and those only because tradition demanded it. He was not having his house lit up like…like…like Santa's Workshop.

"Marlie!"

He didn't wait to see if he'd been heard or if she was running to answer his summons. He spun around and stalked toward the kitchen, smacking the door open with the palm of his hand. "What is all that crap in my living room? I thought I—" The sight before him killed the words in his throat.

It looked like his kitchen was bleeding. Red dripped from everywhere. The countertops, the stove, the windowsill. Marlie.

"I said I would be out in a bit." She waved her hand. "Stay back, it's—"

The pot on the stove erupted and splattered red sauce on what little white space remained.

"Ahh. Drat." Marlie snatched her hand back, cradling it against her arm.

Jacob moved forward, grabbing the pot and shoving it off the burner before turning off the power.

"What happened?"

"It exploded."

"I can see that."

"Then why did you ask?" she snapped. A clump of sauce fell from her hair and landed with a splat on the floor. Her fingers curled slowly into tight fists at her side. "Don't worry," she said though her teeth were clenched together. "I'll get this cleaned up."

"I'll help."

"No! I'll do it. I just want to be alone for a moment."

"But—"

"Please. Go sit in the dining room, I'll bring your dinner in a few minutes."

He opened his mouth, ready to protest, or comfort or something but the firm line of her jaw warned him to walk away. He backed out of the kitchen and went into the dining room, sitting at the table as commanded.

Pans clanked and crashed followed by low growls, which he assumed was Marlie swearing. Listening to her banging around, he turned his attention back to the piles of Christmas decorations waiting to be hung—even that painful thought was better than thinking about the red sauce dripping from his kitchen ceiling. She would destroy his house—if not by spaghetti sauce then with those decorations. He couldn't let her put all that crap on his walls. And based on her performance tonight with dinner, he couldn't let her feed his guests tomorrow night. Poisoning the Board of Directors didn't seem like a good idea right before Christmas. And not right before he wanted their support to buy out Henderson's stores.

"Here." He jumped. Lost in his own thoughts, he hadn't heard her come in. His eyes tracked to Marlie's face—still splattered with sauce—before realizing she held out a plate, piled high with sandwiches. Edible-looking sandwiches. She placed the platter on the table. "Something went wrong with the sauce," she said with a tired shrug. She set a plate in front of him before dropping a bag of potato chips on the table. "One kitchen disaster a day is enough." She picked up one of the sandwiches and placed it on his plate.

"Marlie, we need to talk."

She nodded grimly as if she knew what was coming. "Let me go change. I'll be back." She snagged a sandwich and disappeared into her rooms.

Jacob bit into the sandwich and groaned. The fresh bread surrounding a pile of turkey and, if he guessed right, provolone cheese, cleared any thought of business from his mind. He sighed and reveled in the taste of the simple meal. Deciding he could live on sandwiches for the rest of his life, he took another big bite.

He was almost done when she returned looking damp and flushed. Her hair hung around her shoulders curling into mismatched ringlets. Moisture clung to her neck and it was all he could do not to pull her into his arms and lick it off. The only thing that stopped him was the memory of his living room.

With a sigh, she sat down beside him.

She twisted her fingers together looking remarkably humble for the woman who'd bullied her way into his bed last night.

"I would like to apologize."

"If you'd asked me first, you wouldn't have to apologize."

She straightened and a strange light glowed in her eyes. "You mean if I'd asked permission ahead of time, you wouldn't have been upset?"

"Of course not," he said feeling quite generous. All things in moderation, including Christmas decorations. "I understand there's a place for that…stuff, but we need to keep it subtle."

Her lips squished together. "I'm not sure I can do that. I mean it's fine in theory but it's a problem I've had for years."

"Like a compulsion?" A compulsive Christmas decorator?

"More like an unconscious act, so while I can't guarantee it will work, I'll do my best to stay on my side."

"Your side?" He wondered if he'd missed something and she'd divided up his house.

"Of the bed. Like I said, it's an unconscious thing. I fall asleep where I am but every morning wake up cuddled up to the warmest body near to me." She shrugged. "And this morning that was you."

He finally clicked in to what she was talking about. Wait. Just how many strange men had she cuddled up to? He knew he couldn't ask that question—it wasn't any of his business—but he was curious. Instead he said, "You were planning on sleeping with me again tonight?"

"Well, of course." She laughed. "That's what sharing's all about. I'm so glad you're not upset about this morning." She placed her fingers on his wrist and stroked lightly. It was an unconscious caress that made him think about the same delicate touch on his cock. "I have to say, I was very comfortable when I woke up. You're nice and warm."

He'd felt warm when he'd woken up. Hell, he'd been on fire. Jacob looked at Marlie as she nibbled on another sandwich. She seemed oblivious to the sexual undercurrents between them.

"So, after dinner, shall we start decorating?"

Decorating. That's right, he was going to talk to her about the decorations.

"Yes, Marlie about those decorations—"

"Aren't they wonderful?"

"—and that tree."

"It took me forever to get it home but I managed. Now between the two of us, we can get everything put up."

"No, Marlie we aren't putting anything up."

"But I thought we could—"

"I won't have all those decorations in my house."

The edges of her eyes tightened and the sweet innocent thing she'd appeared to be half the time was gone. Drilling her gaze into him, she leaned forward. "We're having guests here tomorrow night, for a traditional Christmas dinner, right?" Jacob forced his eyes to stay trained on her face, and not drift to her breasts, pushed together by her elbows. He nodded. "We can't have a naked house." *Naked. Wrong word to use.* His body tightened in response. Marlie continued, blind to the torture Jacob was in. He took a few shallow breaths and tried to follow her conversation. "Don't you think our guests will think it's odd if we don't have some decorations?"

"Yes," he finally agreed grudgingly.

Marlie worked to hide her smile. She should have hidden the decorations. They looked a bit overwhelming all stacked together. And she had to admit she went a little overboard. Her idea to buy a few simple decorations had gone out the window when she'd seen all the beautiful choices and then when the store assistant had said Marlie could charge her purchases to Jacob's account…well, she'd overbought just a little.

"Don't worry. It will look lovely," she assured him. "I'm an expert at Christmas decorations." Well, that wasn't exactly true but she'd seen enough elves do it to know what worked.

He held up his hand and shook his head, clearly washing his hands of the situation.

"Fine. Do whatever you want."

He pushed the last bite of his sandwich into his mouth and chewed sullenly.

His glare almost made her laugh. It was a look she'd no doubt flashed at Teresa on more than one occasion. But strangely since coming here, she'd been more cheerful. The thought of decorations or even the dreaded Christmas songs no longer made her wince. She was actually looking forward to decorating. It would be especially fun if Jacob would join her but somehow she didn't think pleading to his joy for Christmas was going to sway him.

"Want to help?"

"No."

"But it's your house. And it's Christmas."

"And if I want to make *my* house look like Christmas, I hire someone to do it." The chill in his voice made the hairs on Marlie's arms stand up. "I'd say it's part of your job."

"And I'll do it. I just need some help." She blinked her eyes and tried to look helpless. "I need help with the lights." She smiled. "That's kind of the traditional male part of decorating, isn't it? If you help me with the lights, then I can do the rest tomorrow." She put another sandwich on his plate—ham and cheese this time—as an offering. He looked at it suspiciously but finally picked it up.

Drat. He hadn't leapt at the chance to help the "little woman". She had to try another tactic.

"If you help me with the lights, I'll cut back on the decorations I had planned."

This time when he looked at her, she could see his businessman's brain working.

"I'll help if you'll agree to only decorate the tree and the front door," he offered.

The negotiations were on.

"No way. I'll do the tree and the downstairs but I won't put any decorations upstairs."

"You were going to decorate upstairs?" He sounded appalled.

"Of course."

"Fine. I'll help with the lights if you only decorate downstairs and you return half of what you bought."

She pressed her lips together and considered the idea. That wouldn't be bad. Even with returning half of them, she'd still have enough to make the house glow.

"It's a deal."

She held out her hand and he readily grabbed it. Prepared this time, she sighed as her cool fingers were enveloped in his palm. Somehow the heat from their bodies combined and multiplied, swelling through her chest. Jacob looked at their hands for a long moment then pulled back. His shoulders straightened and she could see him gathering himself. It was nice to know the touch had the same effect on him.

"And the rest of the decorations...they can't be gaudy or—"

He was obviously searching for the right word so Marlie helped him. "Or tacky. Don't worry. Our guests will have a wonderful time."

He transferred his suspicious stare from the plate to her.

"What about dinner? Am I serving the board sandwiches?"

She blinked her eyes and tipped her head. "Did you want to?" It was hard to keep from laughing when his mouth opened and he stared at her. "I'm only joking. No, we are not serving sandwiches. As requested—through Terry—I'm serving a traditional turkey dinner with all the trimmings. It will be wonderful, it will be delicious."

He didn't look like he believed her but Marlie wasn't dissuaded. All of the food was relatively basic. She'd selected recipes today. She would start early in the day and poof, by eight tomorrow night, she'd have a feast fit for Santa himself. She was determined that this party was perfect. With all

Jacob's friends around him, surely his natural cheerfulness and joy would bubble to the surface.

After he finished eating and Marlie had cleaned the few plates she'd used, she had to convince him once again to come into the living room. The big beautiful tree dominated the room and filled it with the homey scent of pine. A shiver not unlike the intriguing feelings she'd discovered this morning while lying on top of Jacob raced down her spine.

An odd picture crept into her head. Her on top of Jacob—beneath the Christmas tree.

The warmth welled up from deep inside her body at the thought.

Hmm. Definitely something she needed to think about.

Chapter Five

❧

Jacob trudged into the living room behind Marlie. Spending a few minutes hanging lights was a small price to pay to get a slightly more subtle version of Christmas in his house. There was no way a tree that size could be inconspicuous but it could be elegant and simple.

Marlie paused and stared at the tree and he could practically feel the waves of pleasure rolling through her. *She really loves Christmas*, he thought with a shake of his head. She turned her gaze to him—and it looked like more than the joy of Christmas in her eyes. It looked like lust. But as soon as he'd seen it, it was gone and Marlie was handing him a box of lights, fully expecting him to begin. She bent over and grabbed another box. The movement stretched her jeans across her ass.

The night wouldn't be a complete loss, he thought. Marlie would be moving around him. It would give him fuel for his future fantasies. Not that he needed it.

"Where do these go?" he said, sighing. If they got this done quickly, he could do some work before bed.

"On the tree. All of these are for the tree." She indicated the dozen boxes stacked beside her. She couldn't be serious. She'd set the tree on fire.

"That's too many lights."

"No, it's not. It's perfect. You just have to hang them correctly."

"If you put all those lights on, there won't be room for anything else."

"Don't be silly. The ornaments go on the outside, the lights go on the inside." With each of them carrying a box of lights, she led him to the tree and pulled aside the lower branches. "Now, very gently so you don't break the needles, you need to curl the strands around each branch all the way inside. That makes it look like fairy lights."

"You want me to wrap each individual branch in lights?" He couldn't believe what he was hearing. It would take hours. He looked at Marlie to tell her this hadn't been part of the deal but the words never came. It was her eyes. They looked back at him with such confidence—in him. She believed he would do this. That this was the right thing to do.

"Yes. Here." She hooked her strand of lights to his.

It was amazing, he who had avoided Christmas for the past ten years was about to wrap a Christmas tree in lights—and all because of a pair of blue eyes.

The first couple branches were a challenge and quite painful until he got a system down that kept the needles from scratching the hell out of his arms. Marlie kept him supplied with lights and chattered away. He listened as she talked about her shopping trip, fascinated by her view of the world. Everything seemed so new and interesting.

"So, how was your day?" she asked as they moved to the upper half of the tree.

"What? Oh, it was fine." For a day from hell.

"What happened that made it not fine?"

He looked over his shoulder. "I said it was fine."

"Yes, but you didn't mean it."

She was damn perceptive.

"Just work. Holiday stuff I'd rather not deal with."

"Like what?"

"You don't want to hear about it."

"Of course, I do. This is a very important part of sharing."

He pressed down a branch and looked at Marlie. "I think I've done a pretty good job of sharing.

She had the grace to blush but she didn't appear dissuaded.

"And now you have to share the difficult parts of life as well. Then they don't seem so bad. Tell me your problem, and even if I can't help, you'll feel better. Trust me."

He stared into Marlie's eagerly awaiting face. *Trust me.* She wanted him to share a problem. Well, Christmas was his problem. The stores would return to normal as soon as this annoying holiday was over. His latest holiday challenge jumped into his mind. It was one he'd have to deal with first thing tomorrow.

"Well, Santa Claus was drunk today."

Marlie dropped the string of lights she held. Her mouth dropped open and the look in her eye was accusing and pain filled. It cleared an instant later and she released a tense breath. "Oh, sorry. For a minute there I thought you meant the real Santa."

"No, it wasn't the real Santa Claus, Marlie, just the one working at the main store." The words were out of his mouth before he'd realized what he was saying. *The real Santa Claus? There is no real Santa Claus.*

She laughed under her breath. "Thank goodness. I thought things had fallen apart after I'd left." She shook her head and picked up the light string, untwisting them.

"Since you left where?"

Panic walked across her face but she didn't try to think up a lie. "Nowhere." She waved away the idea with a flick of her hand.

"What did you do? Obviously you fired him," she said, stopping him from asking any more questions. "Can't have someone like that spoiling Christmas for the children."

Or irritate that many shopping parents, his retail conscience added silently.

"Yes, I fired him. Third one this season. I had to fire another one yesterday for stealing panties," he explained.

"Where am I going to find a decent Santa this close to Christmas?"

She tilted her head and pinched her lips together in a pose that spoke of deep thought. Her eyes got wide, she drew in a deep breath and directed her gaze back to Jacob.

He shook his head. "Don't even say it. I'm not playing Santa."

Her choked laugh wasn't at all flattering. "Don't be silly. You'd be a terrible Santa. You don't look anything like him and I doubt you could do a belly laugh if you had to."

Jacob plugged in the next strip, his pride stinging a bit that Marlie thought him incapable of being a Santa stand-in.

"Eric."

Jacob looked at Marlie. She couldn't mean *Eric*? "Who?"

"Eric. In Accounting. Terry's boyfriend."

"Eric?" Jacob leaned back to get a clearer view of Marlie. "He has several nervous twitches and he stutters when he speaks."

She shook her head. "It must only be when you're around because he was very funny and sweet to me and he adores Terry." Irritation tightened his jaw muscles. She thought Eric was cute? "I think they're going to get married."

Jacob distracted himself by connecting the final light strand. "How do you know this? I thought you didn't know anyone in town."

"I've been here two days. True love is very obvious." Jacob didn't know how to answer that. He hadn't even known they were dating. "Eric will make a really good Santa."

"No," Jacob answered emphatically.

"Do you have any other choices?"

"I need him in Accounting," he protested.

"No one sees your Accounting department. Everyone sees your Santa."

Damn, she was right.

"Let him try. I just have this feeling about him."

"Fine," he conceded.

"This will make your Christmas season wildly successful."

Housekeeper by day, management consultant by night. How lucky can I get? Jacob grimaced at his own sarcastic and somehow prophetic words.

He shifted his shoulders and realized the pain in his upper back was gone. Damn, she was right. He did feel better after talking with her. Not that he was going to actually ask Eric to play Santa. The idea was insane. On the other hand, reality hadn't been a big requirement in his life since Marlie had arrived.

"Okay, that's it. Step back. Let's see how it looks."

Tendrils of anticipation curled through his chest as he moved to stand beside Marlie. She nodded to him to turn off the lights in the room and then plugged in the Christmas lights.

The tree sparkled—lights of every color, hidden deep in the needles of the tree glowed.

"Oh, Jacob, it's beautiful."

She threw herself in his arms and he had no choice but to catch her. Her body fit against his like it had been designed to match perfectly. Lust had faded in the past hours behind the practical task of putting up Christmas lights but with one touch it returned, rushing through his body, making his cock rebound. His hands squeezed gently as he pulled her closer, her breasts plumping between their bodies.

"Thank you so much," she sighed in that siren's voice. She leaned into the embrace, placing her head on his chest and keeping her arms wrapped loosely around his back. His cock swelled urged on by the desire to lower her to the ground and make love to her by the light of the Christmas tree. The lights would sparkle on her hair, in her eyes as he slid into her, held her. He would take his time, riding her slowly, making the lights turn into stars as he became the center of her world.

How long they stood there, Jacob didn't know. Marlie seemed content and for some reason, Jacob didn't want to disturb her. With a sigh, she finally lifted her head.

"It's late. We should really get to bed." His body leapt to agreement. "Aren't you tired?" Stepping out of his embrace she raised her hands over her head and stretched, groaning as she moved. Unable to speak, he watched her move, that slow sensuality guiding every movement. "Yep, you're definitely tired. You're starting to fade on me."

She picked up his hand in hers and led him toward the door. "All you need is a night in bed and you'll wake up refreshed and ready to face the world."

Jacob silently agreed. A night in bed was what he needed, but sleeping wasn't going to help his problem. A night of long, hot sex might take the edge off, but with the volume of his fantasies, it was looking more like a weekend cure would be needed.

Despite the noise running through his head, he followed Marlie upstairs, feeling unusually comfortable—like they'd done this before many times. Marlie chatted as they walked, telling him her struggles of getting that huge tree home. Her laughter as she recited how she explained to the taxi driver— who spoke very little English—that she wanted to strap a twelve-foot tree to the roof of his cab was contagious. He barely noticed as they entered the bedroom or that Marlie went to his dresser to remove her nightshirt.

When she disappeared into the bathroom, he opened his dresser drawer and saw his underwear and some tiny scraps of satin that certainly weren't designed for his ass.

She bounced out of the bathroom a few minutes later smelling of toothpaste and looking fresh.

"Marlie, what are your clothes doing in here?"

She stopped beside him and peeked over his arm to look into the same drawer. "I had to put them someplace. It seemed silly to have to keep going downstairs just to get clothes. Besides you have so much space..."

"That you decided I could share some of it."

"Exactly."

She sounded pleased that he understood her rationale. As if it was the most normal thing in the world, she crawled into his bed and sat, waiting for him to join her. The path of least resistance seemed to be for him to change into his shorts and lie down beside her. He would wait until she fell asleep and then he'd slip away.

He'd made the same promise last night but he meant it this time.

Laughter that sounded like his conscience echoed in his head.

Marlie sat in bed waiting for Jacob to return from the bathroom. It certainly seemed to take him a long time to get ready for bed. She considered that he might be hiding out but decided that couldn't be true. He didn't seem like the type.

But that was part of her problem. She didn't know his type. She couldn't quite figure him out and he wasn't very forthcoming with information. No one at the store seemed to know him well. They all said he was an excellent businessman, but beyond that, they had little interaction with him. She needed a way to get inside his head—figure out what he wanted, what his dreams were.

Hmmm. Dreams.

It wasn't exactly an accepted practice but she could wish for anything—even access his dreams.

Santa wouldn't approve.

Santa doesn't have to know, she mentally pointed out, silencing her conscience. If she was going to make any progress, she needed some covert information and Jacob's dreams would be a perfect place to start.

She closed her eyes and made her wish. "I wish to share Jacob's dreams tonight." She willed the magic out into the world and opened her eyes. It was a difficult wish and there was no way of knowing whether it would come true until they both fell asleep.

He stepped out of the bathroom, wearing shorts and a T-shirt that clung to his chest. Her gaze fell to just below his waistband and that intriguing body part she'd only glimpsed earlier. Drat. There was no way to see it, not with his shirt covering it. Marlie squirmed beneath the covers as he got into bed.

After a brisk good night, he rolled over, turning his back to her. She sighed and tried to do the same—hoping that whatever filled his dreams would give her an idea of how to make his wishes come true.

Chapter Six

ஒ

Jacob stepped into his living room, the newly lit tree glowing with hundreds of lights. From behind the tree, Marlie appeared, wearing nothing but Christmas lights. The white strands circled her body, cupping her breasts and crisscrossing over her stomach. She sparkled as she stepped toward him.

"Merry Christmas, Jacob," she whispered as she trailed her fingertips down his chest. It was like a path of fire across his skin as she touched him, tracing his stomach muscles and going lower. She blinked those sea-blue eyes—the look of pure lust swelling in her gaze. That dainty tongue peeking out as she glanced down at his naked body. It was the same fascinated look she'd given him earlier as if she wanted to touch him, taste him.

"Yes, I want to taste you," she whispered, her fingers curling around his cock. Jacob gritted his teeth and held on, enduring the delicate touch. So sweet. Did she even know how much he wanted her? She opened her mouth and laved her tongue up across his chest, skimming across his nipple. "Delicious," she whispered. "Can I have more?" Her hand wandered along his cock, stroking his shaft up and down.

Part of his mind knew that something wasn't right, that this couldn't be happening but there was no way to resist her siren's voice. Or the hunger that vibrated through her body. She wanted this. Wanted his cock, in her mouth, her pussy, her ass. Wanted him to fill her.

Slowly, with a seductive smile, she sank to her knees. Jacob held his breath as her mouth opened and she moved closer to his cock. Her tongue flickered out, teasing the head, quick forays as she pushed her hands up his thighs, skimming her fingers between his legs.

"Don't tease me, little one," he commanded, slipping his fingers into her hair. Her eyes glowed with power and pleasure as he tilted her head up. "Take it into your mouth, Marlie." His words were firm and he could see, almost feel the pleasurable little shiver that skated down her spine. She bent her head down and licked one long stroke up the entire length of his cock. When she reached the tip, she hesitated — her eyes daring him to command her. "You'll be punished," he warned and her eyes brightened with the prospect. She twirled her tongue around the thick head one time before she opened her mouth fully and accepted him inside. Heat and wetness surrounded his cock, making it even harder as she swallowed him. The low hum of her groan vibrated through his cock as she began to move, slow languid sucks, pumping her head back and forth, letting him fill her mouth and retreating.

Needing more, needing to move, he held her head still and pulsed his cock deeper into her mouth, shallow strokes. Her lips tightened around his shaft creating a light suction as she pulled back.

"Baby, I'm about to come," he warned. She didn't retreat. She moaned as if she wanted him to come in her mouth. "Marlie, I'm—" He exploded, pouring his cum into her. Her tongue never left him, working him, licking him as his cock wilted.

Slowly, with wicked intent filling her eyes, she rose to her feet and pressed against him, her lighted breasts poking him in the chest. "So delicious. Will you taste me?"

Marlie came awake, gasping for breath, her heart pounding. She blinked into the darkness, letting her eyes adjust as she stared at Jacob. He lay on his side, his eyes closed, his lips slightly open as if he too was having difficulty breathing.

His dream. It had been strange and wonderful. She licked her lips wanting to feel what the dream-Marlie had felt, wanting to give him that incredible pleasure. Beside her, he groaned and shifted rolling toward her. Marlie chewed on her lower lip and tried to see if that strange muscle between his legs was hard as it had been in his dream but it was too dark.

Still locked in his dreams, Jacob moaned. Marlie sank back down on the bed and willed herself to sleep. She didn't know what would happen next but she didn't want to miss a moment of it.

The picture morphed before him, changing until his was on his knees, Marlie standing above him. The lights were gone, leaving her dressed in black leather, a corset binding her breasts high and tight. A black garter belt held up sheer stockings but left her pussy bare. Her foot was propped on the bed leaving her delicious cunt open to him.

Jacob slid his hands up her sleek thighs, spreading them wider, giving him full access to her sex. She watched him as he touched her. Like every other emotion, Marlie wore her pleasure openly. He placed a kiss on the inside of her thigh, flicking his tongue out to taste her. The scent of her pussy, the intoxicating feminine arousal saturated his senses and he pressed upward, needing that flavor on his tongue. He slipped his tongue into the top of her slit, teasing both of them with his delicate caress.

"Do you want my mouth on you?" he whispered, his breath hot on her pussy. "Is that what you want, baby?"

"Yes." Her words were accompanied by a slow roll of her hips, as if she hungered for more.

He flicked his tongue across her pussy lips, capturing a hint of her moisture. "This sweet cunt is wet and eager for me." He placed a kiss on her mound just above her clit. "Only for me."

"Yes, Jacob."

His fingers tightened on her ass as he pulled her to his mouth, urging her legs wider. He kept his touch light, teasing her with soft, fluttering strokes of his tongue, scattered touches everywhere. Her flavor seeped into him as he flicked and licked, sucking on her pussy lips, circling the tight bud of her clit.

All his senses joined in the heady tongue fucking. He listened to her groans, savoring every sound of pleasure, every surprised gasp. Her fingers gripped his head holding him in place as she squirmed, trying to get closer.

He knew what she needed but he held back, loving the slick glide of his tongue across her flesh.

"Jacob, please." Her whimpered plea joined the myriad sounds that echoed in his head. "Please, Jacob, I need you"

He held her hips steady as he pushed his tongue into her pussy, rubbing the tip against the upper wall. Marlie dropped her head back and groaned as he delved deeper, tasting her sweet cunt, loving every inch he could reach with his tongue before drawing back and up, swirling his tongue around her clit. She cried out as he sucked her clit between his lips, working it gently until he heard her gasp and felt the wicked tension zip through her body. He continued, tasting and teasing her until she moaned his name, calling for more, calling for him. He raised his head—her blue eyes glittered with pleasure and hunger. More. He wanted more. He buried his face between her legs and once again pushed her toward—

Marlie's eyes popped open. She lay perfectly still, holding her body in place as she examined the strange sensations that surged through her. The space between her legs—the place that Jacob had licked in his dream—ached. She squeezed her knees together. The tickling zipped through her. *Wow. What is that?* She looked over at Jacob. He was still deep in sleep. Still deep in his dreams.

Strange how humans interacted with each other. She hadn't seen anyone else behave that way. She couldn't exactly ask Jacob. How would she explain what she'd seen in his dreams and how she'd seen it? It was a private moment, private thoughts and she should never have intruded. Santa was no doubt going to be pissed about that wish. Drat. And Jacob's dreams hadn't helped. They'd just confused her more and made her ache. She closed her eyes and reversed the wish, sending a mental apology to Santa.

A little slower this time, she snuggled back under the blankets though the heat inside her body seemed more than enough to keep her warm. And the strange ache between her legs didn't seem to be going away. Whatever Jacob had done in his dreams, there seemed to be some kind of conclusion. Something that made the sparkles burn bright.

Jacob stepped to the side of his bed. Marlie lay before him, her knees bent and her pussy open and wet. He lay down beside her.

"That's it, baby. That's what I want," he whispered. He slipped his finger into her cunt and felt the wet heat close around him. He drew back and added a second finger. She was tight, so tight, so ready for his cock. "Always so wet and hot for me." She whimpered and he pumped in deeper, knowing what she needed. His tongue, his fingers. None of it was enough, she needed his cock, thick and hard and riding her deep. He scraped his teeth along her neck. "Is that what you want, baby? Do you want me to fuck you? Ride this sweet cunt until all you feel is me?"

"Yes, Jacob please."

The plea in her voice tugged on him but he held back. She wasn't going to break his control. Not this time. He wanted to feel her, tease her until she was begging.

"Soon, baby, soon. I'll come inside you. Fuck you until all you feel is me."

"Now, Jacob."

Her pussy quivered around his fingers but he kept his strokes light, reserving that one touch he knew would send her flying. He wanted her to come while he was inside her, his cock claiming that cunt that belonged to him alone.

He placed a kiss on her neck, moving his mouth to her ear. "Are you ready? Shall I fuck this sweet pussy? Is that what you want?"

"Oh yes, Jacob. Jacob!"

He pushed her thighs open and settled himself over her. The heat of her sex flowed between them making him harder.

There were no preliminaries. Neither of them wanted it and they needed this too much. He placed his cock at her entrance and thrust inside. Her cry—pure pleasure—reverberated through his body and drove him on, deeper, harder.

He wrapped his hands in her hair and held her still as he rode her—heavy solid thrusts, filling her over and over again. Open and wet, she whispered his name, pleading for more. Her hot hands were everywhere, stroking and touching, breaking his control far sooner than he wanted.

"Jacob."

He pushed into her again. Just one more stroke, that was all he needed.

"Jacob!" His name was followed by a rough shake on his shoulder jerking him from the dream. He froze—his mind immediately analyzing where he was and what he'd been doing. Had it been a dream? Or had he really been fucking Marlie? He opened his eyes and found himself on top of her, his hips between her legs, her ankle curled around his calf. He braced himself for her wrath and looked into her eyes. His cock twitched. She didn't look angry—she looked curious and eager.

He pushed back, easing his hips away, and looked down. They were both still clothed. His erection was testing the limits of his shorts but he was still covered and so was she—though the tiny scrap of material that hid her pussy wasn't much protection. That's good. It wasn't that fucking Marlie would be a bad thing, he told himself, but he wanted to remember it.

A dark stain marked his shorts and he knew it was from Marlie's pussy. She was wet.

"Uh, Marlie—" Damn, was he going to have to apologize again?

We just need to have sex. Then if we wake up in this position I don't need to apologize, I can just have her again.

Or you could sleep in a different bed. It struck him as odd that this was the second option to come to his mind and how unpalatable it seemed.

Marlie rubbed her hand on his shoulder. "I'm sorry to wake you but your clock keeps ringing and I don't know how to make it stop."

He realized the buzzer alarm on his clock-radio was going off.

She skimmed her fingers through his hair. "It's a very irritating sound," she said, her voice lazy and soft.

"It's supposed to be." Groaning, because once again he was going to start the day with a hard-on that wasn't easily ignored, he rolled off of Marlie and slapped at the alarm. It took a few minutes and a half-dozen deep breaths before he could even consider standing up without embarrassing himself. He'd been on top of her, almost inside her and why wasn't she screaming about it? None of it made sense. The dreams, her response, the fact that she was in his bed in the first place. He inhaled and a foreign, feminine scent clouded his brain.

Inconspicuously as possible, he brushed his fingers beneath his nose. The wicked perfume of feminine arousal covered his hand. He glanced over his shoulder. It hadn't *all* been a dream. He'd obviously had his hand between her legs. In the dream he'd pushed his fingers into her pussy, finger fucked her until she was begging for his cock. His cock lurched forward.

A quick glance at the time added more stress to his morning. Eight-ten. He normally arrived at the office by seven-thirty. No later than eight.

"How long has it been ringing?" He shifted on the mattress to see her better...then almost wished he hadn't. She'd rolled over to her side, her nightshirt crushed up around her waist, her leg bent adding a distinct curve to her ass. Her hair looked tousled and sex teased. It was a seductive picture but she seemed to have no idea of its impact on him.

"A while. As I said it was very irritating."

"Why did you let me sleep?"

"Uhm. Well, you needed the sleep and you were having such exciting dreams—" Her cheeks turned red—as if she actually knew the content of his dreams. "I mean, you seemed to be having really good dreams and I didn't want to disturb you." She shrugged. "But when you rolled on top of me, I couldn't reach it to turn it off."

She said it so casually, as if she was used to men waking up with their cocks almost inside her. And as if the prospect didn't interest her at all. The thought was quite sobering. He'd been two thin layers of cloth from being inside her—and she didn't sound interested.

"I've got to go. I've got to get to work." Work was something he could understand. Something tangible and concrete.

"Oh, good. I'll come along."

Jacob stood up. "No, Marlie, you can't come to work with me." That would be too much. It was his only refuge from the insanity that had become his life. "Besides, don't you have to get ready for the party?" He hesitated, not sure he wanted to go there but said, "You know, a meal to cook?"

"Oh, I'm not worried about that. Got it covered. And I won't stay long at your office. I just need to get a dress for the party." She crawled out of bed, standing up inches away from him. So close her breasts brushed his chest. The dainty caress was like twin fires against his skin but she was completely oblivious. "You wouldn't want me to embarrass you in front of our guests." She pushed past him and left, leaving him once again standing in a daze.

Our guests? Why did it sound like Marlie was coming to the party...not just cooking for it?

And about the cooking...he needed to talk to her again. He hadn't received any explanation about how she was going to prepare a meal when it was glaringly obvious she didn't cook. Her assurances that everything would be fine didn't inspire confidence.

Jacob got ready in record time—after making a quick call to his secretary. He didn't explain why he was late but told her he would be arriving soon. When he got downstairs, Marlie was waiting for him, wearing a pair of jeans that hugged her ass and a short top that showed just a hint of her bare stomach. The unrestrained sway of her breasts gave the top a perfect shape.

The whole outfit was casual and looked comfortable and Jacob wanted to rip it off her body and—

"Ready?"

He nodded not trusting himself to speak. He might finish his thought aloud. She reached into the closet and pulled out the horrid magenta and green coat. "No," he said, finding his voice. "Wear something else. Anything else."

She laughed. "It's hideous, isn't it? Okay." After a few minutes of digging around in the closet, which Jacob spent staring at her ass, she found a coat that—while it didn't fit her—would work. It was one of his old jackets and hung on her like a sack. A very sexy sack. It was the same principle as seeing a woman in a man's shirt. She looked petite and sexual.

Great. Start off another day with the unkillable erection.

"Let's go." He waved to the door.

She cuddled the collar of the jacket around her neck and smiled as she flounced out the door. He stood there watching her for a moment—feeling his own smile creep onto his face. Joy just seemed to hover around her. Somehow his waking up on top of her hadn't started her day off wrong. Unfortunately, she clearly had no inclination to take it any further.

What seemed like mere minutes later, they pulled into the garage at Triumph's and Marlie jumped out of the car.

"Well, have a great day. I'm off to shop."

He looked at the baggy coat and remembered the monstrosity she'd bought the first day. It was too terrifying to imagine what she might come up with on her own.

"Have Anne on floor three help you. She's the personal shopper and she'll find you something appropriate for tonight. Tell her to charge it to my account."

"Great. What time should dinner be ready?"

"Eight." He grabbed her elbow, stopping her escape. "When and how are you going to cook dinner tonight?"

The edges of her eyes tightened and her lips pressed together as if she was holding back some choice words.

"This afternoon. Don't worry. It's under control."

Her words didn't comfort him. He tried to press her for more information but by the time they'd reached the third floor and she prepared to step off, she'd managed to avoid a direct answer.

As the doors opened she turned and looked at him with those wide, innocent eyes. "How do you like your turkey? Medium rare?" The question sunk into his brain as she stepped off the elevator.

"No. Turkey is cooked well done. All poultry is cooked well done."

"Oh." Her eye lids fluttered in rapid succession. "I'll remember that."

The doors began to shut. She was going to poison the Board of Directors. And him.

"Please tell me you're joking," he called as the doors eased closed. A second later they popped open and Marlie was standing there.

"I'm joking. Now don't worry."

The saucy wink she flashed him did great things for his libido but little for his confidence about dinner.

As soon as the doors closed behind her, Marlie released the perky façade she'd struggled to maintain for the past hour. She'd willed herself to be cheerful and pleasant—despite the crazed sensations running through her body. It had taken her a long time to fall back asleep after that strange dream of Jacob licking her—only to be woken up a short time later when he'd rolled on top of her. She'd rather liked that. Especially when he'd eased his fingers inside her. She squeezed her thighs together as the memory reignited the heat. He'd actually touched her there, moved his fingers in and out in slow strokes. It had been incredible. But not quite enough.

There had to be more. Nothing could feel that good but leave her feeling so dissatisfied.

But Jacob hadn't seemed to notice. He'd rolled away like he'd regretted ever being on top of her. It was really too bad. And the way he'd moved against her, pumping his hips. She whimpered at the hot memory. It had been an odd rhythm that she hadn't quite matched when that dratted buzzer had gone off.

"May I help you?"

The cool prim voice lured Marlie from her heated thoughts.

"What? Oh, I'm looking for Anne. She's supposed to help me find a dress. Jacob sent me."

"Jacob?"

"Jacob Triumph. We having a dinner party tonight and I need a dress."

The woman's eyes widened just a fraction before she smiled. "I'm Anne," she said, her tone a little warmer now. "What sort of dress were you looking for?"

The dream returned once again—the tight black corset, those garter things that held her stockings up. Marlie snagged her lower lip between her teeth and considered the idea. Jacob obviously liked that style—if he'd dreamed her in it.

Maybe, just maybe if Jacob saw her in it for real, she'd have a chance to find out what happened next.

"Well," she said looking at Anne. "I'm looking for something kind of specific..."

* * * * *

Marlie released a pent-up breath and leaned her back against the darkened windows of the store. Jacob hadn't arrived yet. If he hurried, they could get home in time for her to take a shower and rest before their guests arrived. She needed a few minutes to get ready before trying to serve dinner for twenty. And the beautiful dress was waiting for her at home. It wasn't *exactly* like Jacob's dream but it was close. The thought made her smile. What would Jacob think when he saw her in that? More importantly, what would he do?

She sighed and let her head hit the window behind her. A stray, straggled lock of hair fell in front of her eyes but she didn't have the strength to push it back. It had been a long day. Shopping had gone well but it had taken longer than she'd anticipated. Anne kept trying to steer her toward more conservative outfits but Marlie had insisted and had finally found the perfect dress.

After she'd left Triumph's—making one more trip to the decorations department to see if there was anything she missed—she'd headed home.

She'd spent the rest of the morning decorating the house and the afternoon destroying dinner.

The last of her energy had drained away when she'd finally put out the fire on the stove. She'd learned two things today—chicken broth caught fire very easily and that the stuff that shot out of the fire extinguisher crept into every crack and crevice and had to be scraped up with a sharp knife. She would have been home in bed right now if it hadn't been for the dinner tonight.

If it were *her* party she would have canceled or ordered pizza, but it was Jacob's party and that was the reason she was still on her feet. She didn't want to ruin it for him. They seemed to be making some slight progress and she didn't want him backsliding. After all, he had helped her put up the Christmas lights and he was doing an excellent job of sharing.

But she had this horrible feeling that if she messed up dinner tonight, the few steps Jacob had made toward a true Christmas spirit would be lost and she'd never get home. The center of her stomach fell away at the thought. She missed her home and friends, but going back to the Workshop meant leaving Jacob. She wasn't ready to do that. He needed more spirit. He needed to smile more. And she wanted to be there to see those smiles.

Tonight he would have something to smile about. Dinner would be edible. After she'd ruined the meal, she'd contacted Terry at Jacob's office and she'd been most helpful. A quick trip through the newspaper ads had revealed a deli that could provide a traditional Christmas dinner on short notice.

Marlie pulled the receipt out of her pocket and looked at it. A complete dinner with turkey, stuffing, mashed potatoes, sweet potatoes, green beans, and pumpkin pie. Enough to serve twenty. Perfect for Jacob's guests. He'd actually sounded relieved when she'd called him and told him she thought they should purchase a pre-cooked meal. He'd even offered to meet her to help get it home.

Anticipation swirled through her insides. He would be here in a few minutes. She spent the time watching the crowd of holiday shoppers. A little boy stepped out of bustling mass to look wide-eyed at the window behind Marlie. The store was closed for the night, but still he stared, the light of a wish glittering in his eyes. Curiosity got the better of her and she turned to look at the window too.

The bright painted window of a tiny neighborhood grocery store held the boy in rapt attention with a huge poster of Christmas dinner adorning the window—a dinner just like the one she'd ordered. The child's threadbare but clean clothes told her more of the story. Then it came to her. His Christmas wish. *My mother would love a dinner like that. I wish I could get it for her.*

A band tightened around Marlie's chest. She'd actually heard a Christmas wish. It was rare for an elf to get a direct wish—most came through letters or whispers to store Santas. But she'd heard it—loud and clear.

The receipt crinkled in her hand. It was an elf imperative to fulfill Christmas wishes whenever possible. Despite holiday traditions, most Christmas wishes weren't fulfilled by magic. Christmas wishes were filled through the careful assistance of others, so it rarely looked like a miracle.

"It looks good, doesn't it?" Marlie asked in a pleasant voice. The little boy nodded but didn't speak. "I'll bet your family would really enjoy a dinner like that, huh?" Again he nodded.

"Marshall." A burly man approached the little boy. "Come on, son. We've got to get home."

"But, Daddy, look." Marshall pointed up to the picture.

"I see it, son. Now come on. Mama's waiting."

"Hi, I'm Marlie." She stepped forward and held out her hand. Marshall's dad put his hand on his son's shoulder, pulling him close to the protection of his body. After a long moment of inspection, he seemed to decide Marlie wasn't a threat accepted her hand in his meaty palm. "And you are?"

"Mitch Taylor."

"I'm not a nut, but I do have a favor to ask. I have this fancy Christmas dinner that I ordered at the deli down the street, already cooked, already paid for, waiting to be eaten and my guests just canceled on me. The store won't give me my money back and I was wondering if you'd like the dinner. It's enough to feed an army but it should have great leftovers." Marshall clasped his father's hand and stared up at her.

Mitch shook his head. "Thanks, but we don't need any charity."

"Oh, it's not charity." Marlie smiled and shrugged. "It will take the dinner off my hands. I'd feel better knowing it wasn't going to waste." She held out the receipt.

Marlie met his eyes and allowed her love and joy to shine through. She watched the tension drain from Mitch's shoulders and he nodded. He took the receipt and looked at it. "If you're sure…"

"I am."

"Are you an angel, lady?" the little boy asked, his voice filled with awe.

She crouched down to his level. "Nothing so exciting. Just a Christmas elf."

"Really?" Marshall's eyes grew even wider. "My daddy needs a job. Will you tell Santa? Maybe he could help."

"Marshall," his father's gentle warning voice quieted the smiling child. Marlie winked at the little boy and stood up.

As she straightened, the skin at the back of her neck began to tingle. *Jacob.*

"Jacob." She smiled his name as she turned around, then grabbed his arm and dragged him forward. "This is Mitch Taylor and this is Marshall." She indicated to Jacob. "This is my friend, Jacob Triumph." She held up one finger. "Wait right here." Tugging Jacob's arm, she pulled him a few steps from Mitch and Marshall. "Mitch needs a job," she whispered.

Jacob was silent for a moment before his lips tightened and he answered in a cold voice, "I'm sorry to hear that."

"Couldn't you help him? Don't you have a job in the store?"

"Marlie, I can't just hire someone off the street."

"Why not? He'd be really good. I just know it." She looked over to the father and son. "Mitch, what did you used to do?"

"I was a longshoreman, before I got hurt."

Marlie smiled and looked at Jacob.

"See?" they said simultaneously.

"Marlie," Jacob gasped. "The only open position is in Men's Clothing. Our clients are used to dealing with designers, upscale salesmen. He'd be horrible."

"He can do it. He was a longshoreman. He's dealt with tough customers before. Please." Marlie hated to beg, but it would be good for Triumph's she could just feel it. And it would be good for Jacob. "Just give him a trial through Christmas. That's fair."

Jacob looked around, trying to avoid looking at Marlie. If he looked into her eyes she'd convince him. Instead his gaze landed on Mitch and his son. Standing alone, together. And as much as he hated to admit it, she'd been right about Eric. From all reports, he'd done a great job as Santa today. The best the store had ever had. With a sigh, he took Marlie's hand in his and walked back to the other father and son.

"Marlie says you're looking for work. I might have a *temporary* opening at Triumph's Department Store," he began a little ungraciously. "It's a sales position in Men's Clothing. Do you have any sales experience?"

Mitch straightened. His fingers tightened its hold on Marshall's small hand and his chin lifted a few inches higher.

"No, but I'm a fast learner," he replied, the confidence clear in his voice. Jacob stared at him for a few seconds before nodding.

"Okay, contact Tyler Nichols at the downtown Triumph's at eight o'clock tomorrow morning. I'll tell him to expect you. The position's open through Christmas. After that, we'll talk again. If you work out for us, and we work out for you, there's a possibility it could become permanent."

Mitch held out his hand. Jacob took it and the men gave two quick handshakes before releasing each other. "Thank you. I'll be there tomorrow." A smile struggled to form on Mitch's lips but he kept restraining it. "Thanks again. Uh, good night." They started to walk away. "Thanks Marlie. For everything." He held up the receipt and, pulling Marshall behind him, walked down the street toward the deli.

Marlie sighed and felt a joyous giggle bubble up in her throat. There was nothing more wonderful for an elf than to see a wish come true. Turning to Jacob, she threw her arms around his neck and her body against his in a tight hug. Heat exploded as their bodies connected and Marlie released the laughter that had tickled her insides. "Thank you, Jacob. That was so wonderful." Jacob's hands lightly closed around her back, but she noticed he didn't pull her close.

"Wonderful," he agreed in a gasping voice. He must be overcome with excitement, she thought. The thrill of helping others was truly an intoxicating experience.

She stepped away and smiled at him, her energy returning in waves.

"Now that I've done my good deed for the day, can we go?" She could tell he meant to be sarcastic but there was too much laughter in his voice for it to work. "Where is this deli?"

"Deli?" Marlie asked, the flush of success distracting her.

"Where we're picking up dinner?" Jacob encouraged with exaggerated patience.

"Oh, dinner." Marlie gasped. She looked around her, as if she'd lost something. "Dinner. Oh, no."

The light that had flickered briefly in his eyes, disappeared. "What's wrong with dinner?" Jacob bit out.

Marlie winced. "I gave it away."

"You what?"

His shout echoed across the street but Marlie didn't back down. "I gave it away. To Mitch and Marshall. I had to. It was Marshall's Christmas wish. I couldn't let it pass."

"We have twenty people coming to our home, *my* home," he corrected. "*I* have twenty important people coming to my home in less than two hours and we don't have anything to feed them? And for a Christmas wish? Who do you think you are? Santa Claus?"

"No, just one of the elves," she muttered. "At least I used be." She wasn't sure Santa was going to let her back in after this.

"Marlie, how could you do something so stupid?"

That was too much. She pulled herself up to her full height and stared into his face. "It wasn't stupid. It was generous. Something a Scrooge like you wouldn't understand."

"I understand generosity, but there's a time and place for it." Jacob pushed back the folds of his coat and jammed his fists onto his hips. He leaned forward, glaring down at Marlie. "And the time is not when I have twenty guests arriving at my house in two hours for a traditional Christmas dinner, which you seem unable to cook."

Marlie acknowledged to herself that there was probably a better way to have fulfilled Marshall's Christmas wish, but she wasn't about to admit that to Jacob.

"There is no reason to get testy," she said primly.

"We're way past testy. I'm full on to pissed."

She held up her hand to ward off any further comments. "Don't get your panties in a bunch. Let's go to the deli and see if they have another meal we can buy," she suggested.

"Now, that's a good idea," he said sarcastically, following Marlie down the crowded street. "And my panties aren't in a bunch," he called after her.

"I'm pleased to hear that," a passerby laughed.

Marlie bit her lips together.

"Laugh, and you're dead," Jacob whispered through clenched teeth as he caught up with her.

Chapter Seven

ഇ

Jacob scanned the dining table one last time. It was everything he'd hoped for—elegant and sophisticated. In fact, the whole house looked great. Overwhelmingly Christmas, but Marlie had done an excellent job decorating. He was a little surprised that she'd been able to tone it down. With everything he'd seen last night he'd feared ceramic Santas on every surface. Instead, it was perfect.

Hopefully it would distract his guests from the fact that dinner would be a little unorthodox.

Nodding one more time to give his final approval to the empty room, he walked back into the foyer. The living room was set up for pre-dinner drinks. The tree glittered with the hundreds of lights he'd installed. Something caught his eye and he looked up. Marlie had hung mistletoe from the doorway. He glanced into the room. Mistletoe hung in random places from the ceiling. *Hmmm.* Could be interesting to get caught under the mistletoe with Marlie.

Despite his dreams and waking up almost inside of her, he'd yet to taste her and the oversight was starting to weigh on him.

The insistent clearing of a throat pulled him back to the hall. He let his eyes follow the sound up the stairs.

Eighties heavy metal music filled his head as Marlie strutted her way down the staircase. Her hips swung in a slow sensual pattern that could only be done by a woman in high heels. Her arms and shoulders were bare except for a layer of glitter that coated her skin. She was bold and wicked and the sexual look in her eye would have put the most hardened porn star to shame.

Jacob swallowed deeply, trying to catch a breath and not choke all at the same time.

"What do you think?" she asked, stopping five feet away from him—close enough for him to smell her subtle, earthy perfume and still see the entire picture presented before him.

The bodice of the dress was a bright red mock corset. He could see from the way she was standing that the material didn't wrap all the way around her back but it still managed to squeeze and plump her breasts until they were half revealed over the top edge. One good tug, a quick flick of his fingers and he could have her out of that and those delicious tits filling his hands. Though the material hid it, he was sure her nipples were tight and hungry.

Jerking his gaze away, he continued his perusal, looking down to the ruffled skirt made of what looked like strips of red cellophane. It was fluffy and didn't cling and it only reached to mid-thigh, emphasizing the surprising length of her legs. She shifted and a strip of red appeared beneath the dress. She was wearing a garter belt to hold up the sheer stockings she wore.

Air seemed to have evaporated from the room. It was almost like his dream. Strip off the skirt and her panties and...damn, was she even wearing panties? His cock twitched inside his trousers.

"So, what do you think?" she prodded when he hadn't answered.

I think I should bend you over the stairs and fuck you until you see stars.

He crushed the words inside him and dragged his gaze back up her body. Her hair was piled casually on her head, with stray strands and ringlets dripping down the sides and back. No doubt it was an intricate style but it made her look as if she'd spent the afternoon fucking and had merely scooped her hair on top of her head when she'd crawled out of bed to find her lover to demand more.

It was difficult to take it all in—the clothes, her hair, the lust. Of course, after the past two nights—and mornings—he had to conclude that the lust was all on his side. She seemed oblivious to it except in rare moments like these when it was easy to imagine her approaching him and demanding he service her. He'd never been overly interested in a woman dominating him in bed but the picture of Marlie ordering him to satisfy her was intriguing. Her blue eyes filled with concern as he hesitated.

"It's amazing." And totally inappropriate for the Board of Director's dinner.

"I'm glad you like it." Her lips bent into a smile that warned she had a secret. "I was thinking of you when I bought it."

For some reason, that didn't surprise him.

"And look, it looks really complicated to get into." She spun around and showed him her back. Two narrow straps met in the back holding on the façade. "It's so easy to get out of."

He gulped in another breath of much needed oxygen—all ability to think had gone south with all his blood—and said, "Where did you get it?"

"Triumph's." She turned around again and skipped closer to him. The sudden movement jarred her breasts and for a moment Jacob was terrified, thrilled that she might pop out. "I did just what you suggested and had Anne help me." Marlie stretched her arms over her head, causing the top limits of her corset to strain then laughed as she lowered them. "At first she kept trying to show me all these long gowns which were beautiful but they looked so heavy. It took a little bit for her to understand what I wanted, but once she did, we found this. Isn't it wonderful?"

It was wonderful. Beautiful and sexy and suited for a night of seduction, not for serving dinner to Triumph's Board of Directors. But how to tell her that without hurting her feelings? She was so excited about this dress.

"Maybe you should—"

The kitchen buzzer sounded. Dinner was ready.

"Oh good." Marlie whipped away before he could stop her. "The lasagnas are done. We just need to make the salad and we're ready to go." She hurried off to the kitchen her ass swishing back and forth like a hypnotist's watch. It was only when she disappeared behind the door that Jacob managed to shake himself free.

After three days of feeling stunned and slightly out of control around Marlie, he was getting used to the sensation. How in the hell was he going to explain her to the board? He wandered into the dining room and quickly counted chairs. Twenty-three. Obviously Marlie intended to join them for dinner. He allowed himself a slight smile when he imagined the reaction of several board members or their spouses when they saw Marlie. The pure entertainment value was almost worth the stress.

The kitchen door popped open and she stuck her head out. "I could use some help."

It was a gentle but insistent nag. The kind a wife would send to her husband when she wasn't yet annoyed but could get there quickly. Jacob laughed quietly to himself and followed her into the kitchen. They weren't married, they didn't even know each other that well but he didn't want to disappoint her.

If nothing else, this would be the first time Christmas dinner with the Board of Directors would not be boring.

It would be interesting to see their reaction when they saw the meal. He was serving frozen lasagna—*store-bought* frozen lasagna. The board would be expecting an elegant Christmas dinner and that would so not be what they were getting.

I can't believe she gave away our dinner. Jacob shook his head. *How could anyone do something so stupid?*

And so generous. She could have picked a better time to do it, he reminded himself, using the logic that there was a time and place for everything and two hours before dinner was not the time to give away their food. Still, that little boy and his father had truly appreciated her gift. Jacob closed his eyes. And now he had a longshoreman working in men's clothing. Nichols had been stoic when Jacob had called to warn him about his new employee, but then Nichols was stoic about most things. That's what made him the perfect sales manager.

Still, Jacob made a mental note to send Nichols a bottle of his favorite scotch to make up for the hassle.

Jacob pushed open the kitchen door and saw Marlie swaying to the slow sounds of Christmas tunes jingling from the radio. Her hips rocked in time to the beat. An unusual emotion formed as he watched her—not the raging lust or stunned confusion—but something different. Pleasure at her pure joy. She smiled at him as he walked in. Not stopping her dance, she pulled out six bags of lettuce from the refrigerator and slapped them on the counter.

"You're on salad duty," she announced then wiggled her way over to the coffeepot. It was half empty. She poured more into her mug and set about making another pot. Marlie, wired on coffee. Interesting was too tame a word for how he was sure the evening would end. "Woohoo. Jacob. We're on a schedule here." She tapped on the counter to get his attention.

While he rinsed the already rinsed lettuce and placed it in a massive bowl, she sliced the dessert—store-bought cheesecake of every variety.

He opened the next salad package—not letting his gaze wander over to Marlie or trying to see how deep her cleavage went.

"I don't get it," Marlie muttered, breaking into his thoughts. He looked up and found her near the kitchen door, staring at the mistletoe hanging above her head.

"Get what?"

He focused his eyes on her face, and fought letting them drift downward as they'd tended to do for the past few days.

She arched her back and stared up. The position pushed her breasts against the tight edge of her top, straining the laws of gravity. He bit back a groan, wanting to feel those mounds in his hands, his mouth. Preferably while he was buried deep inside her. He inhaled through his nose and continued to rinse the lettuce.

"What don't you understand?" Jacob asked, hoping to distract his body from acting on the seductive images his mind was presenting. On top of everything else, he didn't intend to greet the board sporting an erection.

"This mistletoe stuff. The assistant at your store said that when people stand under mistletoe, it's magical." She looked at Jacob with her wide, innocent eyes. The air left his lungs in a rush. She shook her head in disgust. "I don't feel any different. If there's magic in this stuff, it's a very low grade."

A bark of laughter burst from his lips before he could restrain it. Marlie face crumbled.

"Sorry," he apologized quickly. "Didn't you intend that to be a joke?"

A weak smile formed on her face. "I guess," she said, looking cautiously at the plant above her head.

"Marlie, when you stand under mistletoe, you're supposed to get kissed. That's the tradition."

Her eyes crinkled at the edges and her lips pulled up in disgust.

"That's it? You get kissed? Why would someone want to stand underneath this silly plant for that?"

"Not big on kissing, huh?" Too bad. He could spend a lot of time on that mouth. In that mouth.

"Well, it's okay I guess. I kissed one of the other elv — one of the guys at work. It was mildly interesting but I don't know why it would be considered magical." She squished her lips together. "Do you think it depends on who you're kissing?" she asked with intrigued innocence.

"Definitely."

"Really? Hmm. Then I should try it again because I'm looking for all the Christmas magic I can use. Will you kiss me?"

Damn, now she was reading his thoughts. He cleared his throat. "Uhm." *Not appropriate, she's an employee. Even worse, if you start you won't stop.*

Both good logical reasons for not kissing his housekeeper but neither of them seemed to stay in his mind for long.

"Come on." She hadn't moved out from underneath the mistletoe. "I want to see if this stuff really affects a kiss or not."

She has to be stopped and she has to be stopped now, before she does any more damage and I find myself standing under a cold shower the rest of the night.

"I don't think that's a good idea." Jacob locked his legs to keep them from moving across the room. They were no longer taking willing direction from his mind. Like the rest of his body, they were being guided by hormones.

"Maybe the plants I bought are defective. I think we should test them before your friends get here."

It was a simple kiss. That's all it would be. Nothing magical. A kiss. He kissed people all the time. Well, not all the time. He usually kissed Natalie's cheek when he saw her. But a real kiss...

He sighed. He was going to do it. It was becoming painfully obvious that he was only fooling himself. After sleeping next to her, and waking up on top of her the last two mornings, feeling her body wrapped around his, the opportunity to taste her was too much temptation to resist.

Jacob wiped his hands on the dishtowel and threw it on the counter. Determined to get this over with, he walked across the room until he stood mere inches away from her. Pausing, he took a deep breath—and instantly regretted it. The sweet scent Marlie carried with her filled his lungs—it was like a mixture of pine and cinnamon and everything Christmas. And he'd never consumed anything as sexual as that scent. She leaned her head back to look up at him but didn't step away. Almost as if she was afraid to move out from under the mistletoe before she'd been kissed.

Her wide curious eyes stared up at him and he braced himself, clinging to the fact that reality could never compete with his dreams, his fantasies. It would be a simple kiss—and this would prove that she was nothing special and he could get on with his life. He reached for her and began to bend down to her level.

Marlie met him halfway, popping up on her tiptoes and smacking a quick kiss on his lips before dropping back onto her heels. His hand never even made it around her. Jacob pulled back. She scrunched her lips together, her eyes squinted in thought.

Finally she shook her head. "There might have been something there. But I can't tell if it was the mistletoe or just you. You have that nice warmth about you all the time and this was a little warmer than the last time."

That was her idea of kiss?

"Maybe I should try it again." She bounced up on her toes and reached for him. Jacob placed his hands on her shoulders and held her down. Marlie blinked and looked up at him.

"Let's try something different."

"I thought mistletoe was for kissing. That's what I was doing."

"Let's try a different kind of kissing."

"I didn't know there was more than one flavor," she said with a mocking laugh. "But okay, if you want." She puckered lips and waited. And waited.

He wiped his palms on his trousers before reaching for her. He needed a place to put his hands.

Her ass. Grab her ass.

Her shoulders are more appropriate.

But not as much fun. Go for her ass.

Jacob indulged a moment in fantasizing how he'd explain to some future psychotherapist that the voices first appeared in his head when he was preparing to kiss his housekeeper.

"Ca we gea a moo on?" Marlie demanded through pursed lips. "My mouf isf getting dired."

Jacob flexed his hands, spreading his fingers, warming them up for the contact with Marlie. *The waist, that was a good choice.* He couldn't believe he was nervous—like a boy facing his first kiss. He shook out his hands to release the tension and placed them lightly on her hips. He leaned in, moving closer to her mouth.

"Okay." *Friendly. Easy.* "Just sort of relax and follow my lead." He drew her close until their bodies almost touched. "Here goes," he warned as he leaned the short distance down to her level. He paused just before their lips met, breathed in her delicious scent and moved that final fraction of an inch, resting their mouths together, linking them. Jacob pressed no further, giving her a moment to adapt to the sensation. He mentally sighed. It would be okay. *I'm in control. I'm not losing it. I'm...*

Her lips relaxed under his, softening, accepting the light pressure. He turned his head and moved against her. The sweet flavor infiltrated his senses and the light caress wasn't enough. He needed to feel all of her. His mouth moved of its own accord, caressing her lips, drawing her closer. His eyes drifted closed and all thoughts left his mind. There was only Marlie, her taste, her touch, her response. Her touch was shy but eager. Jacob cupped the back of her head and guided her, making their mouths fit, closer, deeper.

He didn't know if it was intentional but she opened her lips ever so slightly, enough to call him inside. Like everything, she welcomed the penetration of his tongue with surprise and trust. He pushed inside, moving slowly, savoring her newness and the way she learned to kiss him back, twining her tongue around his, sucking lightly.

Her fingers dug into his shoulders—as if the sensation had startled her but seconds later she relaxed and wrapped her arms around his neck, holding him tight. Together they learned the rhythm of their kiss, returning each caress and seeking more.

His cock swelled at the warmth and promise of her mouth.

Jacob forced himself to lift his head breaking free of her firm grip and the sensual thrall of their kiss. Damn. It was better than his dreams.

"What was that?" Marlie asked in a breathless voice that proved to Jacob he'd succeeded in making her first real kiss a memorable experience.

Mentally, patting himself on the back, Jacob answered casually. "That was a different kind of kiss."

She blinked her eyes and shook her head as if to clear away the fog. "Now I know why people buy this mistletoe stuff." Marlie launched herself against his chest, wrapping her arms around his neck and pulling his mouth down to hers. Their lips met taking only a moment for their mouths to instinctively align themselves.

He tried to resist, or tried to *convince* himself to resist, but Marlie was too intriguing and he couldn't bring himself to turn away the opportunity.

His hands tightened on her hips, pulling her close. Marlie moved eagerly into him, those tightly bound breasts pressing into his chest. Her fingers slid into his hair, holding and positioning his head as she experimented. Jacob closed her eyes and let her learn, every awkward stroke filled with desire. His control lasted only moments before he took command of the kiss, driving his tongue into her mouth, squeezing her ass and pulling her hard against him. A firestorm erupted in his body.

Heat enveloped his groin. He had the vague awareness of leaving the doorway and pressing Marlie against the wall—his hands under her skirt and holding her bare ass. *Oh fuck, she's not wearing panties.* He pulled her forward, easing her legs apart to make a place for his cock. The warmth from her pussy flowed through his trousers as he eased his erection between her legs, pulsing slowly against her, mimicking the way he wanted to fuck her, deep and long. She groaned into his mouth as he rocked into her.

Marlie snapped her head back and drew in a breathy gasp. Her lips were open and damp, wet from his kisses. Her breasts rose and fell in the tight confines of her top but she made no attempt to move out of his embrace.

She trailed her tongue across her bottom lip. Jacob followed the seductive path with his eyes. "You taste so good," she whispered against his mouth.

He could barely comprehend what she was saying. Her naked ass in his hands, her lips on his, he had to have her. He sealed their lips together, driving his tongue back into the warmth of her mouth—pulsing his hips, showing his need to drive his cock into her in the same way. She whimpered and squeezed her arms around his neck.

His ears began to ring, bells echoing through his senses.

Jacob jerked away. He stared down at Marlie. Her kiss had made him hear bells.

Chapter Eight

It was insane. He was hearing bells. Marlie's sensual smile clouded Jacob's mind even more. Her fingers tightened in his hair and he allowed himself to be drawn back to her. She placed delicate tasting kisses on his mouth, learning quickly to use her tongue and slow bites of her teeth.

The bells rang again. Jacob jerked his head back.

The doorbell. He stared down at their bodies—her knee was wrapped around his hip, his hands were under her skirt and his cock had returned to its favorite place.

"Damn."

Another few minutes and he'd have been inside her. Traces of her moisture teased his fingertip giving him confirmation of what he already knew—she was naked under that dress. Digging deep inside to find the will, he lifted his hands off her ass and pressed down on the inside of her knee to get her to release him. Marlie's disappointment appeared to match his as she reluctantly lowered her leg. Her lips were swollen and sexy. Between the tousled hairstyle and the pouty mouth she looked like a woman recently fucked—and in need of being fucked again.

"The board. They're here," he said though his tongue was thick. "I'd better go let them in." He stepped back, breaking the final connection between their bodies. Looking down at the rumpled sexual woman staring up at him, he groaned. Just a few more minutes and he would have been inside her, enjoying the heat and wetness that flowed from her pussy.

The corners of Marlie's lips turned down and he had to fight himself not to kiss her again and promise he'd be right back. He wouldn't be right back. He was going to spend the next two hours talking business with these people and then probably check himself into the nearest insane asylum because he'd be crazed by frustration by then.

Taking a deep breath, he forced himself to walk away, leaving the kitchen and Marlie behind. The long night ahead tormented him but there was no getting out of it. He straightened his tie and stalked to the door.

A sprig of mistletoe dangled from the doorframe. A distant dread filled his chest.

Marlie had hung the stuff all over the house.

The doorbell chimed again as he reached it. Great, they were impatient to come in, and he was impatient for them to leave. So close. He'd felt her. She'd been willing. He was never more irritated to see the board.

Jacob forced his lips into a stiff smile and opened the door. Natalie stood at the front of a short line of people, her arms tightly crossed on her chest, her eyes blazing with annoyance. Damn, he'd forgotten he'd invited her tonight. At the time, it had seemed like a good idea—a date for the pseudo-social dinner. Natalie knew precisely how to interact with this crowd...but now there was Marlie.

"Welcome." Jacob extended the general greeting to the crowd and stepped back to allow them entrance—and to put a few people between him and Natalie's glare. He'd never considered himself a coward before but Natalie was a complication he didn't want to deal with tonight.

Jacob took coats from everyone, hung them in the closet and directed the people into the living room to find drinks and hors d'oeuvres. Natalie waited at the end of the crowd. She handed her velvet cape to him after the rest of the group had moved away.

"If you'd give me a key, we wouldn't have to wait in situations like that," she said with exaggerated sweetness. Closing her eyes, she tilted her face up to him.

She was waiting for his kiss. He always greeted her with a light kiss, but tonight the concept seemed wholly unappealing. His tongue was still savoring the taste of Marlie and he was reluctant to have any sensation intrude on the physical memory.

The doorbell rang, saving him from having to respond. He waved his hand toward the living room. "If you want to join the others, I'll just get that." The twin fires of Natalie's dagger eyes pierced his back as he pulled the door open to greet the next couple but she was all smiles and welcoming as she led the new arrivals into the living room like it was her right as hostess.

The moment they walked into the living room, Jacob let out the breath he'd been holding but he only got a moment's respite before the doorbell rang again. In truth, it was Marlie's job to greet his guest but he wasn't sure she should be the first thing they saw walking into his house.

In a short time, an elegantly dressed group of people lounged in his living room, sipping drinks and talking quietly. It was a carbon copy of the previous year's Christmas gathering at his house, and probably of the year before that.

But that was about to change.

Marlie walked into the room carrying a platter of mini-quiches fresh from the oven. Almost as a unit every man in the room turned and stared, their eyes going directly to Marlie's displayed breasts. The women looked next and Jacob saw more than one raised eyebrow. But Marlie didn't seem to see any of them. She searched the crowd and found him standing behind the bar. Her eyes still carried the heat from their kisses and the way she licked her lips told him she was remembering as well. A fist of greedy hunger slammed into Jacob's stomach as she strolled through the crowd, greeting board members and introducing herself, her ass swinging in a subtle rhythm that begged a man to fuck her. Muscle by muscle his body tensed, ready to lunge at any man who might touch his little red belle.

But everyone stayed a polite distance away. Good. He didn't like the idea of beating up any of the old men on the board. Marlie bent over, leaning closer to Myron Parish's wife, Jennifer. The movement highlighted both her ass and her breasts and it was all he could do not to fly over the counter and drag her from the room. Instead, he grabbed the nearest bottle of wine and a glass.

He gulped half the glass of wine, then refilled it. *I will not think about Marlie*, he commanded himself.

Marlie. Pressed against him, her hands sliding through his hair, Marlie up against the wall. Her tight hot —

Jacob thunked the wine bottle onto the counter.

A subtle warmth seeped into the left side of his body and he looked. Somehow she'd made it through the room and taken up the space beside him. She stepped into his personal body space and lifted her smiling face to his. He moved by instinct, slipping his arm around her waist, pulling her against him. He bent his head, drawing closer to those lips that tempted him. Closer, closer.

"Jacob, darling," Natalie's sharp voice interrupted his downward path. He jerked away like a child told not to touch the burning candle. "Aren't you going to introduce us to your friend?"

Jacob darling? Darling? Marlie fought the urge to snarl. *He's not your darling*, she mentally growled. She stared at the tall, elegant woman who rested her hand casually on Jacob's arm. Marlie bit her teeth together. *Why is she touching him? He isn't hers to touch.*

Never in her elf life had she felt an instant dislike for someone. Elves liked people. Even at the Workshop, Marlie didn't actively dislike any of the other elves. She found some of them mildly annoying, but this...this overwhelming feeling of ickiness — she didn't know how to react.

I'd like her a lot better if she'd step away from Jacob, Marlie acknowledged. She pinched her lips together and tried to breathe. *Jacob's my human.*

"Who did you say this is, Jacob?" Natalie's cool voice brought Marlie back.

"Oh, yes, Natalie, this is Marlie, my housekeeper." He turned to Marlie and gave her a tight smile. He seemed to be saying something to her in that look, a warning of some sort. She ignored it and waited for the rest of the introduction. "Marlie, this is Natalie Simmons, my, uh, friend."

Marlie sighed. *Fine. If she's a friend of Jacob's, I can be nice.* Although why he'd have such a sour friend she didn't know, but still, sharing the holidays with friends was an important part of a Christmas spirit. Jacob would need all the help he could get. Marlie stuck out her hand to Natalie and tried to sound welcoming.

"It's nice to meet you, Natalie. I'm surprised at how many *friends* Jacob has. You're the third one I've met." Marlie clicked off each one on her fingers. "There's his assistant at the store, and then there's the pretty woman down in Triumph's Christmas store, she really likes him." Natalie's lips tightened. "And of course there's me." She smiled up at Jacob. This could be how she could help him regain his Christmas spirit. "Jacob and I have become very good friends in the past few days. Haven't we?"

"What? Yes, friends." Jacob stared down at her. The emerald green of his eyes melted for a moment before he pulled himself away. "That's what we are," he said to Natalie. "We're friends."

"I think we've established that," Natalie replied in sharp tones.

Okay, new path to take. Marlie jotted it down in her mental notebook. *Get Jacob some new friends.*

"Why, Jacob…"

Marlie's jaw tightened and the sound of her teeth grinding almost drowned out the seductive purring of Natalie's voice. The other woman pouted her ruby-lined lips and leaned forward. Friend or not, Marlie decided she wasn't going to like Natalie much.

"You're standing under mistletoe," Natalie whispered as she stepped closer to Jacob, her shoulders swaying seductively in her strapless evening gown. "I believe that means you get a kiss." She trailed her fingers up the sleeve of Jacob's jacket.

Natalie kiss Jacob? The tiny hairs on the back of Marlie's neck stood straight up. It had been a relatively calm evening so far, but she had this horrible fear that if Natalie kissed Jacob, that was going to change.

"Here, I'll do it," Marlie announced and planted herself between Jacob and Natalie. She smiled over her shoulder to the other woman. "I need the practice." She wrapped her hands around his neck, slid her fingers into his soft hair and pulled his mouth down to hers.

After a momentary resistance, he followed her lead and bent to her level. She touched her lips to his, just as he'd taught her, the barest hint of contact, heightening the anticipation. But she couldn't hold back for long. His mouth was as warm as her recent memories and she moved closer, pressing their bodies together and melding their lips together. Her mouth opened at the first seeking quest of his tongue. It was too wonderful. She loved this kind of kissing. Shivers of pleasure skittered down her spine and settled just south of her stomach, urged on by the warmth of Jacob's hands on her hips.

A warm growl vibrated in Jacob's chest and Marlie caught the sound in her mouth, savoring it.

A harsh, angry throat clearing sound broke through the warm glow around her. With a final taste of his bottom lip, Marlie retreated. For a moment it looked like Jacob was going to kiss her again. Then he pulled back and stared wide-eyed — first at Marlie, then at the rest of room.

Jacob's harsh breath echoed through the room. Marlie froze. *What happened to the party noises?* She peeked at the other guests. Natalie watched them with angry eyes, her arms folded across her chest, her lips pinched so tightly they were turning white. Marlie let her gaze wander beyond Natalie and saw that the whole room was looking at her and Jacob. After a brusque nod, Jacob stepped away from her and stared at the air above her shoulder while he straightened his tie.

Had she done it wrong? Jacob himself had taught her to kiss and surely he knew how to do it right. It seemed right to her.

"So, Jacob, I don't believe I've been introduced to your friend yet." A tall, gray-headed man slapped Jacob on the shoulder and gave him a knowing smile. The slap seemed to be the signal for the rest of the guests to re-animate and quiet conversations and the clinking of glasses once again filled the room.

"My who?" Jacob's voice came out tight and constricted. Marlie jabbed him with her elbow. "Oh, yes, of course. Marlie, this is Patrick Belden. Patrick, this is Marlie."

"His housekeeper," Natalie added through tight teeth from behind Patrick.

Patrick's eyes widened as he looked from Marlie to Jacob and back again. Patrick winked to her and nudged Jacob in the side.

"I had one of those once."

Natalie's eyes shrunk to tiny slits and she glared at Patrick's back as he walked away. Her gaze returned to Marlie and for the first time, Marlie felt the full power of intense dislike. The tiny muscle at the side of Natalie's neck vibrated with tension. Still, when she opened her mouth, her voice was smooth, her words sweet.

"So, Jacob, did your *housekeeper* decorate? It's adorable." The lie in her words oozed through the air. Holding onto her resolve to be nice to Jacob's friends, Marlie tried to summon a smile. And failed.

"Yes, Marlie did this today." The relief was evident in Jacob's voice. Marlie silently shook her head. *He really thinks she's complimenting me on the decorations. Wake up there, Jacob.*

But she had to admit. It did look pretty good.

She'd added ornaments to the well-lit tree and strung more lights around the room, hanging them from every available hook on the walls or in the ceiling. They twinkled like stars on a dark night. The tree dominated the far corner of the living room. It took up a large chunk of the available body space but Marlie had known this was the right tree. And her instincts hadn't failed her. A group of the guests stood near the tree, the admiration evident on their faces. Marlie's shoulders lifted in pride. *Even the Workshop decorators would have approved.*

And then there was the mistletoe. What a wonderful addition that had been. Marlie looked around for the nearest batch and tried to calculate how to get Jacob underneath it.

"But mistletoe is so…mundane, don't you think?" Natalie interrupted Marlie's thoughts with a casual wave at several of the plants hanging from the ceiling. "So common, I would think." Natalie raised an eyebrow in challenge to Marlie. "And dangerous. You know, mistletoe is quite poisonous."

Marlie smiled sweetly and batted her eyelashes. "If you don't nibble on the decorations, we won't have a problem." She stepped in front of Jacob before Natalie could respond. "I think it's time we got dinner ready, don't you?"

She tugged on his hand, dragging him behind her so he couldn't disagree, not stopping until they were in the kitchen. Actually in the kitchen doorway. Under the mistletoe.

"Marlie, you have to be nice to my —"

She silenced his words with a kiss. There was no hesitation this time. His mouth met hers and she opened to welcome his tongue. It was so delicious but she wanted more. She cuddled up close to him, letting her breasts press against his chest and savoring the warmth that seemed to spike through her nipples into her core. Not quite close enough, she edged her hips closer. She wanted more of that wonderful pressure between her legs.

He trailed his mouth down the length of her throat and a whole new world of options popped into Marlie's head. Kisses everywhere. Just like his dream.

"We have to stop this," he muttered against her skin.

"Why?" The question was a groan torn from her throat. Why would he want to stop such wonderful sensations burning through her body? She dropped her head to the side, giving him greater access, even as she pressed against him, her hips falling into a natural pulsing rhythm against his.

"We can't..." he said, lifting his head but not quite separating their bodies. The tight muscles on his neck tempted her and she couldn't resist brushing her tongue across it. A heady masculine scent filled her head as she explored his throat with her lips and tongue, loving the way he tasted and moved. "No, baby, we have to stop."

With that firm statement, Jacob set Marlie away from him. She blinked those intense, explicit eyes up at him, making his cock hard and so ready.

Deep, heavy breaths tortured his lungs. He had to think. He had to think and to do that, he had to stay away from Marlie. The minute she got within two feet of him, all coherent thought disappeared.

"We can't keep doing this," he stated in a harsh whisper. She opened her mouth to respond, but Jacob cut her off. "No, listen we have to stop. I can't concentrate when you kiss me—"

"Really? Me neither." She slipped past his defenses and pressed her lips to base of his throat. "I feel all warm and tingling inside. But why would you want to stop?"

Why stop? Ah fuck he couldn't think of a reason, no, wait, there were twenty-plus reasons standing in his living room waiting for him to serve dinner.

He grabbed her hands in his and pulled them from around his neck and took a step away. Her eyes turned sad, like he'd just stolen her favorite treat.

He took a deep breath and tried to focus. He was in control for now, but knew he was moments away from bending her over the kitchen counter and fucking her until their legs gave out.

No. He forced the most recent fantasy from his mind. "This dinner is very important, and so I'm asking you—" silently he added, *I'm begging you,* "to please not kiss me. In fact I want you to stay away from me for the rest of the night."

Tears appeared in Marlie's eyes and the blatant pain stabbed him in his chest. But his head had finally dominated the lust surging through his body and there was no stopping now. He stared at her—willing her to agree. Finally she sniffed and nodded. With a shuddering sigh, she turned away, her shoulders drooping forward as she walked through the kitchen collecting potholders.

"But what about the mistletoe?" she asked. "Someone is supposed to kiss you when you walk under it. I thought that's what the magic was all about."

Oh, God. She'd hung the stuff all over the downstairs. He'd never be able to avoid it.

"I'll think of something."

"You could always have Natalie kiss you." Marlie bit the words out through clenched teeth. Was Marlie jealous of Natalie? It would be like a rose being jealous of a blade of grass.

"Or—" The clever look on her face seemed to evaporate the tears. "We can hold them on account."

"Hold what on account?"

"The kisses. I'll keep track of how many times you walk under mistletoe and then we'll just make up the kisses later. That will work, right? Unless you just don't want to kiss me."

"No, it's not that," he raced to clarify.

"Well, perfect. I'll keep track and once your friends have left, we'll kiss." She shook her head very seriously. "Christmas magic isn't something you want to mess with."

That seemed to settle it for her and she walked to the oven and began removing the first pan of lasagna. Jacob considered protesting but decided against it. The businessman inside him agreed it was a logical solution. The other half of him viewed it as the perfect idea. He'd be able to kiss Marlie. Later. When everyone was gone. Preferably in a horizontal position. Naked. Naked and horizontal. Naked and upright. Naked and all fours. Didn't really matter at this point.

"Maybe this isn't such a good idea after all," he muttered.

Marlie handed him two oven mitts and a pan of lasagna. "It's too late now. We have nothing else to serve them."

Jacob followed in Marlie's path as she led the way to the formal dining room.

Jacob relaxed as he placed the pan on the table. It wasn't a traditional Christmas dinner but it was food and it looked edible. And now everything would return to normal. They'd sit down have a nice staid dinner and then everyone could go home.

* * * * *

They were never going to leave. Jacob ground his teeth together as Marlie served the final wedges of cheesecake. It hadn't taken the Board of Directors long to fall under Marlie's spell.

Christmas happened no matter what you had or what you ate, she'd announced when she'd presented the unorthodox meal. It wasn't any less Christmas because they were eating lasagna and salad.

124

One by one, each startled board member had begun to smile and enjoy themselves. Only Natalie seemed able to resist. The men still stared at Marlie when she walked by but most of the attention had turned from lust to fatherly affection. All those sexy signals she sent seemed solely direct at him. And if they would all get the hell home, he could do something about it. During the course of dinner, Marlie had been seated four people away from him but her attention still somehow belonged to him. She flashed him teasing smiles or rolled her eyes when someone tried to be too formal.

It was like they were already lovers. And soon they would be. They were going to have sex. That was becoming more and more obvious. It was just a question of when and how. Would he be able to maintain the controlled lust that he'd tolerated over the past ten years or would he find himself digging through the back of his closet looking for a paddle to use on her pert little ass?

Marlie was an excellent hostess. She monitored the table, making sure everyone had enough to eat and plenty of napkins and that no one was trying to be too elegant.

Myron Parish and Patrick Belden, two of the stuffiest, old-fashioned businessmen Jacob had ever worked with, were waving their forks in the air as they led the singing of Christmas carols at their end of the table. Myron's wife sat next to him, draped in a sauce-spotted apron that boldly stated "Get The Hell Out Of My Kitchen". Marlie had found it hanging in the pantry when Mrs. Parish had despaired about the safety of her designer evening dress. She didn't seem too worried now. Jacob watched as she filched the last bite of chocolate cheesecake off her husband's plate.

He didn't know why he was surprised. Marlie had had the same effect on him. Somehow getting him to do things he didn't want to do…and then making him enjoy them.

Marlie had won everyone's heart.

Except Natalie's.

Natalie sat ramrod straight beside him, her arms folded across her stomach. A look of anger and distaste marred her face. She'd spoken few words, and even fewer of them were repeatable. Jacob tried to remember what he'd found attractive or interesting in Natalie but nothing came to mind. She was pretty enough, if you didn't mind cold beauty, but she had none of Marlie's joy and excitement.

Marlie stood up from her place at the formal dining table and reached across the table to pick up the empty salad bowl.

As she walked by him and flashed him a gentle smile. That one smile held an intimacy he'd never felt before. Like they were longtime lovers sharing a private joke. He knew what she was thinking. She glanced up at the mistletoe above the table and winked. His cock twitched. He'd lost count of how many times he'd seen her tick off one more kiss.

When were these people going to leave? He had important business to see to. He had an account he needed to settle.

"So, where did you meet her?"

"What?" Jacob dragged his attention from his frustration back to Natalie. Everyone's focus was on the other end of the table and Natalie was almost whispering so Jacob had to lean closer to hear her.

"Your *housekeeper*. Where did you find her?"

"She's Mrs. Butterstone's niece."

"How lucky for you."

"Yes," he said softly. Strange how in the course of a few hours, he'd gone from irritated to thrilled. When they'd been standing on the street arguing about dinner, he never would have expected the evening to go so well.

"So, should I assume this is just a fling or something more permanent?"

Jacob shook his head absently and then her question registered in his brain. "It's not a fling," he said turning to look at her. "I'm not sleeping with Marlie." *Yet.* He kept his voice low, not sure this was the best place to talk about this. "And it's not permanent. She's just filling in until Mrs. Butterstone gets back."

"So there's nothing between you."

"No," he dismissed, trying not to think about his plans for later. "What would make you say that?"

"The fact that you French kissed her before dinner." Natalie's voice rose slightly above the din but no one seemed interested.

Jacob mentally winced. How was he supposed to explain about Marlie when he didn't quite understand it himself?

Seconds later, Marlie strolled back in. She bent down and whispered in his ear, "That's the last of it." Her low husky voice reminded him of the fascinating sounds she'd made when he kissed her.

She stayed for a long moment, bent over, giving him a direct view of her breasts. As she looked at him, he saw her eyes dip down to his mouth and he knew what she was thinking—kisses. Lots of kisses. Finally she straightened and strolled to the far end of the table to check on their guests. Her ass rocked in a perfect rhythm that held his gaze. Hell, he wasn't even trying to avoid not staring at her as she walked away. She'd dressed for him. He might as well enjoy it. Besides, no one was paying attention to him anyway.

Patrick welcomed Marlie back to his end of the table. He threw his arm over her shoulder, pulling her tight against him, and started singing "White Christmas".

Sending her smile to the whole table, she joined in. Her voice wasn't perfect, wasn't clear, wasn't even always on key but it was filled with such pleasure and joy that the ache in Jacob's chest returned. An invisible band seemed to tighten around his chest making it hard to breathe as he watched her eyes light with a smile. Her sweet smile—even when not directed at him—had the power to affect him.

They finished singing and as the applause cheered them, Patrick slipped his arms around Marlie in a congenial hug. Jacob gripped the table, watching the other man's hands, sure they were going to slide toward her ass. That prime portion of anatomy was *his*. He didn't care if Patrick was on the board, if his hands wandered downward, things were going to get ugly.

"Jacob." At some point in the evening, Natalie had changed his name into a whine. The sound scratched his ears. He dragged his eyes away from Marlie and looked at Natalie, her plate of food untouched. She'd placed several paper napkins on her lap to protect her dress from any stray bit of sauce that might splatter from a neighbor's plate, but she refused to even try the dinner. "Nothing could induce me to eat this," she'd declared and Jacob hadn't tried after that. Personally, he didn't care if she ate. At this point, he didn't care if any of them ate. He just wanted them all to leave.

"Your *housekeeper* is embarrassing you," she whispered, her voice filled with warning.

Jacob glanced at the far end of the table and back to the woman at his side. Her tight mouth was pressed together, emphasizing the tiny frown lines around her lips.

She'd been at his side many times in the last six months. He'd even considered making it a permanent position. It had been a logical decision, based on common interest. They'd been pleasant, equal companions. She fit into his world.

Until he'd met Marlie.

The mere thought of her name and his eyes were drawn to her, watching as she smiled and enchanted his guests. She'd done everything to make sure the board was comfortable and enjoying themselves. And she'd done it for him, only for him. To make him happy.

"Jacob."

"I'm sorry, what?" He shook his head, realizing Natalie was talking to him.

"Never mind." She stood up, letting the napkins flutter to the floor. "I'm leaving."

Jacob jumped to his feet. "You're right," he announced. "It's getting late." Hell, he didn't even know what time it was, but it was time for them to leave.

"Oh my, it is late, isn't it?" Mrs. Parish agreed. She smiled again at Marlie.

"Just one more song," begged her husband, though he stood up along with his wife.

"You can sing in the car," she announced. Their leaving started a general exodus from the table.

Thank you, Natalie. Jacob considered making the obligatory statements of "No, it's early yet. Please stay," but he was afraid they might take him up on his offer. He wanted them gone. All of them. Now. He wanted to be alone. With Marlie.

Jacob escorted them to the door and helped the ladies on with their coats. Marlie hovered as well, making sure everyone was wrapped up tight against the cold and receiving hugs of thanks from the women and some of the men.

"Lovely dinner," Mrs. Parish gushed as she slipped out of her apron and into her fur. "I can't remember when Myron's enjoyed himself more. Isn't that right, Myron?"

In response, Myron started singing "I'll Be Home For Christmas".

Mrs. Parish winked at Jacob. "One too many eggnogs for him." She smiled indulgently at her husband. "I think I'll drive."

"That might be a good idea," Jacob agreed.

"Jacob," Mrs. Parish whispered pulling Jacob away from the crowd. "Wherever did you meet Marlie? She's adorable."

"She's my regular housekeeper's niece."

"Is she from around here?"

"Uhm..." He paused because he had no idea where Marlie was from. "I don't think so."

"Well, wherever she came from, she was an excellent hostess." She tapped his arm. "I think you should consider making it a permanent position for her."

And Jacob knew she didn't mean as a housekeeper.

"Thanks. Well, good night." Jacob stood at the door and watched the last of his guests wander down the drive. No one seemed to be stumbling but they all seemed happy—happy way beyond the effects of alcohol. A happy created by the warmth and joy of a home.

Jacob closed the door with a quiet snap. Marlie had worked magic tonight. *Christmas magic.*

He shook his head. Marlie was affecting more than his hormones. Christmas magic, he scoffed, but the mockery didn't sound real even in his own mind.

The tinkle of plates clanking together drew him back to reality. Marlie and her kisses. His body continued its journey to full hardness, the sweet taste of her soft mouth an easy memory to recall. He shook his head. He'd lost count of how many kisses Marlie had logged, but it looked like the evening was going to heat up a bit.

No longer fighting the fantasy, Jacob allowed his body to respond, enjoying the sensation of desire. He couldn't remember the last time he'd been aroused by the mere thought of making love.

Where did you find her?

Is she from around here?

I have no idea.

The strange conversation repeated through his head and slowed the pace of his heart. What did he really know about her?

Marlie had been very close-mouthed about her previous life. She stumbled over it when he asked her—as if she hadn't had time to prepare an appropriate story. She obviously had a secret that she wasn't willing to share with him. Hints of it seemed to come out when she talked about cuddling up to other men and her old job. A hooker? He laughed at his own thought. She hadn't had much experience with kissing, didn't even seem to realize there were other kisses besides the kind he gave his Aunt Matilda.

Marlie popped out of the kitchen and headed straight toward him. The wide smile and the intent look in her eye warned him what she'd planned. She held a piece of paper in her hand. Dozens of bold check marks covered the page. It was the account. She'd come to settle it.

"I sort of lost track a few times, so I just added a few to the end." She slapped the paper into his hand and stepped close to him, wrapping her arms around his neck. Like before, his body followed her unspoken command and bent to kiss her. Their lips met and his mind went blank.

Why was he resisting this? Her tongue slipped into his mouth—damn, she was a fast learner. The satin feel of her lips caressing his tormented him with thoughts of other places her lips could go.

She slipped away, settling back on her feet. Her breath was as ragged as his as she whispered, "that one doesn't count because you're still standing under mistletoe."

Using control he hadn't exerted in years, he peeled her hands from around his neck and stepped back, holding her hands together, in front of them, between them.

"Marlie, we need to talk."

"Sure, but we have a lot of kisses to catch up on," she said. "And there's still mistletoe hanging all over the house."

"I know, but we really need to talk." He pulled her behind him into the living room. He guided her into a chair before seating himself on the couch nearby, her hands still clasped in his.

"Marlie, what did you do before you came here?"

She blinked and drew back a few inches. She hadn't been expecting that question. "What do you mean?"

"For work. What did you do before you came here?"

"Oh." Her relief was palpable. "I worked in a factory. A toy factory."

He didn't know of any toy makers in town.

"Here?"

"No." Her eyes started to wander as she searched for an answer. "It's in a fairly remote location. Most people haven't heard of it."

"Tell me about it."

"Now?" She leaned forward and the bodice of her dress pulled down, almost spilling her breasts out. With a deep breath, he didn't doubt that she'd be free of the restriction and those hot tight nipples would be available for him. "Couldn't we talk tomorrow? I'd really like to work on the Christmas magic."

Christmas magic. From the mistletoe. Kisses. She thought the kisses brought Christmas magic.

She'd been so sweet with that first kiss—as if she'd truly never been kissed before.

She didn't understand kisses – does she know about sex?

Surely she can't be that innocent.

Under normal circumstances, he would never believe a woman could get to her age without some sort of knowledge about sex but he'd come to accept that much about Marlie wasn't normal.

And if she didn't have a grasp of normal sex, there was no way she was ready for the things he'd been imagining. He mentally put away the paddle. He couldn't take advantage of her.

Kissing was one thing, but naked in bed could definitely be seen as a commitment to someone who didn't understand what was happening. He groaned, feeling the tension return to his body, battling the desire once again.

"Marlie, do you understand, that if we keep kissing the way we are, it's going to lead to sex?" Might as well warn her up front.

She blinked and tilted her head in gentle confusion.

"Is it supposed to?"

"Sometimes." He watched her closely and asked the next question. "Have you ever had sex?"

He tensed, waiting for her indignant response. And waited, while she thought about the question.

Damn it, he had his answer.

Finally she shrugged. "I don't know, where do you get it?"

"No, it's not something you get." He paused. "Well, I guess you do get it in a way. It's something men and women do together." There was no glimmer of recognition in her eyes. Maybe they didn't call it sex where she came from. "It might be called something else. Making love? Consummating a relationship?" She shook her head. "Hooking up?" He sighed. "Okay, let's try this a different way. Do you know where babies come from?"

The look on her face said it all—like he'd just fallen off the turnip truck. "Is this some kind of joke? Of course I know where babies come from."

He eased the ache in his shoulders with a sigh. *Good, now we have something we can work with.* "And do you know how they get there in the first place?"

She rolled her eyes up to the ceiling. "The stork brings them."

A bark of laughter burst from his throat. Trust Marlie to make a joke, lighten the mood. He stared back at her. She wasn't laughing. She wasn't even smiling.

She was serious.

It was insane. A grown woman thought babies were brought by a stork? It had to be a joke. Only Marlie didn't look the least bit amused. She leaned over and kissed him—slow and sweet.

He accepted the kiss but drew back when she tried to deepen it. It was kissing under false pretenses. He wanted to fuck her, had had every intention of fucking her until now.

Instead, he found himself in a rather uncomfortable position. Should he explain sex to Marlie? How could she have gotten to adulthood without knowing about it?

He tried to remember the talk his father had had with him. Somehow, "use a condom and don't get some girl pregnant before you're married" didn't seem appropriate for the situation.

He took a deep breath. "Let me see if I can explain this," he started and began to speak. "Now the man..."

The words stumbled out of his mouth. Marlie listened silently, following his description. She tilted her head in question at his definition of foreplay. Her eyes grew wide as he explained the act of penetration. And she clamped her knees together when he explained about the male climax.

"Any questions?"

"Humans actually do that?"

"Sometimes." Not often enough in his case.

"And if we kiss, we have to do that?"

The appalled, kind of leery, kind of skeptical tone of her voice beat down any hope of that happening anytime soon.

"No, Marlie but that kind of kissing, the way we were doing it, tends to lead to sex."

"Oh." Her mouth formed a tight circle. "Hmm. I need to think about this."

"Good idea."

They both stood up, their bodies almost touching in the tight space between the chairs. She raised her eyes to his even as her tongue peeked out and licked her upper lip.

"But just one more kiss wouldn't make us have the sex right?"

Just one more.

Perfect. Now he could end the day as he'd started it— rock hard.

Chapter Nine

ഗ

Marlie took another sip of her coffee as she wandered through the toy section at Triumph's. Jacob had warned her about drinking too much coffee but she needed the warmth. She'd been freezing the last four days. The only time she was warm was when she was snuggled up to Jacob in the morning. Even after their discussion about the sex, he'd allowed her to sleep with him but he stayed firmly to his side of the bed, gripping the edge so tightly she thought he might fall out.

And she didn't think he was sleeping well. He was getting crabbier as each day passed. This morning when she'd woken up in her usual position—halfway on top of him—he'd barely opened his teeth as he ordered her to slowly, carefully remove her knee from between his legs. He'd hardly spoken to her after that, grunting his agreement to her suggestion of shopping for his parents' Christmas presents today.

She shivered and gulped more coffee. It didn't help. Nothing but Jacob seemed to warm her properly.

It was the sex. It messed up everything.

The day after Jacob had explained it to her, she'd done some research by going to a bookstore and getting the clerk to direct her to the section about sex. Goodness, there were a lot of options out there. And variations. She'd picked one reasonable looking, all-inclusive book and started to read. Now she kept it hidden in the bottom drawer. She didn't want Jacob to know she'd been studying.

A quick glance at her "Elf in the Outside World" handbook that she'd been given at orientation revealed little about the subject. It was one line hidden in the back. "Sex: Contact Santa for more details." She rolled her eyes upward.

Right. After seeing the pictures and reading the book, she wasn't planning to ask Santa about it anytime soon.

No, she had to make the decision on her own. But while she was leaning more toward it every day, Jacob seemed to be pulling back.

She grimaced and knelt down to inspect the teddy bear display. If Jacob had kept his distance before, it was worse now. Well, maybe not worse—he still kissed her, or kissed her back when she initiated it. She had many kisses left on her mistletoe list from the party—though she secretly admitted that she hadn't been as diligent taking them off the list as she had putting them on. The next morning, Jacob had gone through the house and removed all of the mistletoe citing "self-preservation" when Marlie demanded an explanation.

She knew now that mistletoe wasn't required for the kisses but it would have given her an excuse to approach Jacob.

Not that she saw him that much. He'd started spending even more time at work. Each night he'd return home, Marlie would steal a few kisses before he'd disappear into the shower. She'd learned to hunt him down in his study to talk to him each night. Progress on his Christmas spirit was slow but moving forward. He'd stopped complaining about the decorations and she'd even heard him humming a Christmas carol one night as he'd helped clean up her latest mutilation of dinner.

And now, he'd agreed to shop with her. He was supposed to meet her in a few minutes.

"Marlie?" A stunned and startled male voice broke through her thoughts.

She looked up and stared blankly at the man in front of her, trying to place him in her memory. The face looked familiar but...her jaw dropped open.

"Petri?" A grin burst on his face and he looked like he had back at the Workshop. She lunged off the floor and threw herself into his arms. He greeted her with a warm, welcoming hug, as she'd known he would. He *was* an elf, after all. She rested in the comfort of his arms for a moment before pulling back. She couldn't release him completely, so kept hold of his hands. "What are you doing here? What happened to you? You just disappeared." The questions burst forth.

Petri smiled and squeezed her hands. "I was sent on a mission. Is that why you're here?"

Marlie gave him a quick overview of how she'd come to be there. Petri nodded sympathetically.

"Why didn't you return to the Workshop?" she asked.

He shrugged. "I failed in my mission."

The air rushed from Marlie's body. Santa hadn't been kidding. If she failed, she would be here forever. Her heart started to pound.

Petri placed his arm around her shoulders, pulling her close. "Hey, don't worry. I think Santa would have let me come back." He shook his head. "I don't think I was made for Workshop life." Marlie nodded. She'd mentioned him to Jacob the first night she was here. Petri liked to play computer games instead of completing his work.

She looked into his eyes. He looked happy. And she told him so.

"I am happy. I run a Christmas store, if you'd believe it, and I consult with big corporations on their holiday decorations."

"*You* own a Christmas store? But you were worse than I was."

He laughed. "I know but even though I failed my mission, *my* spirit came back in full force."

"What happened to your human?"

The grimace that curled Petri's lips made Marlie laugh. "I'm still working on her. I swear, she is the crabbiest woman, but I haven't given up."

"So you still see her?" Marlie tried to keep the interest out of her voice. That was hopeful.

"I see her about twice a month. She's my sister-in-law."

Marlie felt her mouth sag open. "You're married?"

"Oh, yeah." Again, pure happiness radiated from Petri. He pulled out his wallet and fanned out a series of photos. "Here's my wife Barbara and our kids."

Marlie stared back into his smiling eyes. Peace washed over her. The kind of peace that filled the Workshop, even on the worst days. She clung to Petri's hands and pressed them to her cheek. They'd been friends in the Workshop, kindred spirits.

The stress of the past week and the fear that she would fail, that Jacob would never understand the spirit of Christmas was too much to bear alone. And if she succeeded, she'd have to leave Jacob behind. She couldn't decide which was worse. She needed someone who would understand. She threw her arms around him and held him to her. He'd found his happiness and love. Petri seemed to understand her need for touch and held her as her mind worked through the fear.

"It's going to be all right, Marlie. I promise."

He said it with such confidence that Marlie had to nod even though she wasn't sure she believed it.

Petri pulled her arm through his, keeping their bodies close.

"So, tell me," he said with a conspiratorial whisper as they wandered past the toys. "What do you think of coffee?"

Jacob stepped off the elevator. His heart surprisingly light despite the prospect of Christmas shopping for his parents. He knew it was because of Marlie. He'd done his best to avoid her for the past five days—his libido couldn't take much more pressure—but she'd found a way to take up a portion of his day and strangely, that time had turned out to be his favorite.

Still it was Christmas shopping. In a crowd of people. He'd never been fond of crowds.

Marlie was waiting for him upstairs but wanted to make a quick run by the Men's Clothing department. He'd left Nichols to deal with his new employee long enough. It was time to see what kind of damage Mitch had done to Men's Clothing and the bottom line for the Christmas season. Triumph's was an upscale store and some of the clients were blatant snobs.

He strolled into the department, casually searching for either Mitch or Nichols. A woman stood at the empty checkout counter a Triumph bag in her hand. Returning something before Christmas was never a good sign.

"Are you being helped?" Jacob asked. He'd grown up in the store and worked in every department. He hated to see a customer waiting.

She opened her mouth and looked him up and down before shaking her head. "That's all right. I'm waiting for Mitch."

Jacob bowed his head and backed away just as Mitch walked in from the outside. He brushed a light dusting of snow off his shoulders and hurried to the counter.

"Sorry about that. She just wasn't going to make it to her car with all that stuff." He looked up and saw Jacob. The first look was one of welcome but then his eyes clouded a bit when he saw it was the boss. He nodded briefly to Jacob but turned back to the customer. "Now, what do you have?"

Jacob watched the transaction from a distance. She returned a suit jacket which it appeared from the conversation, Mitch had recommended she not buy in the first place. But instead of losing money, Mitch led her over to another jacket, a little less expensive but still a good purchase.

"He's quite amazing actually."

Jacob tipped his head to the side to hear Nichols' whisper.

"Been here, what? Five days? And already several customers will only deal with him. It appears that he's got that 'every man' feel to him and has an idea for what 'real men' will wear. He's quite a find, Mr. Triumph. I must congratulate you on your intuition."

Jacob chuckled. It had been Marlie. Marlie had been right. Again. Damn, it felt like he was saying that a lot.

With an eagerness he wasn't expecting, he climbed the escalators to the Fourth Floor and followed the noise to the toy section. Normally, Triumph's didn't carry toys at all but they brought in a full section during the holidays. It was a popular place and a moneymaker so Jacob brought it back every year.

He turned the corner and saw Marlie. He opened his mouth to call out to her but before he could, she wrapped her arms around another man. This was no brief hug. They stood together, embracing and whispering intimately to each other to the exclusion of the store around them.

A low burning began in Jacob's stomach. It wasn't jealousy, he told himself. But who was Marlie hugging? And for such a long time. They didn't notice him as they pulled back from their embrace and huddled their heads together, walking arm in arm.

The urge to Christmas shop was quickly overwhelmed by the desire to rip this asshole's head off but Jacob knew he was too civilized for that. What did it matter? She was just his housekeeper after all.

Exhaustion that he'd barely held at bay for the past four days crept up on him and he knew he couldn't face the shops and crowds. The toy clerk walked by, straightening one of the displays.

"Margaret, Marlie's around here somewhere," he said vaguely though he knew she'd just disappeared behind a stack of stuffed lions. "Could you tell her I can't meet her today and I'll see her later at home?"

He didn't stop to see if she agreed to pass on his message. He turned and headed toward the elevators. He had work to do.

* * * * *

Marlie bared her teeth and took out her frustration on the pan, raking the scrubbing pad across the bottom of the skillet, trying to dislodge the final bits of burnt chicken before Jacob got home. She didn't want him to see she'd burned dinner, again. She lifted her head and sighed, willing to concede and let the pan win. Jacob was rich. He could buy another skillet.

It had been one of those days, and she had the burnt dinner and wounded laundry to prove it. And missing out on the chance to see Jacob in the middle of the day had just made it worse. Seeing Petri had been fun but she was still disappointed at missing time with Jacob.

Petri had been a great help to her in many ways. Once she'd heard that Jacob wouldn't be meeting her, they'd sat and talked. She'd asked him about the sex and after his cheeks had stopped turning red, he'd been most informative. He'd warned her not to have the sex with Jacob unless she actually had feelings for him. It still worked without the feelings, he said, but wasn't as good.

Well, she certainly had feelings for Jacob. She liked him, enjoyed him, it hurt to think of leaving him, and drat, she wanted this need inside her to go away. From Petri's description, she was feeling all the right things.

Now she just had to tell Jacob. How did a woman tell a man she wanted the sex with him?

The front door slammed. Jacob was home. Marlie brushed her hair away from her face and headed out of the kitchen.

They met in the hall, their bodies colliding as he tried to walk toward his office. Marlie caught herself against his chest and used the opportunity to give him a quick hug. His arms automatically closed around her but they dropped away before she could enjoy their warmth. Looks like a night without kisses, she thought with a sigh.

"I'm glad you're home. Can we—" She stepped away from him and Jacob shoved a bag of wrapped packages into her hands. "What's this?"

"Christmas presents. For my parents," he sighed. He sounded supremely disinterested in the boxes.

"Oh," she said taking the bag and peeking in the top. The boxes were all neatly wrapped in red and gold foil paper. "I was hoping we could go shopping tonight."

Jacob rubbed his hand across his eyes. "It's done."

Marlie tried to hide her disappointment. Still, if Jacob had taken the initiative to purchase presents, that was all that mattered. It *really* didn't matter that he'd done it without her, she told herself. "What did you buy?" she asked putting more interest into her words than she felt.

He shrugged. "I don't know. Some jewelry and a shirt for my dad, I think. I had Anne do it."

Marlie felt a momentary flash of jealousy. *Some other woman helped Jacob with his Christmas shopping?* It died quickly. Jacob tried to move past her to the right. Marlie stepped in front of him. He swerved to the left. She was there.

"Anne? The Personal Shopper?" Her teeth clenched together. All thoughts of sex disappeared.

Jacob set down his briefcase and turned away, finding an open path into the living room. "Yes."

The weight of the day pressed down on her. "You had a personal shopper pick out your parents' Christmas gifts?" she sputtered. She stalked into the room behind him. Jacob dropped onto the couch, pushed the Christmas pillows onto the floor and stretched out. He folded his arms across his chest and looked coolly at Marlie.

She ran stiff fingers through her hair. How could he do this to her? She was supposed to be instructing Jacob on the ways of a true Christmas spirit and he had a personal shopper pick out presents for his parents? Santa was not going to like this.

"Did you even look at them?"

"Why? Anne's good at her job." He picked up a magazine and covered his face. Marlie plucked it out of his hands and tossed it over her shoulder.

"They aren't Anne's parents," she bit out.

"It's just a Christmas present." He grabbed another magazine from the stack.

Marlie clenched her fists together and released the bloodcurdling scream that welled inside her. It got Jacob's attention. He dropped the magazine and sat up. She propped her fists on her hips and glared down at him.

"What in the hell is wrong with you?" he demanded.

"I'm never going to get home and it's your fault. I'm going to be trapped in this world forever and right now the only things I'm qualified to do are paint toys and clean houses and let me tell you, I am not washing dishes for the rest of my life." She started to turn away, then spun back to face Jacob. "If I'm stuck here, I'm going to haunt you the rest of my days.

She shoved both hands through her hair and began to pace. "Simple assignment. Teach a human the spirit of Christmas. Can't be hard right?" she asked, barely including Jacob in her glance. "I didn't know he was sending me to the original Scrooge." She said the last words right to Jacob. She folded her arms across her chest and continued the next lap around the room. "I don't even get two weeks to fix you. It's going to take *two years* to give you even a glimmer of the meaning of Christmas. Normal people have some feeling but not you, no—"

"You were sent here? To fix me? What the hell does that mean?"

She continued, barely hearing him. "I hope Santa takes into account that you have—"

Jacob jumped up from the couch and planted himself in front of her.

"What are you talking about? Why were you sent here and what does Santa Claus have to do with this?"

Marlie gulped. Oops. She'd said too much. Now, how did she get out of it?

She cursed her temper. Santa had always warned her it would get her into trouble someday. Well, that day had arrived.

I can't lie to him. She stopped. No, she *could* lie to him. She'd done it before. In the beginning. It was different now. She knew him. She liked him. And she didn't think telling a lie would help get his spirit back. She lifted her chin, pushed her shoulders back and stared into his eyes.

"I'm a Christmas elf," she stated defiantly.

He didn't know if it was the tone of her voice or the set of her chin but something stopped his laughter. This wasn't a joke. She really believed this.

"An elf," he finally repeated in a flat voice.

"I work in Santa's Workshop."

"I think you'd better sit down." He moved out of the way. "You're having hallucinations."

"It's the truth. I was sent here to teach you the true spirit of Christmas." Great, her hallucinations were to torment him about the holidays.

"Marlie." Jacob placed a comforting hand on her shoulder. He felt her relax beneath his touch. He'd known she was a little quirky but he'd ignored it. He hadn't expected full on insanity. In as soothing a voice as he could manage he asked, "Is there a doctor that you regularly see?"

"Arrgh!" She screamed and Jacob jumped back.

"I was only trying to help," he defended.

"I am not crazy so stop trying to calm me. I am an elf."

Jacob held up his hands in surrender. He'd done his part. She was crazy and pissed. "Fine. Whatever."

After everything else, and with Christmas so close, he couldn't deal with this. He tried to walk away but Marlie jumped in front of him. She had the knack of being right where he wanted to go.

"I really do work in Santa's workshop," she insisted, the anger disappearing from her voice. "Where they make the toys. I paint red."

"Paint red."

"I paint red. You know, little red wagons, fire trucks. Red," she finished with a forced smile. "Santa sent me to help you."

"Santa?"

"Yes, Santa. You know, the man in the red suit," Marlie snapped, her temper returning quickly. "Do you have to repeat everything I say?" She closed her eyes to calm herself and when she opened them Jacob was gone. He'd slipped past in that brief moment. "I was sent here to help you. You could at least listen," she called after him, following her words down the hall.

He glanced back. "I did. You're crazy."

"It's the truth, you twit," she bit out between clenched teeth. She trailed him back into the entryway. He'd stopped trying to soothe her. And it looked like he intended to ignore her.

He picked up his briefcase before looking at her. "I thought elves were supposed to be cheerful, perky little creatures," he said with a patently false smile.

"I'm being as perky as I know how. This wasn't *my* idea, you know. Santa sent me."

"Why have I been on his naughty list?" Jacob sneered.

"More times than I can count." His eyes widened. *At least he's listening.* "If I'd been Santa, there were times when every piece of footwear you owned would have been coated in soot."

His jaw dropped open. Marlie didn't have time to stop. She finally had his attention and she wasn't going to waste it.

"Forgiven, forgotten." She dismissed it with a brush of her hand. "Now, you're in worse shape. You have no Christmas spirit."

"I can live with that."

"No. It's important. I have the same problem."

"Really?" His cold, mocking tone spurred Marlie on.

"That's why Santa threw me out of the Workshop."

"Oh, this gets even better. Santa doesn't send me a real elf. He sends a delinquent." Jacob walked off, ignoring her.

"Jacob," she called to his back.

"I've got work to do." He stopped at the door to his office. Marlie watched the muscles through the soft material of his shirt tighten. "Get your stuff and get out," he commanded in a soft, steel voice.

"No."

"What?" He whirled around to face her.

"I'm not leaving."

He stalked forward, using his height to intimidate. Marlie stretched to the top of her spine and glared right back at him. She lifted her chin and waited.

"You can't refuse to get kicked out of my house."

"At least let me explain."

"You did, and personally, I think if you were going to have a delusion or a con or whatever it is, you could have come up with something that was supportable."

She pulled the hair away from the side of her face and neck, exposing one ear. The slightly pointed tip was not typical human design. "Look. Tell me humans have naturally pointy ears." Jacob leaned to the side to get a better look at the exposed ear. He straightened and shrugged. "Tell me you've seen ears like this," she demanded.

"No, but I've seen bodies in magazines that aren't natural either. It's amazing what plastic surgery can do these days."

"Why would I change my ears?" She stared at him with the same "you must be insane" look he'd been giving her.

"I don't know," he said with a disinterested sigh. Marlie felt her heart pound. He'd stopped yelling. She was losing him. "Members of some fringe Star Trek fan clubs get their ears surgically altered to look like Spock's. I don't think they're headed for space anytime soon." He turned and walked away, closing his office door behind him.

Marlie sighed and the energy just drained out of her body. She'd failed. She was going to be trapped in the Outside World forever.

And she wouldn't have Jacob. The prospect of being left in this world wouldn't be impossible to face, if she had Jacob.

Pain lanced her heart. *Jacob.* She'd hurt him. The sadness in his eyes, the droop of his shoulders. If she left now, would he regain any amount of trust? *Jacob, alone, with no love.* She couldn't leave him like this. She had to make it better.

She could make a wish for Jacob, one that would help him see the real meaning of Christmas.

A wish. Marlie gasped. *That's it. A Christmas wish.* She was an elf after all. All Jacob had to do was make a wish and when it came true, he'd believe.

She tapped on his door and entered without being asked.

"I've got a solution," she stated as she walked to his desk. He hadn't opened his briefcase. Marlie used it to lever herself up on his desk and folded her legs as she spun around to face him.

Jacob crossed his arms on his chest and leaned back in his chair, the skepticism on his face was only shrouded by the cold disinterest she hadn't seen there since their first meeting.

"After I got in trouble at the Workshop for being overly cranky about Christmas, Santa sent me to you hoping that in helping you regain your Christmas spirit, I'll get mine back as well." Marlie spoke quickly, knowing she only had a few moments of his attention before he realized he'd made a deal with a Christmas elf. "I have proof. That I'm an elf," she rushed on.

"Marlie, let's not go through this again." He closed his eyes and dropped his head against the headrest.

"This is something that's truly magical."

Jacob opened his eyes. The skepticism was still there but so was a hint of hope. "Make a wish," Marlie commanded.

"A wish?"

"Yes, a Christmas wish. I'm a Christmas elf. It's what we do. We grant Christmas wishes. Just begin, 'Dear Santa, all I want for Christmas is…' and I'll make it come true." Jacob opened his mouth then snapped it closed.

She watched his eyes—the distrust faded and she saw heat. His wish came to her in a fiery wave.

Her, naked, kneeling on the ground before him, her hands tied behind her back, her eyes staring at the ground.

"Now, Marlie, you must do precisely as I say. Do you understand?"

"Yes, Jacob."

"And if you don't you'll be punished."

"Yes, Jacob."

"Now, I want you to suck my cock. Does that please you?"

"Oh, yes, Jacob." Along with the visual images, she felt the rush of pleasure that this woman felt, the heat between her thighs.

She gasped and stared open-mouthed at Jacob. That was his wish? She had no idea whether she should fulfill it or not but it was definitely intriguing. Was that part of the sex? She'd seen pictures in her sex book with women in similar positions but hadn't gotten that far yet. Maybe she needed to skip ahead. Later. Now, she had to get Jacob back.

"Uh, maybe you better pick something for someone else."

"I can't make a wish for myself? What kind of wish is that?"

"An unselfish one. That's the whole point. Christmas isn't about getting things. It's about love."

"I thought Santa gave out presents. Why can't I wish for a present?" His eyes mocked her but there was no meanness in his gaze. She resisted the urge to kiss the pout off his face. There would be time for that later, if she could make his wish come true. Besides, she knew Jacob didn't really want to wish, he was playing along just to trip her up.

"You have enough stuff. Santa gives out presents, but love is behind those gifts. That's why I was so upset about your parents' gifts. You didn't buy them with love."

"No, I bought them with money, and a lot of it. Trust me, that's all they care about."

"I'm sure it isn't, Jacob. Love is the ultimate gift but most people can't accept it for what it is." Marlie held her hands open to Jacob, willing him to see the truth behind her words and in her heart. "Most humans haven't figured out how to believe in love, so they have to give and get *things* to make love a visible sign." She cocked her head to one side. "Does this make sense?"

"Unfortunately, yes, you're beginning to." Jacob rubbed his fingers across the tight lines on his forehead. She knew that move. He did it when something was giving him a headache. *That would be me.*

Speaking softly, Marlie continued with her instructions. "So make a wish, and Christmas morning you'll know your wish got to Santa himself because you gave it to a real Christmas elf." Marlie thought for a moment. "If it's going to be proof, you'd better think of something a little outrageous."

Jacob sat up in his chair. He tilted his head to the left.

"Wish, huh? Do I tell you what it is?"

"It's probably best. I can sometimes sense them—" *Like that hot little wish you just made.* "But I don't want to miss this one."

"I always thought if you told someone a wish, it didn't come true."

"That's birthday wishes. This is Christmas. Different celebration, unless you're a Christmas elf, of course."

"Of course," Jacob drawled. He rocked back in his chair. The springs squeaked with the effort. He steepled his fingers in front of his face, his forehead crinkled in thought. He sat back up and smiled. He was ready.

"Okay, just say, 'All I want for Christmas is a blank for', and the person's name and you're done."

"Okay."

Marlie waited.

"All I want for Christmas…" she prompted.

"All I want for Christmas is…" He paused and she had the distinct impression he was drawing out the suspense just to tease her. "A dog for my mother." *That wasn't outrageous.* Marlie inspected the smug look on Jacob's face. Something was up. She put it on her list to run by Santa.

"Okay, come Christmas morning, you'll see."

"Fine," Jacob replied. "Christmas morning, if there's a dog under the tree, I'll apologize."

"And if there's not, I'll…admit I was confused."

She reached out her hand and he took it firmly in his. They'd made a deal. Marlie turned her hand so their fingers were entwined together. It felt like they were back on even footing. She hesitated, then asked, "So, can I stay?"

She waited.

"No more talk about elves and workshops?" he asked, dropping his hands away and breaking from her touch.

Marlie sighed. He wanted to act like it didn't happen. Okay, she could handle that. At least for now.

She nodded and climbed off his desk. Jacob joined her as she went to the kitchen.

He opened the refrigerator and pulled out a soda. Marlie went to the cupboard for glasses while he popped the top on the can. Moving with perfect timing, Marlie dropped ice cubes into the two glasses moments before Jacob poured the soda.

Tension still clung to the air—they might have worked out their first problem but how did they get back to that friendship?

"I didn't cook dinner," Marlie said, breaking the silence. Jacob raised an eyebrow. "Well, I did cook dinner but I ruined it. I thought maybe we could go out."

Jacob hated the tentative sound to her voice. She'd never been tentative before. She'd been in-your-face-and-get-out-of-my-way. Throwing her out of the house had been a dumb idea. He hadn't wanted her to leave but he didn't know what else to do. It really seemed as if she thought she was sent from Santa's workshop. Maybe he could introduce her to a nice psychiatrist who might be able to help her.

He considered the idea that it might be an elaborate con but she hadn't asked him for anything. Not even when she would get paid for the work she'd actually done. He scanned the kitchen. Clutter was growing on the counters. Mrs. Butterstone would have never left it looking like this but Marlie wasn't the best housekeeper.

But he wanted to keep her around his house for a while yet. She'd become a part of his home and his life. Each evening he expected to hear her cheerful greeting and feel her kiss.

Now he had to do something to get them back on an even keel.

"Sure, dinner out sounds fine." It wasn't much of an olive branch but it seemed to work. The starch drained from her body and she jumped into his arms, encasing him in a sweet hug. He breathed deep the scent of her hair, his fingers aching to tangle in her tresses.

Tangle in her tresses? Jacob shook his head. It was a bad sign when he started to wax poetic about a woman's hair.

Instinctively he pulled her close, his head automatically bending to meet hers. His body had learned the feel of hers and settled her into the most comfortable, most arousing position.

Their lips met, a light, promising touch that tasted of more. Marlie opened her mouth beneath his, begging for a deeper caress and Jacob knew he couldn't deny her request. His tongue slipped into the warm cavern of her mouth, loving the way she moved with him. She joined in the dance, tasting him as he tasted her. Her hands smoothed up his chest and wrapped around his neck, holding him with surprising strength.

The sensations swarmed over him, closing his mind to lucid thought. The sweet taste of her mouth, the press of her breasts against his chest, the feel of her hands soft on his skin.

He eased his hands down her hips, drawing her against his hardness, moving her against him in a rhythm designed to drive him insane with pleasure.

A tiny groan escaped Marlie's lips as he trailed his mouth down the column of her neck. He arched again into the cradle of her hips.

Marlie lifted her head and looked at him, her mouth opening to speak. She was going to tell him to back off. She hadn't done so yet but he could tell from the tension in her body that she wasn't comfortable. Jacob dropped his hands and stepped away. He'd promised himself he wouldn't push her. She'd said no to sex so he would accept that. It might drive him insane, but he'd accept it. *Then Marlie and I can share the same cell at the mad house — her thinking she's an elf and me, mindless from frustration.*

He cleared his throat, waiting for his heart to stop pounding and his body to relax enough for him to walk. "I think we'd better go."

"But Jacob…"

Distraction. He needed a distraction. "Let's go get dinner and then we'll go Christmas shopping," he suggested, using the first thing that came to mind. The second the words had escaped his tongue he longed to call them back.

He opened his mouth to offer another suggestion and stopped. The smile that glittered in Marlie's eyes caught his breath. She slipped through his defending hands and threw herself against his chest. A faint whimper slipped from his throat. He was getting addicted to the sensation of her body against his. And the feeling of making Marlie happy. *You've totally lost it, man.*

"I knew it. I knew you would make it." She pulled back from him. His heart constricted as she smiled into his eyes. "Besides, I need to get presents for your parents as well." She turned around and headed out of the kitchen.

"You? Why?" he called to her.

"Aren't we going to their house for Christmas?"

Jacob let his eyes stare at her back. *We?* Marlie was coming with him? *Oh, God, Marlie and his parents.*

Okay, Santa, if you really grant Christmas wishes, ground the planes on Christmas Eve.

"I'm ready," Marlie called as she walked down the hall, pulling on her heavy coat. Pleasure surrounded her. What the hell. He could spend a few hours looking at knickknacks and wall hangings for his parents. Marlie had lights in her eyes. Lights of joy. And he'd helped put them there.

Chapter Ten

ॐ

Marlie stepped off the third floor elevator and scanned the walkways and clothing racks. She only had a few minutes. The store was about to close and Jacob had run upstairs to his office. They'd had a fun evening of shopping. Ignoring the busy Christmas crowds, they'd wandered through shops, talking, more interested in each other than the products around them. Finally, they'd ended up back at Triumph's and Marlie had found a scarf for his mother and a business card holder for his father. She knew they weren't precisely personal gifts but she didn't know them well and they were nice items. Jacob seemed to think his parents would like them.

Overall, she would declare the evening a success. She thought Jacob had actually enjoyed himself.

But now she had a moment to herself and needed to find Anne.

"Thank you, Mr. Jensen. I'm sure your wife will love it."

Marlie turned to see Anne hand a large bag to gentleman. He looked relieved that it was over.

She waited until he'd walked away before hurrying to Anne's side.

"Marlie. What are you doing here? How did the dress work out?"

"It was perfect." She'd looked sparkly and alive—very similar to how she felt when Jacob kissed her. "But I need a couple of quick questions answered." She paused. "Can I ask you about the sex?"

Anne's eyes grew wide. "Uh...uh..."

"You're really the only woman I know in town and I'm just not sure what to do."

"O-kay. What's the question?"

"Well, I'd like to have the sex with Jacob but how do I go about telling him that?"

The garbled sound that came from Anne's throat concerned Marlie that the woman was choking.

"Jacob? As in Jacob Triumph?"

Marlie nodded.

"Well…"

"I've thought about it a lot since he and I discussed it," she continued. "And at first I wasn't sure it would work." She leaned closer. "That part of him seems quite large." Again, Anne choked. "But now, I've decided I can probably handle it."

"Uh, Marlie, I probably shouldn't be hearing this."

"Oh, sorry." Drat, Anne had been her best chance for some guidance.

"It's just that it's such a personal decision. Between you and uh, Mr. Triumph." Her voice sounded strained when she said his name. "If you decide to sleep with him—"

"Oh, I already sleep with him. I'm just curious about the sex."

"Aren't we all?" Anne asked with a quiet laugh.

"So, how do I tell him that I want to have the sex? I mean without actually saying, 'Jacob, can we have the sex?'"

Anne nodded. "I can see how that would be a little abrupt. Well, let's see if we can find something that might give him the idea."

She led Marlie over into the lingerie section and selected two tiny outfits, charging them to Jacob's account and handing them to Marlie without asking her opinion. "My suggestion would be to put one of these on and go to bed. I think he'll handle it from there."

Put them on? I thought it involved taking off clothes. Maybe Anne doesn't understand the process any more than I do.

"Marlie?" Jacob's voice rang through the empty floor. The click of his shoes on the tile floor warned of his imminent arrival. "Are you ready to go?" he asked. Marlie nodded. "Good evening, Anne."

Anne was silent for a long moment. Marlie looked at her. The personal shopper was turning a faint red of shade and her eyes were focused just below Jacob's belt. After a long moment, she seemed to snap out of it and looked up. "Good evening, Mr. Triumph."

"Thanks for your help," Marlie said taking the bag.

"Yes. Well, good luck with that…that project of yours."

Marlie turned and walked away with Jacob.

"What project was she talking about?"

She gripped the straps of the bag tighter. "Nothing."

When they got home, Marlie didn't linger around him as she had in the past week. Instead, she carried her bag into the bedroom he'd originally given her and closed the door.

Jacob went into his study and sat at his desk. His briefcase stood beside him, filled with work. He should be preparing for his meeting with Henderson's tomorrow morning. Terry had managed to find an hour of free time two days before Christmas when they could all meet. The offer was on the table. They just needed to hash out the final details. Details Jacob should have been reviewing, clarifying. During the course of his career at the company, he'd doubled the Triumph's store chain and tripled their income and he'd done it by good business sense and by being prepared for every conversation, every meeting. So why was he sitting on his hands the night before something as important as the Henderson buy out?

It was the same answer to all his questions. Marlie. She wasn't around. Normally by this time she'd be hanging out at his study door reminding him of the time and that it was too late to work and they needed to sleep. But tonight she obviously had things on her mind.

Maybe it was the guy she'd been with this afternoon. Jacob had carefully avoided asking her about him. He didn't want to hear the answer and was trying to convince himself that it wasn't any of his business.

He pushed away from his desk and stood up. He was worthless. He'd just get up a little early and review the final proposal then. Stepping into the hall, he felt strangely isolated, going up to bed on his own. The door at the end of the hall seemed far away and out of reach. Marlie was in there but what was she doing?

"Hey, Marlie, I'm going to bed," he called.

"Uh, okay. I'll be up in a few minutes."

Her voice sounded hesitant and off. Something wasn't right.

"Are you okay?" he asked, walking down the hall.

"Sure. I'm fine. Just go up and I'll be there in a second."

He looked at the doorknob and considered checking it but whatever she was doing, she obviously wanted her privacy. He could accept that. It just took him a few minutes before he could force himself to walk away.

Finally, he went upstairs and got ready for bed, dragging on the hated gym shorts and T-shirt.

Marlie still hadn't come upstairs by the time he came out of the bathroom. He'd gotten used to seeing her there—waiting for him in bed, watching him as he hung up his clothes or took off his watch.

Tonight he did it alone. He stood in front of the dresser for a few minutes trying to convince himself to climb into bed. There was no reason not to. Except that she wasn't there.

Oh, screw it. He yanked back the blankets and flopped down on the mattress. It was the same bed he'd had for two years but tonight, it was uncomfortable. He shifted around, trying to find the right position, finally turning on his side and staring at the empty doorway. Would she even come upstairs? Had she given up on him?

Fifteen minutes later, he heard the creak of the stairs and snapped his eyes shut. No reason for her to know he'd been waiting for her. The bedside light was still on so she had plenty of light. Jacob tracked her movements by the soft patter of her feet on the floor. Was she wearing those ridiculous slippers again? He heard the slide of a drawer opening and took a chance, peeking to get a glimpse of her.

His already hard cock sprang to life and he felt like someone had jabbed him in the throat.

"Marlie?"

She slowly turned around and faced him. Gone was the oversized long-sleeved T-shirt. She wore a bright white lacy camisole-thing that hung to just below her belly button. A matching pair of panties decorated her hips.

She took a deep breath and her breasts stretched the material, defining their shape, highlighting the tight nipples. She stood there—waiting—as if she didn't know what to do next. Was this it? Was she interested in more than sleep?

"Do you like it?"

"Where did you get it?"

"Anne. She picked it out. She seemed to think that if I wanted the sex I should wear this and you'd do the rest."

Jacob was glad he was lying down or his knees would have collapsed. Marlie wanted to have sex. With him. The strain from the past five days flooded his body with energy and it was all he could to stop from leaping out of the bed and grabbing her, and dragging her to him. He might have if it hadn't been for the hint of insecurity in her eyes. She might think she wanted this but she didn't quite know.

"You don't like it?" she asked and her voice held that same uncertainty from downstairs. His bold, energetic Marlie was frightened and he couldn't have that.

"It's lovely. You're lovely." He sat up and held out his hand, letting her come to him. He would go slow. If she wanted this, than he was more than willing to give it to her but he wouldn't rush her. "Come here, honey."

She hesitated for only a second then came to him, placing her fingers in his and allowing herself to be drawn closer.

He took a deep breath and prayed for the strength to keep his vow.

Marlie sighed as Jacob pulled her forward. He cupped his hand around her neck and pulled her to him, placing his lips on hers in the gentlest of kisses. Warmth welled up inside her body. She opened her mouth, silently asking for his tongue. He seemed to hear her and filled her mouth, tasting her with slow deliberation.

"Come to bed, Marlie."

"Are we going to have the sex?"

He smiled against her mouth. "Do you want that?"

"Yes."

"You sound a little unsure. Why don't we just play a bit? Then you can decide."

The books combined most of what she'd already experienced into a section titled "Foreplay". If that was true than she definitely wanted to play. Wanted to feel all the things that had confused her body for the past week. And wanted to see how it ended.

Taking a deep breath, she crawled over him to get to her side of the bed and lay beside him.

It was strange to lie in bed with so few clothes. Her arms and legs were bare. But despite that, she felt decidedly warm with nerves and curiosity. Jacob stretched out beside her on his side. He seemed to take a long time to look up and down her body. The tiny outfits Anne had chosen had done interesting things to her form. The lace bodice of her top plumped her breasts together, making them look larger than they were. The thin material abraded her nipples teasing them every time she inhaled. She rather liked that sensation—she liked it even more with Jacob watching her. His examination paused when he stopped at her groin. The tiny panties that came with the outfit had left most of Marlie naked—barely covering her pussy.

Jacob slowly trailed his eyes back up her body until he looked into her eyes.

She laughed, feeling a little self-conscious. "Done?"

"Barely even started," he warned. The low husky tone of his voice reminded her of the dreams and the way he'd spoken in them. The delightful sparkles pushed away the nerves that had tortured her since she'd made her decision. This was Jacob and he knew what he was doing.

Slowly, as if he didn't want to frighten her, he eased his hand around her waist, pulling her closer. She knew Jacob and she loved being close to him. Loved the way he made her feel. It was her part of the process she wasn't sure about.

He kissed her softly, not retreating far when he pulled his lips away. "Let me know if you want to stop."

"And you'll tell me if I do it wrong, right?"

He smiled but there was no mockery in it. "Don't worry, honey. You can't do it wrong. There's only one rule."

She looked up, pleased to know there were rules for her to follow.

"If it feels good…"

"Yes."

"Do it again."

Marlie's grin matched his. Just playing. That's what he'd said.

"We'll take this slow," he whispered against her lips. "Slow and delicious." He ended the word with his kiss, sliding his tongue into her mouth. She groaned as his warmth and distinct masculine taste filled her senses. She knew this part and loved it—and now she had freedom to touch him. The warm fluttering tingles started low in her body as she smoothed her hands over his back, his shoulders, his chest. Tight muscles flexed beneath her fingers as she touched and explored. The slow drugging kisses Jacob gave her made it difficult to concentrate on where her hands were but she knew one thing—she wanted to feel him. The thin T-shirt he wore was in her way. She struggled for the lower edge, tugging it up and edging her hand under it. Jacob dragged his teeth across her lower lip, a delicate bite before he withdrew. In one quick movement, he reached behind his back and jerked the T-shirt off over his head. The white cotton disappeared as he flung it away.

Marlie licked her lips. Delicious. The strong powerful muscles she'd been so curious about were before her, hers to touch. She placed her hands on his broad chest and stroked down, loving the subtle play of muscles and light scattering of hair.

"See? Anne said I should dress for this but I knew it involved being naked." She reached for the strap of her camisole. "Should I take this off?"

He placed his hand on hers. "Not just yet. Let's enjoy it first." The wicked light in his eyes tempted her.

Jacob splayed his fingers across her stomach on the outside of her camisole and began to draw random circles across the lace, moving closer to her breasts with each stroke. He watched her as he touched her, the desire in his gaze acting as another caress. Her nipples pressed up against the lace, begging for a something, a touch she didn't quite understand.

He cupped her breast, covering it with his broad palm. Warmth flowed into her skin and she felt the peak elongate and press deeper into his hand. He smiled as if the response pleased him then flicked his thumb across her nipple. A quick zing shot into her breast. More followed as he circled the nipple, drawing it higher and tighter.

He bent over her and placed a kiss on her breast—hot and wet, leaving a trace of moisture on her camisole. The delicate bite of her fingernails into his arms made him smile. Her body was so responsive, he had to taste all of her. He placed another welcoming kiss on her other breast. The tight peak seemed made for his mouth. He opened his lips over her nipple, drawing it into his mouth. Using the delicate lace, he rubbed his tongue over the peak, adding a light abrasion and savoring Marlie's startled gasp. The restless movement of her legs and the wicked fragrance of her arousal strained his control. His carefully calculated plan of going slow was quickly disappearing.

His cock pressed against the seam of his shorts but he fought the urge to rip them off and plunge into her. He'd told her they were just playing so he'd give her plenty of room to run—and dozens of reasons to stay.

His self-control held but the hunger, the pure need to see her and touch her naked body wouldn't be ignored. He grabbed the lower edge of her camisole and pulled it up and over her head, throwing it carelessly to the side. It was an expensive piece of material but he didn't care. The dreams, the fantasies about her body had driven him crazy. As the top fluttered the ground he looked at her—her bare breasts round and tight, topped with dusky pink nipples. She was stunning—sleek and curved, a delectable combination. He cupped one breast and plumped it up as he stroked his tongue over the tight nipple. Marlie arched her back, pushing her breast deeper into his mouth. He lavished attention on one peak before moving to the other.

He ran his hands over her body, loving the subtle curve of her hips and the roundness of her ass. Only tight control kept him from sliding his fingers into her sex.

"Jacob."

"What do you need, honey? Tell me." He needed to hear her say it.

"More. Something. I don't know." She grabbed his hand and pushed it between her legs. "There. It aches there."

The heat he knew was there poured onto his hand. The delicate panties she wore were soaking wet. He slipped his finger under the lacy edge and teased her lower lips.

"There?" He dipped his fingertip into her opening and felt her hips rock in response, trying to ease him deeper.

"Oh, yes, that's it."

Her eagerness tore at the control he was so valiantly fighting for. He tugged the thin string that held her panties together—the delicate material tore into two easy pieces that Jacob tossed away. As if the sound freed her, Marlie rolled into him, curling her leg over his hip, unconsciously opening her pussy. Moisture from her cunt dampened his thigh as she rubbed against him. The heat called to his cock. He flipped his head back and drew in a long deep, desperate breath as she moved against him, leaving her sweet juice on his skin as her arousal built.

Her eyes glittered with an intoxicating mixture of lust, pleasure—and innocence.

It was the innocence that slowed him. He didn't want her to regret this but he couldn't leave her—or himself—hanging. Too many nights of dreaming about being buried deep inside her cunt had left its mark. He rolled her onto her back and settled between her legs, pressing his erection against her pussy. His cock pulsed with the need to be inside her but he held back, moving, warning her of his intent. Sweet heaven, she didn't draw back. She moved with him.

Marlie tried to catch her breath as he pumped against her. *Yes, right there.* The ache had spread from one point until it filled her pussy and only Jacob could make it better—and worse. She tried to wrap her leg around his hip to bring him deeper but he pushed away, easing back.

"No." She grabbed the waistband of his shorts and held him close.

Jacob stopped her protest with a kiss. "Soon, baby. I'll be inside you soon." He skimmed his lips across her jaw, her neck, decorating her breasts with kisses as he moved down her body. He swirled his tongue around her belly button and Marlie shivered. She knew what was coming...it was just like his dream. His mouth, on her, licking her.

"I've dreamed about tasting your pussy, honey," he whispered, his breath hot on her skin. He placed a kiss just above her mound.

Her body seemed to know precisely what it wanted. She spread her legs, drawing her knees up—uncertainty tried to insert itself as she opened herself so blatantly but Jacob's soothing whispers and the soft kisses he placed on the insides of her thighs pushed it away. His tongue slid whisper soft across her skin sending a flurry of sparkles through her body. Her eyes widened as a new kind of fire invaded her body.

"Jacob?"

He raised his head. A smile of arrogance and sheer masculine power bent his mouth. He licked the inside edge of his lips. "Delicious." Still watching her, he spread her lower lips and flicked his tongue delicately across her flesh. "Better than the any Christmas candy."

His touch was light and wicked—a flurry strokes scattered across her pussy, making her want, crave more. She never knew where he was going to touch—only that he would leave a trail of fire behind him. The devious pressure built as he slipped his tongue into her opening, a shallow, hot penetration. He licked and kissed her pussy as if he loved what he was doing and knew the intoxicating pleasure that was raging through her body. He lapped her wet flesh, working his way slowly to that point that seemed the center for the brightest sparklers. Her fingernails scratched at the mattress, looking for something to hold on to as he closed his lips over that point and sucked.

Marlie whimpered. She couldn't take any more. Her body was shattering into a million bits of light. It was too much. And there was more.

He slipped two fingers into her opening and began to thrust, a wicked beat in perfect rhythm with his suckling.

The sparklers took over her lower body and Marlie didn't know what to do. She dragged in breath after breath but nothing seemed to cool her. She reached behind her and grabbed the headboard, holding herself still, not wanting to miss anything. The pressure built until she had to move, rocking her hips and driving his fingers deeper. He wiggled the tips inside her and everything exploded.

"Jacob!" Heat and electricity shot through her body, flowing to the very tips of her fingers. Colors swirled before her eyes as she stared up at the blank ceiling trying to find her breath. Her mind was a mixture of hazy pleasure and confusion—what sort of magic did he possess that he could create such feelings inside her? She'd read about orgasms in her book but nothing had quite prepared her for that.

But there was more—he would be inside her, filling her. His fingers still moved in her body but they were slow and shallow. Not nearly enough. She wanted that other part of him, wanted to explore it and taste it.

She opened her eyes and he was there, beside her, over her, staring down at her, his green eyes glittering with undisguised hunger.

He covered her mouth with a kiss that demanded she respond. The warm musky taste of her pussy filled her mouth as he pushed his tongue deep inside. She curled her arms around his neck and tried to hold him close but he pulled away.

"We have to stop, baby." His chest pumped in shallow rough breaths.

"No, please." She wrapped her legs around his hips, creating a trap for him. He didn't try to break free. Instead, he lowered himself down, settling against her pussy, rubbing lightly.

"If we keep going, we're going to fuck. Is that what you want?"

"Yes," she moaned. "That's what I want." She tightened her heels pulling herself up and putting her pussy in full contact with the delicious hard bulge between his legs. Her body moved by instinct, rolling her hips in slow circles. Each swirl carried another tingle into her core.

His hands slid up her thighs, cupping her butt, helping her and guiding her in new ways to move against him.

He changed the rhythm, pushing down against her, hard short thrusts. Marlie groaned at the new sensation. She placed hot kisses on his lips, his jaw, the side of his neck. He tasted and felt delicious.

"That's the part you'll put inside me?" she whispered against his skin.

"Yes." His answer was more groan than spoken word.

"What do you call it again?" There had been so many names and words in the book she'd forgotten. He rocked against her and her entire slit tingled.

"Penis, cock. Oh fuck, you can call it Fred for all I care."

Marlie giggled but the sound turned into a gasp as he pushed against her. "It seems so big. I can't imagine how it will fit."

"Don't worry, honey. You're made for me, made to take me inside you."

She groaned as she heard the words. A part of her deep inside knew it was the truth—she was made for him.

He fought the grip of her legs and pushed back. For a moment, Marlie regretted the loss of his warmth but saw he was taking off the rest of his clothes and decided it was worth it.

He yanked down his shorts and let them join the rest of their clothes on the floor. As he turned back to face her, Marlie was there, her eyes, her hands reaching toward his cock. Pure fascination and intrigue filled her gaze as she swirled her fingers around the thick head—her touch light as she explored. Jacob groaned. It was better than any of his dreams–too good, in fact. He was on the verge of exploding and her dainty strokes were too much.

He pulled her hands away. "But I want to—"

"Later, baby." He soothed the disappointed look on her face with a kiss. "Your touch is driving me crazy and I want to be inside you."

Her lips bent upward in a brazen feminine smile—as if the thought that she could push him to the edge pleased her. His wicked little innocent liked the idea of seducing him. He moved over her, strangely battling nerves he hadn't felt since his youth. He wanted to make this good for her. Wanted her to want it again. With him. But beyond the nerves was the hunger. Too many nights of dreaming about fucking her followed by too many mornings waking up beside her, almost inside her had torn down his defenses. Now that she was before him, naked and eager, he had to have her.

She stared up at him with those wide trusting eyes and Jacob felt himself melt. He could do this. He would make it good for her.

He leaned over her leg and reached for the bedside table and the supply of condoms he'd put there after the first morning. It had been fairly obvious from the start that they would end up in this position and now he was glad he'd planned ahead. He opened the packet and began to roll the sheath up. Marlie's hand slipped between his and began to stroke him as well. The delicate caress was a wicked temptation as she smoothed her hand up his shaft.

"Why do you do that?" she asked.

"Protection."

She blinked and looked into his face. "From what?"

"All sorts of things. I'll explain tomorrow."

"Hmm." She smoothed her hand down his full length. "I liked it better without."

The thin layer of latex did little to muffle her touch and he curled his hands into fists trying to contain the sensation.

"Me too, honey, but don't worry, it will feel good inside." Again he pulled her hand away from his cock and eased her back so he was above her. He pushed his fingers into her pussy to make sure she was still with him but couldn't wait any longer. He placed the head of his cock to her opening and began a slow thrust.

She gasped as the first inch filled her and Jacob bit back a groan. She was tight and wet and gripped him like a fist. Heat poured into his cock, drawing him deeper but the tight clasp of her pussy slowed his penetration. He didn't want to hurt her. He started to retreat.

"No!" she said. "Don't stop."

"I'm not leaving you, honey." He couldn't if he'd wanted to. "I'm still here." Slowly he pulsed into her, deeper each time. He watched her face as he entered her, each penetration painting new sensations across her skin—her eyes drooped low and heavy, her lips hung open, giving voice to those soft delicious moans as he filled her, slowly in and out until he was almost there.

He rubbed his thumb across her clit, massaging the point until he felt her relax enough to drive the last inch into her. Her gasp was drowned out by his groan. Her pussy held him like a vise of pure silk. He clenched his hands on the mattress, holding himself still as he looked down at Marlie—her eyes wide and a bit startled. "Are you all right?"

She nodded. "You?"

He smiled. "Yes." He was better than all right. He was great. Now he just had to find a way to make her feel the same thing.

"Is that all of it? Because I'm not sure I can take any more," she warned.

"That's it, baby." His eyes lit with laughter. She shifted her hips and the laughter changed to lust. "Kiss me."

Marlie followed his lead, returning the slow, languid kisses as she adapted to the sensation of having him inside her. The pain eased as he kissed her and touched her, stroking his fingers across her breasts, teasing her nipples with gentle flicks.

After long moments the familiar ache returned and she knew she needed Jacob to finish it, to move inside her. She slipped her hand down his back and curled her palm over his backside. He lifted his head and smiled as she pressed him into her.

He took the initiative and withdrew just a bit before sliding deeper. "Is that what you want? Shall I move?"

She groaned her response as he pulled all the way back and filled her in one long thrust. It was a delicious sensation—full and stretched by his cock. Pain whispered through her again but it faded quickly and all that was left was the pleasure and the hunger for more.

"More, Jacob. Give me more."

He tossed his had back, lengthening his neck as if he was fighting some inner pain. Her knees curled up, cuddling his hips between her thighs, needing to balance the rhythm he set. The pure heat of his cock moving inside her spread that delight warmth through her whole body. He placed his hands on the mattress beside her and moved inside her, slow at first and then faster, each stroke taking him deep.

Marlie clutched at his arms, spreading kisses across his chest, nipping at his shoulder, needing that release that was just outside her reach. Her thighs tightened as she pumped against him, her body finding the rhythm to match his. Each time he entered her, the pressure built, higher and faster until she couldn't think anymore, could only whisper his name, pleading for more, for release.

And then it was gone. The pressure, the ache evaporated in a bolt of intense pleasure. The wild sensation flowed from her pussy in warm streams, pouring into the rest of her body. Jacob continued to move inside her again and again until the same wicked tension bound his body. He cried out and drove himself one more time into her, his cock buried deep her like he wanted to stay. Long seconds later, the strength of his arms gave out and he sank down, settling his weight onto Marlie.

Marlie hummed softly and rolled with him as he pulled his cock from her wet haven. With his remaining strength, he wrapped his arm around her back and drew her closer. Her sigh was pure contentment as she dropped her head onto his chest. "Jacob?"

"Hmm?"

"Remember that rule you taught me?"

His eyes snapped open. "Yes."

She pushed herself up on his chest and looked down into his eyes. "That felt good." She blinked. "We should do it again."

Chapter Eleven

ℰℴ

"Jacob?"

He grunted, unable to speak, every muscle loose and relaxed. Marlie had managed to fuck the strength from his body. The edges of his mouth curled up in a weak smile. He couldn't remember the last time he'd been this wrung out after sex. Of course, he also didn't remember the last time his partner had inspired such a need for a second round. After that first time, he'd taken her again. A little faster, a little harder. It was fast becoming obvious that once—even twice—wasn't going to be enough. And she'd been with him, returning every caress—her confidence growing and with it her desires. His smiled broadened. He had a feeling Marlie would prove to be a demanding lover.

He tightened his hand on her ass, holding her close. The warmth from her pussy heated his thigh and gave rise to all sorts of ways he could have her but he knew he needed to wait. His cock would take awhile to recover and she was probably getting sore. He'd ridden her pretty hard the second time. He licked his lips imagining riding her from behind, that tight ass pressed against him. Oh, yes there was much more he wanted to do Marlie but he had to give her a chance to recover.

"I think we should go to your parents' house tomorrow."

"Hmm?"

There was something worrisome in that statement but since the only portion of his brain that seemed to be functioning was focused on ways to fuck Marlie, he couldn't figure out what it was. She ran her hand up the center of his chest and circled her finger over his nipple. The flat pad tightened at her light touch. The caress was followed by the slow lapping of her tongue across the same spot. She mimicked the motions he'd applied to her nipples, circling and sucking. His cock twitched and he moved instinctively closer, pulling her leg over his hip. Heat and moisture welcomed him as he snuggled his growing erection between her thighs.

"We should drive to your parents tomorrow."

He tried to listen to what she was saying but she spoke between hot, sexy kisses and it was difficult to concentrate. "Aren't we scheduled to fly out on Christmas Eve?"

"Yes, but a drive would be so much prettier and then Jack could spend Christmas Eve with his family."

"Who?"

He shifted, moving on top of her, instinctively sliding between her legs. She groaned as he nudged his cock against her pussy. The functioning part of his brain was fading. There was a reason he wasn't going to fuck her again but right now, he couldn't think of what it was. He needed to be back inside her. Feeling all that heat that seemed just for him.

"Your pilot. He has a new baby and I thought it would be nice if we didn't make him work on Christmas Eve." The sentence ended with a gasp as he slipped the first inch inside. The heat was there, waiting for him, calling him inside. Marlie scraped her teeth along the line of his neck as she curled her leg behind his back.

"So can we, Jacob?"

"Sure." He couldn't remember what he was agreeing to and didn't care. He was fucking Marlie again and that's all that mattered.

"Good." She groaned as he pushed into, giving her more and more of his cock. "Oh yes, that's very good." She giggled. "Fred is most interesting."

"Fred?" Another man's name jolted him out of his daze. He looked down and realized what she was talking about. Great. He'd always avoided naming his penis. Now, it was named Fred and honestly he had no one to blame but himself.

"Glad you like him." He withdrew and sank back in, filling her with every inch.

"Oooh, especially when you do that."

* * * * *

Morning sunlight brightened the room and dragged Marlie reluctantly from her sleep. She came awake slowly with an overall sense of peace and warmth, and the growing awareness of heat between her legs. She smiled even before she opened her eyes. Jacob. She recognized his touch as he slid his finger into her pussy, holding herself still, savoring the slow penetration, the teasing stroke of his fingertip each time he withdrew.

"I know you're not asleep, Marlie," he said.

"It's just such a delicious way to wake up. All warm and…"

"…and wet." He drew his hand back and thrust two fingers into her. More familiar now with the sensation, she groaned, feeling her body ease to take him.

"Are you sore?" he asked though he continued the slow strokes inside her.

"No, it just feels…oh, like I want more."

They moved together, rolling until he was on top of her, his cock poised. She tilted her hips up, wanting him inside her, wanting more of the—

The annoying ring of his cell phone shattered the breathless silence between them. Jacob closed his eyes and dropped his head forward.

"I have to get that."

Cursing all the way, he slipped out of Marlie's grip and grabbed his cell off the dresser. "Triumph," he barked into the phone. Left without his warmth, Marlie rolled to the edge and watched him. He was so beautiful standing there, all strong muscles and hard delicious cock. She turned onto her stomach, pressing her cheek against the heat left behind by his body. Her pussy rubbed against the mattress and sent delightful tickles into her core. She repeated the motion. It wasn't as strong as when Jacob touched her but ooh, it was nice. Watching him, she moved her hips in slow circles, searching for that elusive caress.

Jacob held the phone to his ear but didn't comprehend a word of what was said. All his attention was on Marlie — slowly humping the mattress, her ass pumping up and down. He felt his mouth drop open as she slipped her hand underneath her body and between her legs. Her low groan told him that she'd discovered her clit and was exploring. His cock stretched to the point of pain. He'd never seen anything so sexual as Marlie naked and masturbating on his bed.

"Jacob!"

The strident voice burst from the phone so loud even Marlie flinched. She glared at him as if he'd disturbed her pleasure.

Jacob stared at the phone trying to recognize the voice. "Natalie?"

"Well, who else did you think it was? I've been talking for five minutes. Have you heard a word I've said?"

"No. Sorry." He knew he should look away but couldn't convince himself to miss one moment. "What were you saying?" he asked vaguely, not caring.

"We had a meeting. Thirty minutes ago. Where are you? My father is ready to put this deal to bed."

Yes, to bed.

Marlie rolled onto her back, her hand between her legs. The deep pink of her cunt glittered with her moisture. Wet and hot. She eased one finger into her pussy and slowly began to pump.

"Jacob, we're waiting. When will you be here?"

"Yes, I remembered. I'll be there in thirty." Marlie's hips rocked up, driving her finger deeper. "Maybe an hour. Talk to you then."

He snapped the phone shut and dropped it on the floor, moving toward the sexy woman on his bed. He grabbed a condom as he placed his knee on the mattress and knelt between her legs.

"Jacob," she moaned. "It feels better when you do it."

"Then let me."

Part of his mind screamed he had to get to work but the rest of his mind, body and soul shouted down the one lone voice. There was no way he could miss this, deny either of them. Natalie and her father and the rest of the world could wait.

He eased Marlie's fingers out of her pussy and carried them to his mouth, licking the moisture from her skin. Someday soon he might be able to fuck her slowly—but the warm taste of her pussy and the sexy finger fuck destroyed his chances of that happening now. He sucked on her fingers then grabbed her hips, pulling her high onto his thighs. She was spread wide open before him, barely able to move, his to fuck. He placed his cock at her entrance and drove forward, filling her in one deep thrust. He struggled to contain his shout. She felt so good, so hot.

"Am I hurting you, honey?" he asked, hoping she denied it. Heat flowed from her center and poured into his cock.

"A little, no, don't stop. It feels good." Her breasts shimmied with each breath.

"Touch your breasts," he commanded. Her eyes grew wide but she slowly slid her hands up her body, cupping the full mounds. "That's it, baby," he encouraged. "Play with those tight nipples. Let me see how much you like it." Her hands moved in slow circles, massaging and caressing her beautiful breasts. The sight hardened his cock even further—

176

her body splayed out before him, his cock buried deep in her cunt.

"Jacob, please."

He tightened his hold on her hips and drove into her, riding her in fast deep strokes.

"You squeeze me so tight, honey, like you'll never let me go," he said as he pushed into her. Her eyes were the color of the night sea as she stared at him. Tiny flutters were beginning deep in her cunt and he knew she was about to come. He slipped his thumb into her slit and teased the side of her clit, massaging the tight nub in rhythm to his thrusts.

He watched as he drove her higher, the glorious pleasure on her face as she came — long vibrations moving through her pussy that translated to his cock. He bit his teeth together and groaned as he followed her over.

Despite the urgency, the fact that people were waiting for him in his office — and he'd taken time for a morning quickie — Jacob felt relaxed and energized as he dressed. That's what a night — and morning — of great sex did for you. He stared at the rumpled blankets and scattered sheets. The fitted sheet was pulled back at the corner. They'd certainly done some damage to his bed last night. He hummed softly as he fastened his watch, mentally constructing plans for tonight. Maybe he'd bring home dinner so Marlie didn't have to worry about cooking and they could spend the evening in front of the fireplace, the Christmas tree lit up. Marlie would like that.

She walked in as he was buttoning his shirt. She handed him a cup of coffee but leaned forward to kiss him before he could drink it. It wasn't a friendly kiss — it was one of seduction and Jacob felt himself falling under its spell.

He cursed the people waiting at his office and the plan to take over Hendersons and everything that kept him from crawling back into bed with Marlie. But he had responsibilities. People relying on him. His father would demand an accounting.

With willpower he hadn't known he possessed, he lifted his head. "I've got to go. I've got Natalie and her father waiting for me in my office."

Marlie's eyes squinted and her fingers curled into his collar, crushing the material and holding him place. "Natalie? Do you have the sex with her, too?"

He opened his mouth to deny it—he didn't talk about previous lovers—but he couldn't lie to her. "Yes. Sometimes. Not often. Not for a while," he felt compelled to clarify.

"So, you've made her feel that same way?" Marlie seemed quite offended at the idea.

Jacob shook his head and answered with absolute honesty. "I don't think I've ever made Natalie feel what you felt last night. Not the same way." He knew Natalie came when they were together—or he assumed she did—but she obviously didn't feel the same joy or thrill that Marlie had. Or eagerness and energy.

Marlie nodded but he could tell she wasn't completely satisfied with his answers. "I guess that's okay then." She paused and he could see her mind working. "I don't want to dislike anyone but I don't care for her and I don't want you giving her that kind of magic."

"I won't."

"You won't have the sex with Natalie anymore?"

"No."

Marlie's eyes lit up with her smile and pleasure. "Thank you." She wrapped her arms around his neck and planted her mouth on his.

"I've got to go," he said reluctantly pulling away.

"I know." She patted his chest and took the coffee cup away from him. "But don't forget we're driving to your parents' house tonight. We should probably leave a little early."

He nodded then froze. What? Driving to his parents' house? When had he agreed to that?

He racked his brain as he walked to his car. There was a hazy memory of an even hazier conversation about driving instead of flying. And he'd agreed to it.

Sex had confused his brain. He stopped. No, sex had never done that to him before. It was Marlie. She'd confused his brain.

He stared up at his house for a long time before deciding he'd have to institute another rule into their lovemaking—no talking to him after the sex.

Chapter Twelve

ଛଠ

Jacob dropped his pen on the desk. He sighed, puffing his cheeks out as the air slipped between his lips. With a final glance at the clock, he stood and pulled on his suit jacket. Marlie would be expecting him soon. His meeting with Henderson and Natalie had gone about as expected — considering he'd been over an hour late and his mind was back at home in bed with Marlie.

And now this?

How had he ever agreed to it? Not only was he *driving* down to see his parents instead of taking the company jet, he was going down *early*. Again, he asked himself how he'd gotten here.

Marlie. She looked at him with those deep blue eyes and suddenly he was agreeing to her every wish.

Wishes. Ha. A fond smile settled on his face as he tossed a stack of papers into his briefcase. Marlie and her wishes. The line of his lips flattened. Christmas morning she wouldn't be staring up at him with lights in her eyes. They were going to be filled with tears. And all because he'd made some stupid Christmas wish.

Damn, Marlie was going to be so disappointed when there wasn't a puppy under the tree for his mother.

He snapped his briefcase shut and opened his office door. Ms. Benson was typing, concentrating on the screen in front of her. She glanced over her shoulder as he walked into the reception area. Ever efficient, she turned from the keyboard and picked up her pen, ready to take any final notes he might have before he left.

She's always here. The thought struck him as he looked at his secretary — as if he was seeing her for the first time. She'd worked for him for four years and, except for a major flu epidemic, had never missed a day of work. She arrived before him in the morning and often left after him at night. Always making sure he had everything he needed or wanted. He didn't know how he would function if she wasn't around.

"Mr. Triumph, are you okay?"

"Yes. I'm fine." He rubbed his fingers across his forehead, trying to understand what he was about to do. "I'm leaving for the rest of the week. Why don't you do the same thing?"

She stared back at him, her eyes stuck open with shock. "Pardon me?"

"Clear your desk. Take off the rest of the week. Close down the office. There's nothing that won't wait." Jacob thought about. There *wasn't* anything that wouldn't hold. The Henderson deal was on the rocks, thanks to his late arrival at this morning's meeting — and Natalie's irritation with him after the party last week. She'd been hoping for an all-around merger — business and personal.

Normally the thought of losing a deal would have him at his desk but he was surprised to find himself eager to get home. And see Marlie.

"Take off next week, too. With pay of course," he announced, warming up to the subject. "I'll see you the Monday after New Years."

"But...but..." Jacob didn't know how to react to the shock on her face. It had clearly been too long since he'd done something nice for his employees.

"You've been working a lot of hours lately. Take the time." He picked up his briefcase and headed to the door.

"Thank you, Mr. Triumph."

"And after four years, maybe you could start calling me Jacob. If you don't mind...Terry."

"No, that's fine."

"Have a good vacation."

He let the door drop behind him noticing that his shoulders felt light and a glow of satisfaction settled in his stomach.

"Good night, Mr. Triumph," the pretty clerk from women's clothing greeted as he walked by.

"Good night." He nodded and smiled. Marlie was rubbing off on him. Not that he intended to let her see that. She seemed to enjoy reforming his Christmas spirit and he was going to let her keep on doing that.

If she thinks I'm a hard case, wait until she meets my parents. What would they think of her? She was definitely not like any of the other women he'd brought with him. Every woman in the past who'd met his parents had instantly fallen under their spell, become like them. Somehow, he couldn't see that happening with Marlie.

Marlie taking on his parents—the King and Queen of Superficial Holidays. He grimaced as he watched the floors in the elevator light. His father had bred into him the retail spirit of Christmas, while his mother had demonstrated the importance of expensive presents. Holidays at his parents' house were of perfectly orchestrated events. Each move, each gift, was designed to impress friends and family. And the parties. Jacob suppressed a shudder. As a child he'd been dragged out of his room, dressed in a tuxedo and paraded in front of friends until it was time to be hidden away again. As an adult, the parties became one long blur of polite talk.

But for the first time in almost twenty years, he was looking forward to the holiday. Just the thought of his parents' faces when they met Marlie made him smile. The Board of Directors had succumbed to her charm, but Jacob knew his parents were made of stronger stuff. It was almost worth the holiday nonsense.

He stepped into the garage, walking the short distance to his car. Marlie would survive his parents. It was the Christmas wish-thing that had him worried. It was an impossible wish.

His mother had never let animals in the house. He'd begged for a pet when he was ten, and eleven and for years after that but nothing could convince his mother to have an animal in the house. It might mess up the carpets.

Even if there is a Santa Claus, which there isn't, Jacob reminded himself, *he's never going to be able to make this Christmas wish happen.*

Jacob sat inside his car and stared at the garage wall. Marlie was going to be crushed. Stupid, stupid. *You should have wished for a nice diamond necklace. Mom always gets one of those.*

His heart thudded deep in his chest and his hands warmed on the steering wheel. He hated to support her delusion but he couldn't watch Marlie's eyes on Christmas morning when no dog showed up. He looked at his watch. He had enough time to make one stop before he went home.

He had a Christmas wish to make come true.

* * * * *

Marlie shivered and settled into the soft leather of the seats. She knew from experience that Jacob's car would soon warm up, but until it did, she wasn't moving. Wasn't going to waste any of her precious body heat. The luscious warmth of the sex had faded away and now she cold again.

Jacob pulled open his door and folded his body into the driver's seat. He looked over at her and stopped.

"You can't be cold."

"I'm freezing. Shut the door." She tightened her grip around her shoulder and tried to bury deeper into the warmth of Jacob's coat.

"How can you be cold? It's barely cold enough to snow."

"It's always cold enough to snow," Marlie groused. She knew this was a poor way to start their trip but dang it, she *was* cold. And despite her anticipation of spending the next two days with Jacob, when those two days were over, it would be Christmas. And she'd be gone. She just knew it. Somehow, blundering though she'd been, and even though she couldn't cook, she'd succeeded. Jacob was learning the meaning of Christmas.

The car door snapped shut. Jacob didn't turn on the engine. Marlie finally looked up from staring at the floor of the car to see what he was waiting for.

"If you're really a…a…well, what you say you are, how can you not like the cold? Isn't this workshop at the North Pole?"

"The word is elf, and yes, it's at the North Pole, and yes, I was always cold. I think that's what made me so crabby."

"What's your excuse here?" Jacob asked innocently.

"Ha-ha. Now drive." It took all of Marlie's control not to smile, though she knew it shined through her eyes. *Jacob was making jokes.* Her glow of success was tinged with sadness. She wanted Jacob to find the meaning of Christmas, she really did, but when he succeeded, she would leave.

Jacob's gentle laugh followed her command. He started the engine and a blast of heat billowed across Marlie's cold toes. Her eyes opened wide and she smiled as she turned back to Jacob.

"I warmed it up before you came out."

Her sadness forgotten, she leaned across the car and wrapped her arms around his neck. Jacob's hand slipped around her back and squeezed her to his side.

A warm glow settled in her heart as she dropped back to her seat.

Jacob guided the car down the driveway. Tears pricked her eyes as she watched the house fade into the distance. If things went as planned, she'd never see it again.

Her basic cheerful nature warded off the tears and within a few minutes, her anticipation for their trip had returned.

She tried not to stare at him as he drove but it was a challenge. It amazed her. In a short space of time, she'd learned to read his emotions in the tiny variations in his facial expressions. A small crinkle on his forehead meant he was startled, but too contained to stare wide-eyed. He clenched his jaw muscles when annoyed or frustrated. Marlie almost laughed. She'd learned that one very early on.

The tree-lined driveways of the other houses disappeared as the car ate up the miles, taking them out of the city. The sun dropped below the horizon, a steady reminder of the passing of another day. Her time with Jacob now measured in hours and minutes.

Snow began to fall as they left the highway. Light flakes that grew in size until they were splattering across the front window.

Surrounded by heat, Marlie lost herself in her own thoughts. The truth had been haunting her for days but now—after last night—it seemed more important than ever that she face it. She loved Jacob—but it wasn't the love she was used to. The love she felt for the other elves was a distant, "wanting the best for you" kind of love. Friendly, but oddly impersonal. This was love specific to Jacob.

The words that had been hanging just below her subconscious, now clamored to be released, to be spoken.

"I love you," she said feeling relieved that she'd said it aloud. She turned in her seat and looked at his profile.

Jacob gripped the steering wheel and tried to convince himself he was hallucinating. His heart started to pound, filling his throat and moving up to his ears. She hadn't really said it, right? It couldn't be true. She couldn't love him. *Could she?* A strange flash of hope whipped through his chest before he knocked it away.

"I think we'd better find a place to stay for the night," he said focusing on the falling snow. "The signs showed a bed-and-breakfast up here. Let's try there."

"That's your answer?" She laughed softly as if his avoidance of the topic amused her. Any normal woman would have blushed and let it go—like it had never been spoken. Not Marlie. "I tell you I love you and you ignore it? You didn't even say thank you."

"Forgive me for forgetting my manners," he replied, his voice ringing with sarcasm. "I didn't know Emily Post had a rule on this."

Marlie stared out the window while Jacob seemed to be the only one who recognized the tension that had suddenly filled his car.

"You can't," Jacob finally answered with a sigh.

"Can't what?"

"Can't love me."

She laughed softly and tipped her head to the side to look at him. The wisdom in her eyes seemed so counter to the blazing innocence that usually lived there. "Why can't I?" she asked.

He stared at the road. "You don't know anything about me."

"I know enough." She shrugged. "And I love you."

He glanced at her, curled up in the front seat of his car, watching him. He really did need to give her some kind of reply. His knuckles turned white as he squeezed the steering wheel. "I-um-I…"

The words caught in his throat. He hadn't said those words to anyone, except the high-school cheerleader with whom he'd lost his virginity. And he'd only said it then because she wouldn't "do it" without the words. It wasn't his most honorable memory, but it was the last time he'd told a woman he loved her just to get her into bed.

"You don't have to say anything." Gentle laughter rumbled beneath Marlie's voice. "It's a gift, Jacob. Accept it, but you don't have to give anything in return."

"Uh—thank you." They drove along in silence, watching as the dark woods passed by, marking each mile.

Marlie loved him? The idea was outrageous. They'd known each other less than two weeks.

If he did fall in love, how would he know? Not having been in love before he didn't have a point of reference. He did a quick review of his five senses. Nothing seemed completely out of whack. He didn't hear angels when she spoke and the touch of her hand didn't make him melt. A grim smile formed. Her touch had the opposite affect, making him rock hard. But that was lust. That didn't have anything to do with love.

Marlie was obviously feeling something or she wouldn't have said it.

It's lust. That was the truth of it. She didn't love him. *That's all it is. She's too new to sex to understand the difference.* He relaxed in his seat, determined to be happy with his mental explanation.

The light from the B and B came into view and Jacob slowed to take the turnoff. The snow was coming down at a rapid enough clip that they needed to stop for the night.

They pulled down the long driveway and saw the quaint B and B.

"What do you think?" he asked. Marlie looked up at the name—Noel's Nook—and he watched with some satisfaction as she smiled.

"It's perfect."

The parking lot in front of the building was empty. Jacob stopped the car and helped Marlie out. Her hand stayed clasped in his as they walked through the snow. Knowing her tendency to get cold, he urged her toward the door but she lingered, turning her face up to catch snowflakes on her tongue.

187

The simple joy and beauty stunned him—and left a foreign ache around his heart. She'd said she loved him and he'd brushed it aside. The pain near his heart turned into a slow sickening roll of his stomach.

Marlie felt the snowflakes on her cheeks and smiled. Even the snow felt warmer when she was with Jacob. She looked at him, sad to see the shadow in his eyes, knowing she'd put them there by blurting out her feelings. He obviously wasn't used to people saying they loved him.

She closed her eyes and made a wish. *I wish that Jacob finds a woman who loves him and tells him so often.* She gathered her elf magic into her and sent the wish out to the world.

When she opened her eyes, Jacob was staring at her. He tilted his head to the side in silent question. Love welled up inside her even though she knew she couldn't speak of it. Instead she threw her arms around him and kissed him. Snow floated down around them, cold penetrated her boots and she'd never been happier. He caught her to him. The heat from their bodies warming the air.

When he finally pulled back, she was breathless but she'd grown used to the sensation in the past few days. She looked at the sign. Noel's Nook Bed and Breakfast. They had beds. That meant she and Jacob could have more of the sex.

"We should get in before we freeze in place," he said though his voice had lost its gruffness from the car.

She hooked her arm in his, keeping him close and walked inside.

Noel was a sweet woman who offered them a light dinner along with their room. Before they knew it, they were seated at her dining room table with sandwiches and chips in front of them. Their hostess smiled and left them alone.

After eating dinner, they moved into the living room, sitting by the fire and sipping cold white wine. Marlie had shed her coat and was using Jacob as her warmth. He didn't mind. They sat cuddled together on the couch, their toes touching as they watched the flames. Noel moved silently about the house, cleaning up the small remains of dinner.

It was well dark by the time she walked into the living room and said good night. "I have my own suite of rooms so the run of the house is yours. I'll take care of the fire after you go up." She looked at Marlie and winked. "Have a good night."

When the innkeeper had left, Marlie shifted in Jacob's arms, looking up at him. "She thinks were going to have the sex."

"Yes." He paused and asked in all seriousness. "Are we?"

Marlie flinched. "I hope so."

Her comment seemed to spur Jacob to action and within minutes they were headed up to their room. Jacob left her at the door and said he needed to get something out of the car.

Marlie was glad to have a moment alone. Her emotions had been on a pendulum today—love and sadness. She loved Jacob but knew she would be leaving him in two days. Two days until Christmas.

And she wasn't going waste a minute of it.

She looked at the beautiful room and the huge bed. It was so easy to imagine Jacob and her on that bed.

She quickly changed into the second outfit Anne had picked out for her. The first one had worked so well, she couldn't wait to see what happened with the second. Last night had been amazing but she knew there was still so much for her to learn and try. Like that dream of Jacob's where she'd licked his cock. She ran her tongue across her lips. That seemed quite interesting. Similar to the way he'd tasted her last night. Her pussy twitched and she could feel the rising warmth.

She heard footsteps on the stairs and knew Jacob was returning. She smoothed her hands over the skimpy outfit she wore. This one was red and almost see-through, hanging loosely from her breasts to the tops of her thighs. The material fluttered across her skin feeling like angel wings.

She walked to the side of the bed and leaned against the high post, waiting as Jacob opened the door and came in. His eyes lit up with a dangerous heat when he saw her.

I love you. The words echoed in her head but she couldn't say them. Jacob didn't want to hear them. Didn't believe them.

The center of her chest ached. How did she teach him to believe in love?

He shrugged off the heavy coat and tossed it casually over the arm of the chair then quickly brushed the snow from his hair. He didn't look around, his attention locked on her. He walked to her side and cupped her face in his hand, bending down to kiss her. His lips were slow and delicious, cool and soft against her mouth.

"You look beautiful," he said whispering the caress across her lips. A low sensuous need built inside her sex. The driving hard ache from last night was still there but subdued and slowed. Tonight, she wanted to touch him, taste him. Moving together—their lips locked in their kiss—they removed his shirt and let it fall to the floor. Marlie moaned into his mouth as she smoothed her hands up his chest. His hands slid down her back and cupped her ass, pulling her against him, his erection pressing against her stomach as he skimmed his lips down her neck. His hands began the long lovely strokes that warmed her and inspired those delicious sensations in her body.

"No." She pushed against his shoulders and after a moment's hesitation he released her. Caution—and maybe a hint of pain—flared in his gaze. She flashed him a gentle smile to soothe his ego. "I didn't get to touch you last night. I want to feel you." She followed up her words with a quick brush of her lips across his chest. "Taste you." It was like the shutters had opened on his eyes and the pure, devastating hunger returned.

Wicked sensual power flowed through her. He wanted her, wanted her touch. She flicked her finger across the top button of his jeans. "You should probably get rid of those."

He lifted his chin toward her barely covered breasts. "You first."

It was only fair, after all. He was topless. She reached down and pulled the off the top of her outfit and tossed it aside. Strange, for something that cost so much, she didn't end up wearing them long.

Jacob nodded in approval as he stared at her breasts. She'd seen pictures of women with much larger breasts but Jacob didn't seem to mind. The memory of their morning loving came back to her and she smoothed her hands up her body, capturing her breasts in her palms. His gaze heated up and he reached for her but she backed away, shaking her head.

"The jeans. Take 'em off." It felt wicked and wild to be commanding him to strip and Marlie loved every second of it. Still caressing herself, she stayed out of reach as he undid the button fly and pushed the jeans and his shorts to his ankles. As if daring her to comment on his body, he stood there, his feet trapped in his pants, naked from the ankles up. She took a moment to look at him. He was so beautiful. Strong and powerful. And his cock. The thick rod was hard and rising, a trickle of liquid adorning the tip.

She didn't speak but she did lick her lips, telling him what she wanted.

The edge of his mouth kicked up in a half smile.

"Now you," he said indicating her panties, daring her to defy him.

She hooked her fingers into the sides of her panties and began to push them down. Some latent instinct told her to go slow, to let him wait to see her. Slowly, she turned, giving him a view of her profile as she bent over and slid the scrap of material down until it rested around her ankles. She didn't need to look at him to know he was watching her, staring at her ass. Her hips pressed back as she allowed her body to straighten but kept one hand over her pussy, covering it as she faced him. The warning glint in his eye made her smile but she didn't move her hand.

"This is my show tonight. Get on the bed." For a moment she thought he would refuse but finally, his body relaxed and he stepped out of his jeans and followed her instructions. Heat warmed her fingers as she waited and watched, his muscles so graceful and strong.

She crawled up beside him and stared down at the delectable buffet before her. So many options and choices. Hmmm. Where to start? Head to toe. She glanced down at his hard cock. Well, she doubted she'd make it all the way to his toes but it would be fun to try.

She cuddled close, letting her whole body feel his. She curled her leg over his hip, letting her pussy settle against him even as she began to stroke him. Her fingers wandered across his chest and down but soon in became clear that wasn't enough—she needed to taste him, wanted to feel him beneath her tongue. As she moved down his body, touching and tasting him, the hunger built inside her. His body was a delicious treat just made for her.

Jacob ground his teeth together and endured every stroke of her hands. Her exploration dragged him to hell and back. Every whispered touch of her fingers was followed by a slow lap of her tongue—his chest, his nipples, the tight muscles of his stomach. Time and the torture she was putting on him didn't seem to matter to her but Jacob was at the breaking point. He gripped the headboard, and held on, fighting the urge to grab her head and plunge his cock into her mouth.

The sweet torment of her hands ripped at his control as she worked her way down his body. She trailed her fingers down his stomach to his thighs, painting swirls of fire across his skin. Slowly she drew closer to his cock. Her tongue was like a brand on his skin—hot and permanent.

Her hands curled around his shaft, light delicate strokes, as if she was afraid to hurt him.

The first brush of her tongue sent a lightning bolt through his body. He couldn't do it. He wasn't strong enough. If she sucked him off, he'd lose control, pound himself into her until she begged for mercy.

"No, baby, not that." He grabbed her arms and pulled her up, dragging her onto his chest, the gentle mounds of her breasts hot against his skin.

"But I wanted to kiss Fred," she said, laughter and passion competing her eyes. "Don't you like that?"

Fuck yes. He liked that. Wanted it. Wanted her mouth crammed full of his cock—but he couldn't. Not tonight. He was struggling to keep his urges under control. And there was just too much temptation with the fantasy of her sucking him off.

"I do, baby, but tonight, I want to be inside you." He coaxed a deep kiss out of her and moved her up and over him, her legs straddling his hips. Her eyes were filled with excitement as she pushed herself up and saw him beneath her, his cock stretching long and hard toward her pussy.

"Oooh, I read about this in the book." Her voice was filled with awe. "I can be on top."

"Yes."

The strain in his voice comforted her. She could see his struggles—as if he was fighting to grab her. Instead he let her have her way. She took his cock in her hands and raised it, placing the broad tip to her opening. Touching him had been wonderful but it had left her aching for more.

She slowly lowered herself down, letting his cock fill her. A light soreness slowed her descent but it wasn't enough to make her stop, the need was too great. Remembering the way he'd filled her last night, she took him in shallow pulses, deeper and deeper.

"That's it, baby, ride me." His hands tightened on the headboard as he held himself still, letting her move. She didn't have much experience but she knew what this was costing him. Needing more of his taste, she bent down and dragged her tongue across his nipple, ending the caress with a gentle bite. He groaned and pumped his hips upward, forcing him deeper into her pussy. More, she needed more. She placed her hands beside his chest and began to move, sliding his cock in and out, feeling every delicious inch. She tried to go slow — there was too much to enjoy to rush it — but her body wouldn't let her.

Pushing back her with her hands, she sat up tall, pumping up and down on him, shallow steady pulsed deep in her pussy, needing more, just a little more.

Her breasts bounced in time to the quick pumps as she rode him, faster and faster toward her climax.

"That's it. Take it, honey. Let me feel it."

His words seemed to ignite the latent need inside her. She cried out as the delicate ripples moved through her pussy.

He watched the orgasm shoot through her body and couldn't stop his own. He held her hips, feeling the flutters of her cunt as she came, the pulses moving through his cock.

As if the climax had drained the strength from her body, she sagged forward, collapsing onto his chest. He let her stay there for a long time before he finally shifted her off, keeping her close to his side. Slowly she raised her head and looked at him.

The dazed pleasure in her eyes made him smile.

"Like that?" he asked, teasing her.

She licked her lips and nodded. "Wonderful." She snuggled against his chest, her mouth reaching up for his, her hand sliding down his waist.

"I can still feel you inside me." She curled her hand around his cock, reawakening the sated muscles. "So thick and long."

Jacob was sure he'd never seen anything more beautiful than her eyes as she looked up at him—pure joy, pure love stared back at him.

And the wicked smile of intent that lit her eyes.

He was in for a long night.

Chapter Thirteen

৪৩

The sharp stabbing pain in Jacob's shoulders increased with each rotation of the tires that brought him closer to his parents' home. *This is a really bad idea.* He should have canceled. Or come alone. He could have flown down Christmas Eve and been back to share what was left of Christmas with Marlie. Christmas with Marlie. A reluctant smile turned up the corners of his mouth. Next Christmas they could spend alone, in front of the fireplace, sipping hot chocolate, listening to Christmas—*whoa.*

His mind slammed a door on that image but his body jerked in response. A quick glance told him Marlie hadn't noticed. She stayed in her same position, staring out the window, knees curled up in the seat, a slight frown on her lips.

Breath passed through his lips in a tortured gasp. Planning a year ahead? What was he thinking? Not only would he probably not be with Marlie next year, there was no way in hell he was going to suddenly start living a Norman Rockwell Christmas.

On the other hand, he debated with himself, if, by some odd chance, Marlie *was* still around, then a Christmas like that would make her happy. His eyes flicked over to her. She looked...confused and sad. Maybe the stress of going to his parents' house wasn't only on his part.

Or maybe she'd realized the truth. She didn't love him. It was just lust. Jacob's hands tightened on the wheel. *She didn't say she loved you when you made love. She finally figured out it was just good sex.*

"You cold? I can turn up the heat," he offered, finding it odd that she'd been silent for so long. They'd left the bed and breakfast almost two hours ago and she'd said very little.

Marlie shook her head. "I'm fine."

"You know, we could still turn around, and go back to the B and B." He wiggled his eyebrows with teasing intent.

"Oh, no," Marlie answered quickly. *Too quickly.* "Then you wouldn't get to see your parents for Christmas." No big loss, Jacob mentally added. She snuggled down, curling against the seat and smiling lazily at him. "Will you be recovered by then?" she asked innocently.

"Recovered?"

"This morning you said we couldn't have the sex again because you had to recover."

Jacob remembered that conversation. He hadn't explained the limitations on the male anatomy and would have to do that one day soon.

"I'll be fine by tonight."

"So we can have the sex then?" Jacob nodded. "Oh goody." She squished her lips together. "Who decides if you're recovered?"

"Nature," he replied, not even unnerved by their unusual conversation. *Par for the course.*

"You humans have rules for everything," she said with a shake of her head and returned to her silence.

Jacob concentrated on the road. The painted yellow lines served only to hypnotize him as they clicked by.

Images of his parents' annual Christmas Eve party drifted through his dulled mind. Elaborate dresses, men in tuxes, subdued and elegant Christmas decorations. Jacob tried to insert Marlie into the scene. His imagination dropped her into the picture under a strand of mistletoe.

He'd better warn his parents that he might be dragging Marlie from the party early. The mistletoe would start it off, but if she got it into her mind she wanted to make love, who knew what would happen? He couldn't stop the smile that curved his mouth. His parents had never met someone like Marlie. This was going to be interesting.

"Why don't you like Christmas?" Marlie's voice dampened his pleasant thoughts. Most people just accepted his surly behavior during the holidays and let it go at that. Not Marlie.

"I work in retail," he said, adding as much casualness as he could summon. Marlie didn't laugh. She waited, not interrupting, not prompting him.

"I wasn't emotionally scarred as child or anything," he finally began. "It's just that everything at my parents house was there for show—even me. Christmas is a time to display, not to enjoy. If it was comfortable, it wasn't posh enough." The memory of dressing in a tux every Christmas and having his feet crammed into dress shoes assaulted him. "We open our presents on Christmas Eve, so the guests from the party can watch. Trust me, the presents are always elaborate and expensive. When I was young, I was kept upstairs until it was time to open presents then I was dressed in my little tux and brought downstairs.

"A very elegant Christmas, I guess you could say, but not much fun."

Marlie listened then filled the silence with her soft voice.

"Christmas is more than that. It's about love, about the ultimate love," she said with assurance. "Uh, isn't that your parents' address?" Marlie asked pointing to the driveway they were passing.

Jacob slammed on the brakes, thankful the road wasn't icy, and made the turn down the long driveway. It was almost a relief to arrive. The imposing house at the end of the road never failed to impress visitors. It should keep Marlie from any more probing questions.

Marlie sat up in the seat and looked out the window, the house being the only thing today that had drawn her attention away from Jacob. It was a beautiful home. The curved driveway rolled past the front door but Jacob stopped the car when they reached the arc. Even before he'd shut off the engine, the front door opened and a grim-faced, elderly gentleman in a prim black suit came out to greet them.

"He doesn't look anything like you," Marlie whispered as Jacob opened her door and helped her out. He smiled.

"That's good, because he's the butler."

"Oh." Marlie turned to the newcomer. "Hello, I'm Marlie." She held out her hand to him. The butler hesitated for a moment. He looked at Jacob as if seeking permission before he reached out and accepted her hand.

"How do you do, miss? I'm Balford."

"I'm fine, Mr. Balford. You have a lovely house."

"It's just Balford, miss, and it isn't my house."

"You take care of it, don't you? So that makes it as much yours as anyone else's, and it looks like you've done a wonderful job," she finished with sincerity.

Balford's shoulders straightened with pride and he presented her with a tiny bow of thanks. "It's my pleasure, miss." He nodded to Jacob. "I'll see to your bags, sir."

"Oh, don't bother yourself." Marlie slipped her arm through Balford's and guided him toward the door. "Jacob can carry them. He's very strong, you know."

Marlie walked with Balford inside, her eyes bouncing from curiosity to curiosity. Silver bells dangled from the door and jingled as she walked through. "Another angel got its wings," Marlie said with a smile and her heart fluttered with joy.

She stopped dead in her tracks, pulling Balford to a halt with her. "It's back," she whispered.

"What's back?" Balford answered, his concerned face staring down into hers.

"My Christmas spirit. It's back." She felt her eyes widen.

"Had you lost it?"

Marlie nodded in response, too caught up in the truth to speak. If hers was back, what about Jacob's? Santa had indicated she'd get her spirit back if she helped Jacob get his.

The heavy front door swung open and Jacob trudged in carrying their overnight bags and their box of Christmas presents. Despite the weighty burden, he was smiling. Tiny flakes of snow melted in his soft brown hair. She watched him as he walked past her into another room. As he disappeared she heard his clear whistle blowing to the tune "It's Beginning To Look A Lot Like Christmas".

Her heart sank like a stone in her chest. She had confirmation. She'd succeeded. And soon, it would be time to leave.

"Where is everyone, Balford?" Jacob's return interrupted her grim thoughts.

"Your parents are upstairs."

"Usually at this point the house is filled with people cleaning and decorating for tonight."

"I'm sure your parents can explain."

Jacob wanted to prompt Balford for more information, but having grown up in this household, Jacob knew he'd get nothing more out of the tight-lipped butler.

He didn't have to wait long. His parents glided down the stairs moments later. Jacob greeted his father with a handshake and gave his mother a quick kiss on the cheek, before stepping back to introduce Marlie. He never got the chance. She rushed past him and wrapped her arms his father.

"It's so good to meet you," she gushed. Her eyes sparkled with joy and Jacob couldn't help but smile. His father accepted Marlie's embrace and returned it lightly. She sprung out of his arms and lunged into his mother's. Jacob watched his parents' faces closely. They were clearly shocked but they didn't seem upset.

After Marlie had stepped away, Jacob began the introductions.

"Mom, Dad, this is Marlie. Marlie, the people you just hugged are my parents, Nate and Genevieve Triumph."

Marlie gave him a playful slap on the arm. "I know that. I didn't think I was hugging strangers." She turned back to his parents. "I am so excited to be here."

The sincerity of her words struck Jacob as clearly as they did his parents. The tension eased from his shoulders. They'd passed the first hurdle. Now they just had to make it through dinner and the party.

* * * * *

Jacob finished the last bite of apple pie and placed his fork on the plate. The pie had been the only part of the evening that hadn't been a surprise. First came the shock that there was no party at the house. They were spending the evening quietly, just the four of them.

Jacob even sensed a difference in his parents. The sweet, loving looks he'd seen pass between them was a shock. His parents had welcomed Marlie with open arms—literally—falling under her spell as easily as the board had done. And Jacob. Sitting at dinner, watching her chat and laugh with his parents, he could admit it. He'd fallen under Marlie's spell as well. It had taken him a little longer than some but still, she'd worked some kind of magic.

But something was still bothering Marlie. She looked...sad. At least he assumed it was sadness. In his brief acquaintance with Marlie, he wasn't sure he'd ever seen her look sad but if ever there was a solemn face, it was hers. She tried to hide it but something in the way her smile didn't stay on her lips, her pale skin and the light fading from her eyes, made Jacob realize she was faking happiness. Maybe she was worried about impressing his parents, he thought for a moment. She didn't have to worry.

She'd certainly won them over in quick order. He hadn't seen his father smile as much since...Jacob paused. He'd *never* seen his father smile this much. After a brief reticence, his mother had warmed up to Marlie and had settled in to tell tales of Jacob as a child, warm memories that Jacob himself had forgotten.

"And every Christmas—" his mother continued, "We'd have these elaborate parties, each year bigger than the last." Jacob nodded in agreement. "And every year, Jacob would hide in his room until we absolutely forced him to come down. He was so shy so we didn't make him stay long." She smiled at Jacob and he responded in kind.

He'd always thought they were hiding him away, and she thought he was the one doing the hiding. *Odd.*

"We were so proud of him and our friends heard so much about him, but never saw him so this was the one time each year we'd insist he join us. And he looked so handsome in his tux." His mother sighed with that oh-wasn't-he-cute memory. "I could tell even then he'd be handsome. And I was right, wasn't I?"

Marlie nodded her agreement while Jacob felt his ears turn red.

"Why didn't you have the party this year?" Marlie asked.

His parents looked at each other and shrugged. "It was just too much," Nate finally said. "And we just wanted an evening alone with family." He included Marlie in his definition of family and Jacob could see her glow from where he sat.

"It was as if we both came up with the same idea at the same time," Genevieve added. "I don't know where it came from, but I'm glad we did it. So, dear, you two drove down instead of flying," his mother said to Marlie. "It's a good thing you did. All of the planes were grounded."

"Freak snow storm," Nate interjected.

Jacob remembered the silent wish he'd made about planes being grounded on Christmas Eve. *Impossible. Santa Claus does not make wishes come true. Marlie is getting to you,* he silently challenged himself. He nodded. She *was* getting to him. In every way.

"I love that drive," his mother continued. "Nate and I used to drive it just for the fun of it."

"The weather got bad and we stayed the night at a little B and B," Jacob said.

"Is there a place on the side roads?" His father looked to his wife for confirmation. "We've never seen any inns along the road."

"Yes, it's a place called Noel's Nook," Marlie said, her eyes twinkling.

"Humph. Must be new."

Jacob took a sip of his coffee, relieved, at last, to see Marlie's joyous smile.

"It was wonderful," Marlie agreed eagerly. "The drive was beautiful and last night we had the sex and I got to be on top."

Coffee sputtered from Jacob's lips, spraying across the white tablecloth. His mother's quick intake of breath was a sure sign he hadn't imagined the comment.

"That's very nice, dear," his mother said with unfailing politeness.

"It was more than nice. It was incredible. Did you know you could...?"

She was planning a blow-by-blow description of last night.

"Marlie," Jacob snapped. She looked over at him and he continued in more gentle tones. "My parents don't want to hear about last night."

Her eyelids fluttered and her face held that adorable blank look. "Why?"

"Some things aren't general topics of conversation. This is one of those things."

Her eyes widened and her mouth formed an O. She was so open and honest about everything, every emotion visible on her face. "I'm sorry." Her eyes fluttered between his parents, the apology written in her gaze.

"Not to worry, dear, we weren't shocked in the least." His mother shook her head and brushed away Marlie's concern.

"Of course not," Nate popped in. "Don't even worry about it."

Marlie glowed under his parents' words.

Jacob could barely take it all in. He'd never seen his parents take such time with someone to make sure they were comfortable and at ease.

The rumble of voices at the table stopped as Marlie and his mother pushed their chairs away and stood up. Jacob responded by reflex and joined his father in standing. If they'd said where they were going, Jacob had missed that part of the conversation.

"I want to apologize again for bringing up the sex between Jacob and me," Marlie said to his mother as they moved to the door. Jacob picked up his coffee cup and took a small sip. "It's just, he made it so wonderful, I wanted to share it."

"It's nice to know he takes after his father," his mother answered. Jacob witnessed the seductive wink she sent to her husband as she guided Marlie out the door. Jacob choked on the hot coffee sliding down this throat. The satisfied, slightly smug look on his father's face made Jacob shake his head.

"I don't want know, Dad," he said before his father could speak. He waited. Now was typically when they'd discuss business, review the plans for the new store, but Jacob was hesitant to bring work into the conversation.

"She seems like a lovely young woman," his father began. Jacob nodded.

"Yes," he agreed, with one little problem. He'd done his best to ignore it over the past twenty-four hours. What was a little insanity compared to great sex? he justified. Jacob sighed and stared into his coffee cup.

"So what's the issue?" his father questioned, obviously reading the tension on Jacob's face.

He hesitated. He'd never discussed personal relationships with his father, never asked his advice. Jacob had decided from an early age to make his own decisions but in truth, he wasn't doing so hot on this one. Maybe his father could provide a little guidance.

"She's crazy, Dad," Jacob blurted out. His father's eyes popped open wide. "I mean I think she's wonderful, but she's nuts. She thinks she's a Christmas elf."

"A what?"

"An elf. You know, building toys in Santa's workshop. That kind of Christmas elf." He watched his father pause. The idea took a moment to settle into anyone's brain.

Jacob could relate.

"Hmm."

"Exactly," agreed Jacob to his father's unspoken comment.

His dad seemed to come to a decision after a moment more of thought. "There are worse delusions she could have."

"What?" Jacob felt his mouth sag open as he stared at his logical, staid businessman father.

Nate looked slightly offended at Jacob's outburst. "She doesn't think she's an ax murderer with instructions to kill her lovers. That would be worse."

It was kind of hard to fight that sort of logic. "You're right, Dad, that would be worse, but still…"

"And she doesn't tell everyone about it, does she? She didn't walk in here and say 'Hi I'm Marlie and I'm a Christmas elf'."

"She thinks she can grant Christmas wishes, Dad." Jacob's voice became more insistent as he realized his father was still encouraging the relationship.

"Maybe she can," Nate answered, his voice tinged with awe.

Jacob didn't reply. He didn't know *how* to reply. He just sat and stared at his father.

"Your mother and I wanted a Christmas just like this, and look how it's turned out. It's nice to have just family around, and your mother didn't need the stress of a big party."

"How is Mom doing?" He knew she'd been taking medicine for high blood pressure but whenever he asked about her condition, the standard reply was, "She's fine, not to worry."

This time, he watched his father's shoulders droop.

"She's still doing too much. She's not taking her medicine regularly. She's not exercising. The doctor said if she doesn't get her blood pressure down, it could be serious."

Again Jacob didn't know how to react, both to his mother's medical condition and to the honesty in his father's answer. His parents had never lied to him but they'd not told him much of what was going on.

"So, we're taking it easy. We've been talking and the holidays have become so overwhelming around here we decided to just do a quiet Christmas." His father's face lit up. "And now that we've met Marlie, it's even better. When you called and said you were bringing a date, we thought it would be Natalie." Nate took a drink of coffee, and asked with exaggerated casualness, "Are you still seeing Natalie?"

"I don't think she's real fond of me right now," he said with a grimace, then proceeded to tell his father about the dinner party-mistletoe incident which somehow led to him telling his father about the Henderson deal being on the rocks because Jacob had spent the morning in bed with Marlie. Expecting a reprimand and a reminder of how many people depended on them, he was stunned to realize his father was barely containing his laughter.

"Dad?"

That simple word seemed to break Nate's control and he started to chuckle.

"Dad, what is so funny? I might have screwed up a deal because I was having sex." He put it in the bluntest terms.

"Glad to see you have your priorities in order, son." Nate wiped the tears of laughter away from his cheeks and said, "Can't wait to tell your mother." With a few more gasping laughs, his father calmed enough to speak. "She's a lovely girl, Jacob. So, she has a few quirks, they aren't anything that will get you thrown out of the Better Business Bureau."

"But, Dad…"

"Is this serious? If she's just another girlfriend, then don't worry about it. If she's something more permanent, well then…"

Jacob waited. His father had to have some wisdom of the ages that would get him through this situation.

"Yes," he finally prodded when his dad didn't finish his thought.

"I still wouldn't worry about it." Jacob stared at his father. Where was the stern man who spoke about proper lineage and finding the perfect wife for a corporate executive? His father actually seemed to be giving his blessing on a relationship to a woman who believed she was an elf from Santa's workshop. "I'd make a list of pros and cons," his father finally said. Jacob relaxed. That was more like the man he knew. Make a list. Numbers, facts don't lie. "Of course, from what I can see the only negative is this little elf thing and compared to the list of positives, I'd say go for it."

Go for it? Jacob looked around the room to see if he'd fallen into a parallel universe where everything was opposite from this world. No, the room was normal. He felt the same. It was only his father who had changed.

"Balford," Nate called. "We're basically finished for the evening. Why don't you and Nancy call it a night? We'll be getting up late so don't worry about breakfast."

"Thank you, Mr. Triumph." He nodded his head to both men seated. "Mr. Triumph. Have a Merry Christmas Eve."

"Same to you, Balford."

"Good night, Balford," Jacob mumbled, his mind still whirling with the strange revelations he'd learned tonight.

It had been so long since he'd spent time with his parents, alone with them. Had they changed so dramatically since the last time? Or had he?

Jacob peered into the bottom of his china coffee cup and considered the idea. It all came back to Marlie. He knew with certainty that he wouldn't have been sitting at the table after dinner alone with his father if it hadn't been for her.

"Jacob," his mother's voice pulled him from his thoughts. "It's almost time for bed," she announced, a smile teasing the corner of her lips.

He raised his eyebrows in question and leaned back from the table. He hadn't been sent to bed since he was ten years old. "I didn't know I had a set bedtime."

"Oh, this request is from Marlie."

His heart leapt in his chest. He placed his hands on the table and started to stand.

"No, you're supposed to wait for ten minutes and go up." His mother winked. "I think she might have something special planned."

The image of Marlie in the tiny scraps of lace that Anne had selected came to him in a rush of blood straight to his groin. Was she up there, even now, putting on some sexy bit of lingerie to lure him into bed?

He sat back in his chair and tapped his fingers on the table, trying to maintain the outward sign of calm. No need for his parents to know his mind was on ripping off his housekeeper's clothes and fucking her until she screamed.

A quick glance at his father—and the barely constrained laughter—told him he wasn't fooling anyone.

The ten minutes passed with relative external calm and Jacob was pleased that at the end of it, he didn't run from the room. He stood and calmly said good night to his parents.

"Yes. It's not polite to keep a lady waiting," his father added. Jacob looked into his father's eyes. They sparkled with joy. Marlie was contagious.

"Well, since you've raised me to be polite," Jacob answered with mock formality. "I will leave you now. And see you in the morning." He stopped at the doorway and turned back to his parents. They sat together at the table, their fingers loosely entwined. His voice was soft as he spoke. "Merry Christmas."

Chapter Fourteen

Jacob stopped at the bedroom door and listened to his heart pound. Anticipation urged him on but he held back. He had to maintain control. The past two nights had been hot and sexual and more than exotic enough. It finally seemed possible that he could live a life with relatively vanilla sex—if that sex was with Marlie.

Marlie. He focused on her and willed the control into his veins.

He knocked softly and pushed the door open. The first thing that hit him was the sight of the small Christmas tree in the corner and the fresh scent of pine. So this was what Marlie and his mother had done after dinner. Jacob smiled softly. Marlie was intent on bringing Christmas into every part of his life.

He walked farther into the room, smiling as the lights twinkled in the almost dark.

He looked to the foot of the bed and saw Marlie—naked and kneeling, her hands clasped behind her back and her eyes lowered in a classic submissive's pose. Her thighs were spread just enough to hint—teasing him with shadows—of her pussy.

Power surged through his body making his cock rock hard.

"Marlie?"

She raised her head, her eyes glowing with the desire.

"Merry Christmas...sir." She lowered her gaze. "I hope you find me pleasing."

He didn't know what to think. Here she was, offering herself.

He crouched down in front of her and placed two fingers beneath her chin, drawing her eyes up to him. The warm scent of her skin, her sex and the tree surrounded him.

"Marlie, do you know what you're doing?"

She nodded. "Granting your Christmas wish."

How had she known that?

"Do you know what I'm going to do to you?"

Again she nodded. "I'm to do whatever you tell me."

"And you want this?"

"Oh yes." Her breathless agreement was like a warm hand around his cock. She was here, offering him what he wanted. What he'd denied himself for so long.

"If I do anything that frightens you or that you don't like, you must tell me."

"All right but I don't think that will happen." She stared straight into his eyes and there was no hint of submission in her gaze—only heat. "I've enjoyed everything you've done to me so far."

He nodded and backed away, standing up and taking a good look at her. He stared at her for a long moment before she seemed to hear his silent command and dropped her gaze.

"Do you enjoy this, Marlie? Being naked and before me."

"Yes...sir." She hesitated on the "sir" but he wouldn't punish her for that. Not yet. He'd never been fond of "Master" but "sir" was just enough.

"Do you like knowing I'm staring at your pretty tits?"

"Yes, sir."

"Does it make you wet?"

She took a deep breath before she answered. "Yes."

"You must address me appropriately. Either call me Jacob or Sir. Do you understand?" His voice was firm but loving and Marlie shivered as the words washed over her.

"Yes, sir," she responded, hoping she sounded sufficiently submissive, loving the game they played. Her body was tingling with the pleasure and it was becoming difficult to breathe. It had taken her a little time to find a book that contained the images like those in Jacob's wish but once she'd found it, she'd been quite intrigued and tonight was the perfect night to grant him his wish.

"Show me," he commanded. "Put your fingers between your legs and show me how wet it's made you to display yourself like this."

She released the grip she had on one wrist and pulled her arms around front. A sudden shyness came over her but she knew she wasn't ready to stop. She slipped one hand between her legs. The wet heat from her pussy immediately coated her fingers but she couldn't resist sliding her hand farther, dipping into her opening that she hoped Jacob would fill soon. She tickled the very entrance and felt a warm flutter of the sparkles that Jacob so often created.

"Marlie, stop." She froze at the sound of his harsh command. "Remove your hand." She paused. She had never been good at taking orders—just ask Santa—but she had said she would do what Jacob told her to do. Already missing the warmth of her own sex, she drew her hand out. Jacob crouched down before her. He didn't touch her but she could feel him surrounding her. "You were not given permission to pleasure yourself. This pussy." He cupped his hand over her sex. "This sweet little cunt is mine to pleasure tonight. Do you understand?"

Her back arched instinctively moving into the caress. His fingers fluttered along her slit.

"Yes, Jacob."

"Good." He pulled his hand up. He was coated in her moisture. He offered his hand to her mouth. "Taste yourself. Taste what pure desire is."

With his eyes drilling into her, heating her body with a simple stare, there was nothing she could do but open her mouth and stroke her tongue across the tip of his finger. The warm musky flavor was foreign but not unpleasant. Heat exploded in Jacob's gaze as he watched her. Wanting more of that, she repeated the motion, dragging her tongue across the flat of his finger.

"Now, let me taste." He sealed their lips together in slow drugging kiss that sent a flood to her pussy. "Delicious," he whispered. Jacob drew his hand back and held his finger up to his lips. "The other night, when I put my mouth on your cunt, and licked you—you liked that didn't you?"

"Yes, sir."

"Good." He stood up and she let her eyes wander up, all the way up his body, stopping at his crotch. The telltale sign of his erection tempted her to smile but she resisted.

He stroked his fingers along the side of her jaw and across her lower lip.

"Have you ever taken a man's cock in your mouth?"

She slowly shook her head. "No, sir." She glanced up at the distinct bulge in his trousers and couldn't resist licking her lips. Her whole body was practically vibrating. When she'd decided to grant his wish this way, she'd expected him to be pleased but she'd never expected the desire inside *her* to build so rapidly. There was something so delicious about kneeling before him, letting him command her. Her breasts were tight and heavy and she wanted to touch them but didn't think that was allowed.

The almost silent rasp of his zipper being lowered made her heart pound.

"Now, Marlie." Jacob's fingers again tilted her chin up. The hard thick erection stood between his legs. "You may pleasure me with your mouth." His words sent another delicious shiver up her spine. Struggling to keep her hands behind her back, she leaned forward and lapped her tongue across the curve of his shaft. He tensed beneath the tiny caress and Marlie knew she could drive him crazy, make him hunger the way she did.

She remembered the way he'd licked her pussy and tried to mimic the motions, hot little flutters of her tongue countered by long delicious strokes up the whole massive length. But her mouth just wasn't enough. There was too much of him. She wanted to hold him and stroke him.

Barely pulling her mouth from his cock, she whispered. "May I use my hands...sir?"

He heard the deliberate delay in her voice and vowed she would receive a very sensual punishment for it but now, he needed this too much.

"Yes," he growled. Her eyes glowed with power and Jacob thought he'd come right there. His little elf was enjoying this, loving it in fact. The sweet way she moved her body as she lapped at his cock, the teasing touches—she knew just how far she was pushing him. At first her touch had been shy, exploring but she'd quickly learned what and where to touch to make him groan.

He braced himself when she dipped her fingers between his legs and cupped his balls. The hot, intoxicating strokes of her tongue didn't stop.

"Take it into your mouth, Marlie," he commanded, pleased that his voice didn't trembled. "All of it." This time her eyes widened and he almost laughed. "As much as you can, darling."

She opened her lips and lapped at the thick head before taking it inside. The heat was incredible, filling his shaft, sinking into his balls. She groaned as he slipped deeper into the warmth of her mouth and the sound sent dozens of shock waves through his cock. He couldn't stop the slow roll of his hips, needing to move. Her tongue rubbed against the underside of his cock as she slowly retreated. The light, dainty suction as she pulled back made his eyes burn and he clenched his teeth to keep from crying out. She reached the tip and returned, accepting him until he touched the back of her throat.

The sweet torture grew a hundredfold as she slowly pumped her mouth on him, working the end of his cock in shallow pulsing strokes. "Suck me," he growled. "Make me come."

Her gaze met his and he could see the devious smile in them. Vowing to punish her, after, he slipped his fingers into her hair and gripped her head and urged her to move, faster, a little deeper.

Fighting the urge to thrust, he held himself still, feeling the pressure rise inside him until it was too much. His shout filled the room as his cum pulsed from his body, filling Marlie's mouth.

It took him long moments before he felt his control return. He looked down — Marlie still knelt at his feet. A satisfied, cat-just-ate-the-cream smile curved her lips and knew he couldn't let her get away with.

"Arrogance is not permitted in a sex slave." He held out his hand and helped her to her feet. "You must be punished."

Her breath caught in her throat and her eyes widened. "Punished?" If he'd seen a hint of fear, he would have stopped but there was only curiosity and unquenched heat in her gaze.

"To teach you proper respect." He nodded toward the end of the bed. "Bend over, Marlie. Rest your elbows and hips on the bed." She slowly turned, peering over her shoulder to watch him as she positioned her body on the bed. "Eyes forward, Marlie. You must trust me."

"I do," she whispered.

He stepped back and stared at the perfect image presented before him — Marlie bent over the bed, her rounded ass his to warm. His cock twitched. It wouldn't take long for him to recover, not with such a delightful inducement before him.

"Open your legs. Let me see your cunt while you accept your punishment."

As she followed his command, he slipped his hand down her backside and into the space between her thighs. Slick, hot liquid coated his fingers.

"You're soaking wet, baby. Sucking me off got you hot, didn't it?"

"Yes, Jacob." The breathless anticipation in her voice reached into his chest and pulled at his heart. This was a woman who could take all of him and would love all he had to give.

He took a step back and paused a moment, needing all his control so that he didn't hurt her. He wanted her to enjoy this, a little burst of pain with all the pleasure he planned to give her. Raising his hand, he brought it down in a short smart tap across her ass. Her body jolted as if she'd been shocked.

"Jacob!" He pushed his fingers between her legs, driving two fingers into her cunt. "Oooh, Jacob."

"That's a good girl. Stay still and take your punishment."

Marlie nodded and stared at the bedcovers, bracing herself for the next stroke. It came seconds later—a quick little shock of pain followed by a warm flood of heat in her pussy. It was strange and amazing. She'd never had a spanking in her life—and it was strangely pleasurable. The urge to move was too much to resist and she pressed her hips against the bed, looking for something to rub against.

"Now, Marlie, you know better. This cunt is mine to pleasure tonight."

She shivered at his words and tried to hold still but it was so hard. He smacked his hand across her ass again, a little harder and she groaned, dropping her head forward and fighting every instinct in her body to move.

"That's good. You're learning, trying to please me."

"Yes, Jacob, but please, I need you."

"Soon." He smoothed his hand between her legs, teasing her opening and her clit. "That first night when you crawled into bed, I almost came in my pants seeing this tight ass." His teeth nipped at the side of her throat adding to the layers of sensation already swamping her. "And every night since, I've dreamed about fucking you like this, feeling your ass press against me while I'm deep inside you."

Marlie moaned, loving his low sexy words—words meant just for her.

"Is that what you want?"

"Yes, Jacob, please."

"I'll feel huge inside you when I fuck you this way. I'll touch every part of you," he promised. "Filling your sweet cunt, loving every inch." He stroked her pussy lips, teasing her flesh as he guided his cock between her legs, not entering her, but sliding against her wet flesh. Her moisture flowed over his shaft, coating him. "Is that what you want, baby?"

"Yes, Jacob. Please, put it inside me."

The blatant need in her voice tore at his control and he knew he wouldn't last much longer. The hot liquid pouring from her pussy and drenching his hand combined the warm pink of her ass was too much for him to resist.

He lifted her hips and pulled her to the edge of the bed, draping her over the corner so she straddled it. She cried out and he knew she was feeling the thick soft surface pressing against her clit.

He placed the thick head of his cock to her opening and pushed, slow, steady, hard—he didn't stop, just drove forward until he was balls deep inside her, her pussy gripping his shaft, squeezing him.

She lowered her forehead against the mattress and groaned even as she pushed back against him.

He gripped her hips and held her still as he began to move inside her, long deep strokes—slow at first, letting it build—knowing the mattress was pressing against her clit, teasing her from that side. He worked his cock inside her, loving every stroke and retreat. It was like every inch of his cock was submersed in molten gold. Marlie quickly learned how to move against him until their bodies were rocking and he was doing just what he'd promised—fucking her hard and deep, claiming her cunt as his.

And she took him, accepting every inch he put into her. More than that—she wanted him, welcomed him, thrusting back to drive him deeper. His balls pulled up tight and he knew he wouldn't last much longer. He curled his hand around her hips and found her clit, stroking her as he'd learned last night, knowing where to touch to send her.

"Jacob!" Her cunt fluttered along his cock as she came. He dug his fingers into her hips and pounded into her again and again until he couldn't take it anymore and poured himself out—flooding her with his cum.

"Come on, baby. You can't sleep here." He tapped her ass and then slipped his fingers between her legs, letting her moisture coat his fingers. With a groan, she lifted her head and looked at him, her eyes glowing with sexy satiation.

"That felt really good," she said though her words were hazy and slow. "Can we do it again?"

His cock was limp and she was exhausted. "Not right now, honey, but some time soon, definitely." And a whole host of other things. "Now let's get you into bed."

He watched as she dragged herself up the mattress, his cum trickling from between her thighs. It should have worried him. He hadn't fucked anyone without a condom since—well, never. The risk had never seemed worth the pleasure but no other woman had ever driven him to the point of distraction just by walking into a room.

The image of Marlie pregnant with his child was strangely satisfying and he held on to it as he crawled into bed beside her.

"Jacob?" she muttered as he settled her against his chest.

"Hmm?"

"This is one wish we don't have to tell Santa about."

He smiled in the dark. "No. We won't tell anyone."

As if that satisfied her, she cuddled close and let her eyes drift shut. He buried his face in her neck and breathed in the heady scent of her shampoo.

I love you. He heard the words in his head but didn't know where they came from — inside him or the memory of Marlie yesterday.

In the distance, the tall clock in the hall chimed midnight. It was Christmas.

He looked down at the beautiful woman beside him. In a few short days, she'd changed his life and Christmas would never be the same.

* * * * *

Marlie stared at the note clutched in the tight grip of her palm. It had been harder to write than she could have imagined. Saying goodbye to the man she loved proved the biggest challenge of her life. Tears had clogged her eyes and smudged the ink on the page, but it had to be done. Santa would be here soon. She could hear the sleigh bells in the distance. In moments the tapping of the reindeers' hooves would signal his arrival at the Triumph household, and it would be time to leave. Time to leave Jacob.

She watched him sleep. He lay on his stomach, his bare back a pale contrast against the dark sheets. His arm reached to her side of the bed where she'd lain until he'd fallen into a deep sleep.

It would be cold at the North Pole without Jacob.

I love you.

She closed her eyes. She wanted him to believe that so much. That was *her* Christmas wish, that Jacob believe in her love.

She memorized his face. It wasn't supposed to be like this. She was supposed to teach *Jacob* the meaning of Christmas—teach him that love existed but this kind of love hurt. She knew it was best for Jacob. He would take what he'd learned from her and rejoin life. But she wouldn't be there to see it.

The almost silent skid of the sleigh runners trailed across the roof. Eight sets of hooves pattered on the snow. Santa was here and it was time for her to go.

She looked at Jacob one last time. He'd been handsome when she'd met him. He was so beautiful to her now. A bittersweet smile curved her lips. She'd done her job. She'd taught Jacob that love existed. And she'd learned it for herself.

She set the note on the bedside table and trailed her fingers down the smooth skin of his hand. She knew it was right, the Workshop was where she belonged, but oh, she didn't want to leave.

Sleigh bells jingled. Santa was getting impatient. Marlie walked to the window, pulled open the curtains and disappeared into the night.

* * * * *

Jacob rolled over and reached for Marlie. Her side of the bed was definitely empty and decidedly cool. She never got up before him. For the past two weeks he'd woken up with Marlie on top of him. Now that he could actually do something about that, she was gone. Jacob sank back onto the pillow. He'd become accustomed to Marlie being the first thing he saw each morning.

Maybe she was in the bathroom.

"Marlie?" he called out. The room was silent. A chill settled into his chest. The room *felt* empty. He sat up in the bed and looked to where their overnight bags were stashed. His remained. Hers was gone.

She was gone. She'd left him. *She can't be gone.* She said she loved him. Why would she do that and then leave?

The pink envelope on the table next to him caught his attention. He tore it open, his heart already knowing its contents.

Dear Jacob,

It's time for me to leave. I have a job back at the Workshop that needs my attention. Thank you for the most wonderful Christmas ever. I love you and will hold you in my heart always. Believe in love,

Marlie.

He crumpled the note in his hand. *Love, right.* If she loved him, she wouldn't have left. Had he scared her with their sex games last night? She hadn't seemed frightened. Hell, she'd asked to do it again—so why would she leave in the middle of the night? He'd better have Balford check the silver to make sure none of it was missing. The cynical thought didn't sit well with Jacob and he leapt from the bed, no longer comfortable in its warmth, warmth that reminded him too much of Marlie.

Damn, everything was going to remind him of Marlie, the house, his office, even the store. She'd been there for less than two weeks and had infiltrated every part of his life. He jerked his clothes on, deciding he needed to be fully dressed to face his parents. She'd even won them over, now he had to tell them the truth about Marlie.

If only he knew what that was.

Jacob trudged down the stairs and found his parents in the family room. The bright lights of the Christmas tree sparkled like the light in Marlie's eyes. The ache around Jacob's heart increased. He had to leave. Had to get away from Christmas. Everything Christmas reminded him of Marlie.

"Good morning, Jacob," his mother's cheerful greeting grated on his already stretched nerves. "How did you sleep?" She rested back in her recliner, a cup of tea held in one hand.

Nate stood by the fireplace, tending the tiny blaze. He greeted Jacob and took his traditional seat across from his wife.

"Fine, uh, —" he started to answer. He shoved his hands into the pockets of his trousers, steeling himself for what was to come.

"Where's Marlie?"

"She's gone."

"Gone where?" His mother's shocked expression was a mirror to his own hidden thoughts.

"Gone. She left in the middle of the night." He glanced around the room, unwilling to see the pity in his parent's eyes. He just wanted to get Christmas over with and get back to town. "Could we open our presents now?" The cold that had settled in his heart came through in his voice. "I have to get back to town. I've got work to do."

"Of-of course." His mother and father exchanged curious looks but neither asked the obvious question, and he was thankful. He wasn't prepared to answer questions. He didn't know why Marlie left or where she'd gone or if he'd done something wrong. All he knew was she was gone and her love hadn't been real after all.

With only three of them, it took mere moments to hand out the presents. Jacob stared at the tiny pile in front of him. He thought about the coat he'd bought for Marlie—something to keep her warm when he wasn't around. He'd be returning it to Triumph's on Monday. With a sigh, he reached for the first box, feeling none of the Christmas joy he knew he was supposed to feel. The truth was, he didn't care what was in the boxes. It could be the crown jewels and he didn't care.

He didn't want presents. He wanted Marlie. Tears tickled the corners of his eyes. He forced them away. He hadn't cried in years, he certainly wasn't going to do so now.

"Why darling, thank you," Jacob's mother gushed. "It's wonderful."

The presents. His Christmas wish. Against all logic, hope flared in his heart. Maybe she was right, maybe she was real. He whipped his head up to see his mother's gift.

A new, tiny diamond bracelet dangled from her wrist. She smiled at her husband. "It's truly beautiful."

"I'm glad you like it," Nate answered. He opened the box on his lap. His eyes brightened. Slipping two fingers into the box, he pulled out a new blue and red tie, so similar to last year's gift, Jacob wasn't sure he could tell them apart. "It's lovely, my dear, thank you."

Jacob's mother lowered her eyes at the kind words and reached for her next box.

Jacob sighed and pulled the paper from around his packages. Marlie was gone and for a moment there he'd dropped into her insanity and thought she might be a real elf. But nothing ever changed and wishes didn't come true.

The cold that had settled around his heart collapsed and extinguished the final tiny flame of hope.

"Why Jacob," his mother sighed. "It's adorable." He looked up at his mother's call. She cuddled the stuffed puppy he'd purchased to her cheek. It had been his attempt to fill his own Christmas wish. Try as he might, he couldn't deny the spark of joy in his heart. His mother's face glowed with her happiness.

"Just something I picked up." He shrugged.

"Well, I'll just have to kick your father out of bed so there's room," she said with a gentle laugh.

"Hey," Nate playfully warned.

How odd that he'd never seen it before—the loving way his parents treated each other. So much of his life had been spent in front of others when they'd been formal and stiff. But last night and today, it was obvious they loved each other. Jacob felt like he was intruding on an intimate moment between them.

It would be nice to share his life with someone, as his parents did. Jacob stared at the torn wrappings and empty boxes in front of him. *Christmas isn't about presents, it's about love. People have to give and get things to make love visible but it's all about what's in your heart.*

Her words came back to Jacob. Presents were the way humans had of showing love. He glanced at the pale blue shirt he'd given his father. What kind of love did that show? His father didn't need another blue shirt. Jacob wasn't even sure his father wanted another blue shirt.

"That's everything," Genevieve said.

Jacob nodded and stared at the pile of papers, not wanting to move, suddenly not wanting the moment to end.

"Actually, there is one more present," his father said with a hesitant clearing of his throat. Genevieve and Jacob looked around the room. No package was left unopened. Nate walked to the door and cracked it open. He slipped out into the hall, returning moments later holding a small fluffy brown puppy.

Jacob's jaw dropped open and for a moment he was unable to breathe.

His father looked embarrassed as the energetic puppy squirmed in his arms but he walked to his mother's side and placed the dog in her lap.

"I know we've never had a pet before but the doctor said you should exercise more, maybe walk. I thought a dog would give you a reason to be outside." The brown little ball of fur lifted its head and blinked up at Jacob's mother. Pushing its tiny body up on all fours, it wavered a moment then stretched up on its hind legs and placed its paws on her chest.

"Now, if you truly don't want it, I have a good home for it," Nate continued. He looked over to Jacob. "They say that's a problem with Christmas puppies." Jacob nodded barely comprehending his father's words. It was a puppy, a real live puppy.

Jacob crawled across the carpet on his hands and knees to his mother's side. Genevieve picked up the dog and cuddled it under her chin. Jacob followed each movement with his eyes. He inched closer, needing to see that it was real.

"Jacob, are you all right?" his father's worried question shook him.

"It's a puppy," he answered, his voice filled with awe.

"I know."

"Just like my wish."

"You wished for a puppy?" his mother asked. His parents exchanged curious glances. Genevieve shook her head. "Was this when you were younger? I think back now and I can't think of a good reason why we didn't have a dog."

"No, I wished for it last week," he whispered, his dazed voice reflecting his confusion. Jacob continued to stare at the puppy that had settled himself securely in Genevieve's lap, its nose resting on her arm. "To Marlie." He stared up at his father, wonder filling his eyes.

"Well, however he got here, whoever wished for him, I'm thankful," Genevieve said with a real, joyous smile. She petted the top of the puppy's head. "And I will take him for walks every day, just like the doctor ordered," she concluded with a gentle look at her husband.

The present made her happy, Jacob thought, not because of what it was, but because of the love it showed from his father.

She'd done it. Marlie had actually made his Christmas wish come true. She was real. An elf who worked in Santa's Workshop. His logical mind battled the very concept of it. Santa was a made-up creation to bribe children's good behavior, he reminded himself.

The puppy jumped down from his mother's lap to investigate the room. His parents shared a secret smile as they watched the puppy's antics.

Jacob felt a little envious of his parents. They had each other. Love swelled in his heart. *Marlie was right.*

Marlie. He had to find Marlie.

He jumped to his feet. "I-I have to go," he stuttered.

"Oh, of course, dear. You have to get back to work," his mother agreed, a tinge of sadness in her voice.

"I have to find Marlie." He looked at his parents and shrugged. "How do I get to the North Pole from here?"

* * * * *

Jacob stared down at the blank piece of paper. He couldn't believe he was contemplating writing this letter. It was insane. He knew that, but he couldn't think of anything else. He'd searched for her, even knowing she had truly gone back to the North Pole. Gone forever from his life.

He'd searched every toy section in every department store in the city. Everyone remembered Marlie but no one had seen her since before Christmas.

She'd taught him how to love and then she'd left.

The flash of anger at her disappearance no longer tormented his soul. In its place was a kind of peace. She was gone and he would continue to mourn her but he wouldn't have missed knowing her. *It's better to have loved and lost than never to have loved at all.* Jacob sighed. He was becoming a walking, talking cliché. He couldn't resist a slight smile. Marlie would have laughed if she could hear his thoughts.

She was magic. She'd made all his Christmas wishes come true. He smiled at the memory of Christmas, his mother's joy at the simple and wonderful gift of a puppy.

He picked up his pen. There was only one thing left to do. He had to let her go. He had to make one more Christmas wish.

She had a life back at the Workshop, a place she'd longed for even while she was with him. He was going to wish for what she wanted most. A bittersweet smile turned his mouth. *Painting red. Red on fire trucks. Red on the little red wagons.*

He tightened his fingers on the pen and began to write.

Dear Santa…

* * * * *

"Marlie?"

She lifted her eyes from the tiny truck she was building. Santa waited. "How are you, Marlie?" She could hear the concern in his voice, could see the worry in his eyes. He'd looked at her like that since Christmas Eve. Only three weeks had passed but it seemed like forever.

She forced a smile and nodded. "I'm fine." It wasn't exactly a lie. She was glad to be home. Glad to be around the other elves and glad to be doing a new job. But she missed Jacob and even having the new job in the Workshop designing little toy trucks wasn't enough to keep her thoughts away from him. She pulled her sweater tightly around her. The ever-present cold was seeping into her skin.

Santa's observant gaze stared into her soul. She turned her face away to avoid his too-seeing eyes.

"I heard from your charge today," he interrupted the silence of the workroom.

My charge? Who? Jacob!

"Jacob? Is everything okay?" Marlie dropped her carving knife and jumped to her feet. "Is he hurt?"

Santa held up a silencing hand. "He's fine. He just sent me a rather unusual Christmas wish and I'm not really sure how to fix it." He pulled a crumpled envelope from his pocket and handed it to Marlie. The address was simply "Santa Claus, North Pole". She peeled the flap back and pulled out the letter. Jacob's scrawling handwriting covered the page. Tears formed in her eyes as the memories rushed back to her. The sound of his voice echoed in her ears as she read the words.

Dear Santa,

I know this is a little late for this year, but this is the kind of Christmas wish you can make come true at any time. So here is my wish...that Marlie know how much she means to me and that she's happy wherever she is. She taught me the true spirit of Christmas. Thank you for sending her to me. I never would have learned it without her.

Sincerely,

Jacob Triumph

A smear covered the last letters of Triumph, as if a tear had fallen unnoticed. Her heart maintained a steady, loud thud in her chest. She'd succeeded. She deserved to be back in the Workshop. She hadn't known if Jacob had forgotten how to love as soon as she'd left. Now she knew. Yes, she deserved to be here, but she didn't want to be.

"So, Marlie, are you happy?"

She lifted her head. "Sure." Her shoulders twitched in an involuntary shrug. How did she tell the big guy that she'd rather be in the Outside World with all its problems than in his cozy, loving Workshop?

"I see," Santa said with a nod. "I'll handle it then."

* * * * *

Jacob picked at the casserole Mrs. Butterstone had made for his dinner. It was one of his favorites. She'd been making a lot of his favorite foods lately. Anything to get him to eat. He appreciated her efforts so tried to eat but he just had no desire for food. No desire for anything, except Marlie. That was one desire that never went away. He raised the fork to his lips. Everything reminded him of Marlie, even dinner, which was one time when he was thankful she wasn't in his kitchen. She never did learn how to cook.

He dropped the fork back to his plate. Damn, he would have hired a thousand cooks if he could have one Marlie back.

And worse, it was his own damn fault. He'd hoped the letter to Santa would be the end of it—but he hadn't been able to let go. Christmas still decorated his home. The only part of the decorations he'd permitted to be taken down was the Christmas tree—after it had become a fire hazard. It was silly, but the decorations and the Christmas carols he played in his car stereo reminded him of Marlie and he wasn't ready yet to lose her memory.

"Mr. Triumph?" Jacob slowly lifted his head at the call of his housekeeper. "There's a gentleman at the door. I told him you were not home, but he seems to know I'm lying. He insists on seeing you."

"What does he want?"

"I don't know. I think he's a little off." She touched one finger to her temple. "He says he's Santa Claus."

Jacob leapt out of his chair, sending it to the floor. He grabbed Mrs. Butterstone's shoulders and held her in front of him. "Did you say Santa Claus?"

"Y-Yes, should I call the police?"

"No." He walked past her, ignoring her startled look. *Santa is here.* His heart raced. The idea that, as a grown man, he was excited about meeting Santa Claus momentarily struck him as odd, but he brushed the worry aside. He had proof. Santa existed and really had elves. Beautiful, lovely, loving elves. Jacob picked up the pace of his steps and jerked the door open.

He wasn't sure what he expected, maybe a red suit and a reindeer-pulled sleigh in his driveway, but the man standing in front of Jacob didn't look like any Santa Claus picture he'd ever seen. He looked like a slightly portly, white-bearded casually dressed man on the street. Then he smiled. The classic twinkle in his eyes glittered and the rosy cheeks puffed out.

"Jacob, it's good to see you again," Santa greeted, as he stepped inside. He stopped in the entryway, looking at the decorations Marlie had put up and Jacob hadn't been able to take down. "I like your house. Marlie did a good job."

"Thanks, uh—" He couldn't do it. Everyone knew Santa Claus was a myth. Jacob's tongue caught in his mouth.

"Santa, will do," the bearded man called as he walked into the living room. "No need to be formal after all these years."

"All these years?" Jacob followed Santa into the room, in time to see the older gentleman sink into the couch.

Santa rubbed his hand across the soft material. He looked across the room. "Is that coffee?" he asked, indicating the silver service set behind Jacob. Jacob nodded.

"Would you like a cup?"

"I'd love one." Jacob was surprised by the vehemence behind the old man's words. "We don't have coffee at the North Pole," Santa explained as Jacob handed him a cup of the steaming black liquid. "Nothing with caffeine," Santa concluded with a shake of his head. "Can you imagine a workshop full of wired elves?" A gentle shudder went through his body. "They are perky enough without any help." He took a sip from the coffee cup and released a contented sigh. "But back to the business at hand. I've been watching you for years, Jacob." He fingered his beard. "You were ruining Christmas for a lot of people, and for yourself, of course. I had to do something."

Jacob wanted to deny the accusations, but he couldn't. Santa was right. His office was a different place now. Marlie had been right about Eric being a wonderful Santa. And now Eric had blossomed and was leading the Accounting department to new productivity and morale. They were the happiest department in the store. Two days ago Jacob had heard Christmas music sounding from behind the door to Accounting. And Mitch had turned into the number one sales rep in Men's Clothing. Jacob suppressed a smile. *I could use Marlie in my personnel department.*

"So, I sent you Marlie." Santa's words interrupted Jacob's thoughts.

He nodded.

"She did a good job, didn't she?"

Again Jacob nodded. "She did a great job." He did nothing to hide the wistful longing in his voice. He missed Marlie. He loved Marlie.

"Yes, but now, I have to tell you. She's pretty worthless as an elf. Oh, she makes an effort, a good effort, but her heart just isn't in it, you know what I mean?"

"I know what you mean," Jacob agreed. He'd been living the same existence.

"I'm glad you wrote to me, son," Santa said as he stood. He took the few steps needed to put him in front of the fireplace and set the coffee cup on the mantle. "It's a little late for Christmas, but the gift of love can be given at any time."

Like a pianist warming up before a concert, he rolled his shoulders, clasped his fingers together and turned his hands inside out. After a quick stretch, he raised his hands like a conductor preparing a symphony start. Jacob caught his breath. Santa lowered his hands and looked at Jacob.

"Do you like kids?"

"Sure."

"Do you want to have several of your own?"

Again Jacob shrugged. "Sure."

"Good. Elves are notoriously fertile," he smiled.

Jacob's heart began to pound. Breath lodged in his throat. *Elves. Did that mean…?*

With a final shoulder roll, Santa lifted his arms, and clapped his hands together twice.

A pile of ashes burst into a dust cloud that swelled in the room, blocking Jacob's vision. Santa and Jacob coughed in unison. As the ashes sank to the ground, Jacob noticed a large burlap sack, about four feet high, tied at the top and struggling. Well, the bag wasn't struggling but whatever was inside was certainly trying to get out.

Santa looked around at the ash-covered carpet. "Sorry about the mess. Wasn't one of my best landings." He reached out and untied the top of the moving sack. Jacob stepped forward. His heart thudded in his chest. The string slid away and the burlap bag sank to the floor, revealing Marlie. Crouched down, hands tied in front and a neck-cloth tied around her mouth.

Santa had brought her back—but for how long? Was she going to disappear again? No matter. Jacob would enjoy the time they had together.

Marlie stood up, the bag around her feet. She didn't see Jacob. She only had eyes for Santa. He released the gag first. *Bad move.*

"Have you lost your mind?" she shouted as Santa bent to untie her feet. "You've gone completely nuts. Wait until the history books hear about this one."

"Marlie?" Jacob asked, walking toward her. It was really her. She was back.

She swung her head toward him.

"Just a second, Jacob. I'm not done with him yet." She looked back at Santa. "You tied me up, you kidnapped me—" Her eyes widened. She dropped her hands as Santa released her bonds. "Jacob?" She looked from him to Santa. "Santa?"

Santa smiled and shrugged. "Merry Christmas?"

A joyous squeak erupted from Marlie as she launched herself into Santa's arms. "Oh thank you, Santa, thank you so much." Jacob continued to walk forward, trying to figure out what had happened. He knew what physically had happened, but why was Marlie hugging Santa Claus?

With a quick pat on her back, Santa released Marlie from his embrace. He placed a gentle hand on Jacob's shoulder and whispered into the younger man's ear.

"Remember, elves are fertile." Jacob jerked away trying to look into Santa's face. What was he talking about? "You'll see," Santa smiled as he answered Jacob's unspoken question. "Be happy," he called to both of them as he walked back to the fireplace. With a quick word, he disappeared, leaving tiny tornadoes of twirling dust in his wake.

Marlie and Jacob were alone.

He stared at her, absorbing everything about her, frightened she might disappear.

"You don't have to worry," Marlie began. She stepped closer to Jacob, dying to touch him, but she couldn't. His hands were firmly clenched by his side. His letter hadn't said anything about wanting her back, just that he wanted her to be happy. Santa had seen to that, but what if Jacob didn't want her here. She knew he wouldn't want her back as a housekeeper. She scanned the room out of the corner of her eye and could tell even from that quick glance that the house was back to its impeccable condition.

This was supposed to be the answer to Jacob's Christmas wish. How was she supposed to be happy if Jacob didn't want her back?

"I don't expect anything," she added bravely and lying through her teeth. Jacob still didn't touch her. "If you don't want me to stay, I can find someplace else to go." She thought about it for a second. "I don't know where, but I can leave…if you want."

She waited. Jacob continued to stare at her, but kept his hands by his side and his lips firmly closed. He looked at the fireplace where Santa had disappeared.

"Is he coming back?" Jacob indicated to the spot where Santa had stood.

Oh, no. He doesn't want me. "I don't think so," Marlie said honestly.

The tension eased out of Jacob's body. "Good." He made the single step to her and pulled her against his body.

She wrapped her arms around his neck and opened her mouth.

"Wait," he stopped her. "Let me say this first." Jacob took a deep breath. "I love you and I don't want you to ever leave again."

A smile exploded in Marlie's heart. "I love you, too. And I'm not going anywhere."

Jacob pulled her close. "Then I have all I want for Christmas."

Epilogue

ଔ

Marlie stood in front of the Christmas tree—illuminated with the power of hundreds of lights. Jacob had once again done a wonderful job. She looked at the mix of homemade and store-bought ornaments scattered unevenly about the tree.

She had no doubt that the "tree fairy" would come through in the middle of the night and rearrange the items. The kids had tendency to clump the ornaments, which threw off Jacob's sense of balance, but he waited until they were in bed to readjust them.

It was all part of their day after Thanksgiving tradition. Put up the tree and everyone from their three kids to the Board of Directors helped with the decorating.

*Dear Santa. All I want for Christmas...*she felt the words inside her heart moments before the explicit, erotic image popped into her head. Marlie, spread-eagle on their bed, her hands and feet tied to the corners. Jacob, kneeling between her open thighs, his cock riding slowly, ever so slowly into her pussy.

She glanced over her shoulder and smiled at her husband.

"You always wish for the same thing," she said.

"I'm a simple man with simple tastes." He strolled into the living room, wrapping his arms around her waist and pulling her back against him. "The children are in bed, the guests are gone." He nipped her earlobe. "I say we welcome the holiday season in appropriate fashion."

She tipped her head to the side. "Why do I think that means naked and making love beside the Christmas tree?"

"Can I help it if the scent of pine is an aphrodisiac to me?" He placed his hands on her hips and held her still as he rubbed his already hardening cock against her ass. "Blame it on the fact that I married a very sexy Christmas elf who insists on celebrating Christmas all year long."

Marlie wanted to think of a comeback but her mind was clouded, as so often happened when Jacob touched her. "What about your Christmas wish?"

"We'll save that for later. For now..."

"For now, I should give you your Christmas present." After five Christmases together, she'd come prepared. She stepped out of Jacob's arms. She reached beneath the bulky sweater she wore and undid the button of her jeans. She slipped them down and kicked them out of the way before pulling the heavy sweater off. She held it in front of her just long enough to tease her husband then tossed it aside.

The white lace top cupped her breasts and added a little extra lift. Like much of her lingerie, it stopped just south of her pussy, giving him just a hint of what was beneath.

"Do you like your Christmas present?" she asked, picking up the strap of her top.

"Is this for me?"

She nodded. "I thought you might like it." She undid one button in the center and shimmied as the straps slid down and off, leaving her dressed in the tiniest pair of panties imaginable. "Anne helped me pick it out."

"Anne's getting a raise."

"Anne gets a raise every Christmas."

He winked and pulled Marlie into his arms. "So do I."

Marlie laughed and wrapped her arms around his neck, savoring the warmth of his body, so familiar and so exciting.

"I love you," he whispered.

"I love you."

Marlie kissed him, knowing she had everything she could have wished for.

Why an electronic book?

We live in the Information Age—an exciting time in the history of human civilization, in which technology rules supreme and continues to progress in leaps and bounds every minute of every day. For a multitude of reasons, more and more avid literary fans are opting to purchase e-books instead of paper books. The question from those not yet initiated into the world of electronic reading is simply: *Why?*

1. *Price.* An electronic title at Ellora's Cave Publishing and Cerridwen Press runs anywhere from 40% to 75% less than the cover price of the exact same title in paperback format. Why? Basic mathematics and cost. It is less expensive to publish an e-book (no paper and printing, no warehousing and shipping) than it is to publish a paperback, so the savings are passed along to the consumer.

2. *Space.* Running out of room in your house for your books? That is one worry you will never have with electronic books. For a low one-time cost, you can purchase a handheld device specifically designed for e-reading. Many e-readers have large, convenient screens for viewing. Better yet, hundreds of titles can be stored within your new library—on a single microchip. There are a variety of e-readers from different manufacturers. You can also read e-books on your PC or laptop computer. (Please note that Ellora's Cave does not endorse any specific brands.

You can check our websites at www.elloracave.com or www.cerridwenpress.com for information we make available to new consumers.)

3. *Mobility.* Because your new e-library consists of only a microchip within a small, easily transportable e-reader, your entire cache of books can be taken with you wherever you go.

4. ***Personal Viewing Preferences.*** Are the words you are currently reading too small? Too large? Too… ANNOYING? Paperback books cannot be modified according to personal preferences, but e-books can.

5. ***Instant Gratification.*** Is it the middle of the night and all the bookstores near you are closed? Are you tired of waiting days, sometimes weeks, for bookstores to ship the novels you bought? Ellora's Cave Publishing sells instantaneous downloads twenty-four hours a day, seven days a week, every day of the year. Our webstore is never closed. Our e-book delivery system is 100% automated, meaning your order is filled as soon as you pay for it.

Those are a few of the top reasons why electronic books are replacing paperbacks for many avid readers.

As always, Ellora's Cave and Cerridwen Press welcome your questions and comments. We invite you to email us at Comments@ellorascave.com or write to us directly at Ellora's Cave Publishing Inc., 1056 Home Avenue, Akron, OH 44310-3502.

COMING TO A BOOKSTORE NEAR YOU!

ELLORA'S CAVE

Bestselling Authors Tour

UPDATES AVAILABLE AT

WWW.ELLORASCAVE.COM

erridwen, the Celtic Goddess
of wisdom, was the muse who
brought inspiration to storytellers and those in the creative arts.
Cerridwen Press encompasses the best
and most innovative stories in all
genres of today's fiction. Visit our site
and discover the newest titles by
talented authors who still get inspired -
much like the ancient storytellers did,
once upon a time.

Cerridwen Press

www.cerridwenpress.com